L♥VE S♥ME B♥DY

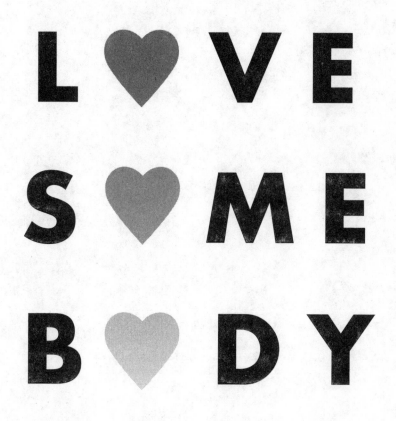

L♥VE S♥ME B♥DY

RACHEL ROASEK

Farrar Straus Giroux
New York

Farrar Straus Giroux Books for Young Readers
An imprint of Macmillan Publishing Group, LLC
120 Broadway, New York, NY 10271
fiercereads.com

Our books may be purchased in bulk for promotional, educational, or business use.
Please contact your local bookseller or the Macmillan Corporate and Premium Sales Department
at (800) 221-7945 ext. 5442 or by email at MacmillanSpecialMarkets@macmillan.com.

Library of Congress Cataloging-in-Publication Data is available.

First edition, 2022
Book design by Michelle Gengaro-Kokmen
Printed in the United States of America

ISBN 978-0-374-38896-6 (hardcover)
1   3   5   7   9   10   8   6   4   2

To the kids still figuring out who they are

L♥VE S♥ME B♥DY

SAM

A WHOLE LOT OF MY PERSONAL SUCCESS IS riding on my ex-boyfriend right now.

The front room at Flannery's is even more crowded than usual. It's an artsy college town coffee shop, the kind that sells indie zines and has free lollipops at the register like it's a doctor's office. It hosts local musicians or poets or other events from time to time, and it has a stage set up in one corner specifically for that purpose. Right now, Flannery's is hosting *me*. Chairs and tables have been pushed together and clustered around the small stage to form something like an audience. The usual café chatter is gone, except for the occasional hiss from the espresso machine or the *ting* of the outdated cash register. I'm standing in what could loosely be called the wings, which is really just a few haphazardly draped curtains lined against one wall, watching

Christian stumble through the monologue I wrote him like it's the hardest thing he's ever done. It almost hurts to watch.

This play is, hands down, one of the most ambitious things I've taken on in all three years of high school. The acting and playwriting side of things is familiar, but actually producing a show is completely new territory. It required a lot more work than I first thought. Mom used to joke over the phone that she should have gone into producing instead of acting, since "that's where the money is," and now I kind of see her point. Still, there's something really satisfying about having my hands on every part of the project—of taking the steps to make it come to life, instead of only joining up when most of the work is already done. I wrote the play, secured the venue, organized the cast, bribed one of the techs from school to run the sound and lights, *and* did the marketing and made the programs. We even rehearsed over Christmas break, and now, with school finally back in for January, I'm bringing this thing to life. You can say what you want, but this project is mine, from start to finish, and I might actually die if it doesn't go perfectly.

I'm pitching this play as a true story—or at least based on one, since doing a whole play as myself would be a little narcissistic, even for me. Especially with my playing the main character. So instead of Sam, the main character is a girl named Sara. Her lifelong dream is to get out of her boring existence in Toledo, Ohio, and make something important of herself. She's smart, passionate, driven—everything a small town doesn't deserve. She wants out, but the people in her life keep holding her back.

Christian, of course, had to be one of the main characters.

His doppelgänger, Chris, is Sara's well-meaning but hopelessly average boyfriend. He likes Toledo and doesn't see the point in leaving. Sara loves him, but the two of them get into it fairly often over the course of the play. (That's an exaggeration on my part. Christian's and my relationship was never as juicy as that. Still, what's a good story without some heavy drama?)

Finally, a break comes for Sara—admission to a prestigious art school in New York. It's the last nail in the coffin for her and Chris. They get into one big argument, where Sara lets out her feelings about him, and then she leaves to start her new life.

So now, technically, my part of the show is done. All I have to do is watch as Christian and my other friend Aria carry out the last scene. Somehow, this is even more scary than being onstage. I don't like having to rely on other people to make sure things go well.

CHRISTIAN

There's something special about Sam that gives her the power to drag me into the craziest things.

To be honest, we haven't actually known each other that long. We've been going to the same schools since third grade, same classes, some shared friends, but it didn't go further than that for a long time. We officially met in the second semester of sophomore year, when she decided to ask me out.

I said yes—because why wouldn't I? She's gorgeous, smart, and surprisingly persuasive. Ever since, it's been one ridiculous scheme after another. Like roping me into this show, for example.

Theater and art, in general, have never been my thing. I've played soccer since I was five, and that's pretty much been my life ever since. Most of my friends are from the team, too. Sam was the outlier—more creative than me, more outgoing, and so completely far out of my league that I was shocked she ever showed me any interest.

Even now that we're just friends, that interest hasn't gone away. It's just changed direction. Now it's more like she's my sister or my guidance counselor. She could have picked any of the theater guys to play my character, but she insisted it had to be me. "I based the character on you," she said with the usual stubbornness that I've learned is baked into Sam's personality. "What's the point of choosing someone else?"

Sometimes, I think she has bigger dreams for me than my parents do, and that's saying something. I hope I don't let her down.

The play is almost over. It's the last scene, after Sam's character leaves Toledo without really saying goodbye. It's only me and another actor onstage now, Sam's friend and fellow theater kid Aria. But I can feel Sam watching me from the sidelines, and it's starting to make me nervous.

"Why would she leave you behind?" the other girl asks me.

"She said I was holding her back." I resist the urge to glance back at Sam. Instead, I look out over the crowd. My mom's out there, sitting in the middle of the crowd. Sam's grandma, Nana Bea, is right up front, and she grins and gives me a thumbs-up. I swallow hard. "I've been trying to keep up with her for so long, trying so hard to be what she wanted, but in the end, I couldn't."

"Did she at least say goodbye?"

"She came to see me. But there wasn't a real goodbye. That wouldn't be like her. She sent me a letter instead. Only one sentence."

Aria raises an eyebrow. "What did it say?"

I have to remind myself to pause. This is it: the last line of the play. Sam told me to give it "gravitas," let it hang in the air for a minute to make the moment more significant. Still, I'm eager for this thing to be over. Right as I open my mouth, though, a noise from the audience distracts me. It sounds like crinkling paper. My eyes shoot toward the source.

Sam drilled me over and over about not getting distracted during the performance. "It's not going to be as quiet as a regular theater," she said. "There's going to be noise and people talking. You have to tune it out." I did okay with that during the rehearsals, but this is different. This time it's not just Sam and Aria watching me, and as much faith as Sam puts in me, I'm still not much of an actor. So yeah, when somebody pulls a sucker out of their pocket and unwraps it as loudly as they possibly can, that's probably going to throw me off. I catch the flash of colorful paper in the hands of someone near the front and stare at it for a second before realizing that *I'm still in a play*. That's almost enough to make me recover, too . . . until I see the person holding it.

It's a girl around my age, with long brown hair and a black sweater. Her dark eyelashes almost completely hide her eyes from this angle, and the lights shining in my face don't exactly help. But even from here, I can tell she's gorgeous.

She crumples the wrapper up in her fist, lifting the sucker to her mouth, and then, for whatever reason, she locks eyes with me.

The rest of the world phases out.

I can't explain it much better than that. I'm still talking; I know I am, because I can hear myself saying my last line—or at least something close to it. But suddenly all thoughts about acting or getting this right or even Sam don't feel that important anymore.

My vision tunnels and focuses on her face, on *her*, and who cares about some play? Why would I care about literally anything else, right at this moment, other than the fact that this girl is looking at me?

Maybe Sam's got a point. Sometimes it feels really good to be the center of someone's attention.

ROS

As nice as this job is going to look on my résumé, it's times like these when I wish I were getting paid. *Art Pulse* isn't a big magazine—more the indie type, perfect for an area like Worcester—and it pretty much covers only smaller local events.

Official Broadway tours or appearances by big-name artists don't interest *Art Pulse*. They'd rather talk about community theater productions, concerts by little hipster bands no one has heard of, and installations by unknown artists. I'm all for supporting the arts, obviously, and as one of *Art Pulse*'s theater critics, I might not get paid, but I do get to see amazing pieces of work.

This, though? Isn't one of them.

I look back down at the program. A foreword on one of the inside pages mentions something about this play being "based on the experiences of the playwright," which is just a fancy way of saying this is an autobiography with different people's names slapped on for flavor. Still, something tells me that very little about *this* play is real. It's all I can do not to actually roll my eyes when the main character—a two-dimensional cutout of someone's idea of a "strong female character," played by a girl who looks like she wishes she were halfway to Hollywood already—has the nerve to say anything about her "dreams."

Honestly, this girl's dreams are the only thing we really know about her. Her personality can be boiled down to a few basic aspects: driven, ambitious, and determined, which are all different ways to say the exact same thing. The actual plot of this play (what little there is) isn't bad, and the acting is surprisingly well-rounded for what is basically a high school play, but this main character is just . . . a walking piece of ambition. No flaws, no insecurities, nothing. If this girl were anything like the girl she's playing, then she would be the most boring person in the world.

The actress's name, Sam Dickson, is all over this program: "Written by," "Directed by," "Produced by," and "Starring." There isn't a single part of this play this girl hasn't had her hands in. Maybe she's more like this character than I thought.

I force my attention back to the stage. Of all the people in this play, the male lead's acting is definitely the weakest. I think I recognize him—he goes to Northeastern High School with me, but we've never talked. His name's Christian. He seems like one of the athletic types, and they aren't the kind to stop and speak to someone like me. Not that I'd want them to. I'm happy over here in my own little corner, with my books and my unpaid internship at an overly pretentious indie art zine. I've never doubted that I'm going to end up a hermit academic like my dad one day, and the closer I get to graduation, the more sure of it I am. He would say that that's not necessarily a good thing, but why not? The life of a hermit academic sounds a whole lot more appealing than being surrounded by superficial people, talking about superficial things, never bothering to get to know one another beyond the surface level. I've lived through two and a half years of high school already, thanks. I'd rather not keep doing *that* for the rest of my life.

The girl playing the main character leaves the stage after some sort of argument, and internally I breathe a sigh of relief. That has to be her final exit, right? It's only a one-act, and we're coming up on an hour. It's the homestretch, then. I adjust the notebook on my lap. I pride myself on taking fairly detailed notes, and even something like this is no exception. I'm taking this gig as seriously as I can, and with any luck, I can be home and completely roasting this whole play within the hour.

The play keeps going, though. Apparently, there's more the esteemed playwright has to say.

I resist the urge to sigh loudly. This *has* to be wrapping up soon. I fiddle with the lining of my coat. There's something hard in one of the pockets, and desperate for some distraction from what's in front of me, I pull it out. It's a lollipop, I realize. I grabbed one from a little bowl up at the register when I got my coffee.

Might as well. I unwrap it and pop it into my mouth, letting the artificial, oversweetened taste cover my tongue.

Come to think of it, I've never really liked this coffee shop, either. It's marketed to appeal to all the cool, hipster kids from the local high school and universities, but the music is too loud, and the decorations are so busy they make my eyes hurt. The people are weird, too, constantly acting like they have something to prove just by being there or looking at you sideways like they're trying to figure out if you belong there.

Like right now.

Because this guy onstage will not stop staring at me.

2

SAM

OKAY, THAT *DEFINITELY* WASN'T PART OF THE script.

I know what I wrote. The last line was supposed to be "So long, sweetheart." It was Sara's final, poignant farewell to Chris, a nod to her old feelings for him while still acknowledging that she had to move on. I agonized for days over the writing of it. Except the line that left Christian's mouth isn't what I wrote.

What was *that*?

He's just stopped, staring at some girl near the front. I recognize her: Rosalyn Shew—Ros for short—one of the pretentious faux intellectuals at Northeastern. She's got a reputation for being ruthlessly smart and nearly impossible to impress. I've also heard she's a critic for a local arts magazine. That can't be a coincidence. She's here to review my play, and Christian's staring at her, and now she thinks I wrote that completely ridiculous last line.

Maybe I can still save this. Maybe Aria will say something else or Christian will realize his mistake and fix it. Maybe I won't have to look like a complete screwup in front of everyone who came to see my play. Turns out, though, nobody gets the chance, because at least *one* person here knows how to do their job. The tech guy, hearing something close enough to the last line to make it count, brings the lights onstage down, and the music that usually plays in the background of the café cranks up. That's our cue for the curtain call. I jump onto the tiny stage as the audience starts to applaud. I hear Nana Bea's signature hoarse whistle and shoot her a grin as I join hands with the others for the bows. Maybe I squeeze Christian's hand a little too tight, but that's beside the point.

As the audience starts to rise and filter away, I head off to the side with the rest of the cast.

Aria gives me a hug. "Great job, lady."

"You too. Thanks so much for agreeing to do this."

She winks at me. "Not like Mr. Campbell was gonna cast me in anything."

"Well, he's a racist prick and we know it. And as your promised payment for your hard work, you get coffee on me until the end of the semester."

"Sounds great. I'm gonna catch up with my parents now, but I'll see you later, okay?"

With one last wave, she breaks away and vanishes into the crowd. I watch her go for a second, then turn back to Christian.

13

I'm expecting—I'm *hoping* for—some sort of apology or explanation, but I don't get one. Instead, he's staring off into the crowd of people heading for the door, craning his neck like he's looking for someone specific.

I shove him. "Seriously?"

He jumps. "What?"

"'So long, *dum-dum*'?"

He frowns at me for a second and then goes pale. "I . . . is that what I said?"

"Take a wild guess."

Christian flinches. "I'm sorry, Sam. A girl in the audience unwrapped a lollipop or something, and it completely threw me off. I didn't even realize I'd said it."

"What are you, five? Nobody says *dum-dum* anymore, Christian. You might have even gotten away with 'sucker,' but apparently, pretty girls turn your brain into soup or something."

"I said I'm sorry!"

I really don't have the energy for this right now. Performing takes a lot out of me, and I can feel the adrenaline starting to wear off already. The show is over, and there's nothing I can do now to change how it went. Better to just go home and forget about it.

I shake my head. "Never mind. Thanks for doing this, but I'm going home. Have fun with Lollipop Girl."

Christian blushes bright red. "I really didn't mean to space out like that, Sam. I'm sorry. Was it that noticeable?"

"It was enough. Look, it doesn't matter now. The show went fine. I'll see you on Monday, all right?"

He's still only half listening to me. He keeps glancing around the rest of the café, like maybe Ros stuck around to talk to my leading man. No such luck—I don't see her anywhere.

"Yeah, see you Monday," he says absently. "You did really well, Sam."

"You too, Chris." And he *did* actually do pretty well, I guess. Except for the flub at the end.

He waves a distracted goodbye, and I let him wander off into the crowd. No sooner is he gone than Nana manages to find me, fighting past a group of people loitering in front of the stage and grinning from ear to ear. "That was fantastic, sweet pea," she says, wrapping me up in a huge hug that smells like laundry detergent and her favorite Dior perfume.

I return the hug. "It could have been better."

"Oh, hush. I was emotional the whole way through. Everything was perfect."

As a grandmother, Nana is contractually obligated to say that, but it feels good to hear. "Thanks, Nana."

"Where'd Christian get to? I wanted to congratulate him as well."

"He's already heading out."

"Too bad. You tell him for me, then." She gives me another quick hug. "Good job again, baby. You want me to pick up ice cream on the way home as a treat?"

Ice cream after shows is a tradition between Nana and me, spanning all the way back to elementary school, when I played Dorothy in my school's version of *The Wizard of Oz*. I'm still disappointed with the line screwup at the end, but Moose Tracks would definitely help with that.

"You know it," I say.

"I'll see you at home, then. Drive safe."

She heads to the door, and I walk back onstage to pick up the props and costume pieces I scrounged together for the show. While I do, a few people from school stop to congratulate me as well. They seemed to like it—they came to see the show in the first place, which speaks to either my reputation or just how much they want me to like them. I'll take either, at this point.

All things considered, this wasn't actually a disaster. One dropped line doesn't ruin a show, and I can guarantee that the work I put in was the best it could possibly be. But there's always that nagging voice in the back of my head that tells me things could always be better. I could have tried harder, done a little more. Maybe then I'd be satisfied.

Or maybe not. I've tried my best for years, and my inner critic has never once been happy with me.

I shake my head, stuffing the props and clothing into a duffel bag. The coffee shop is going to close soon, and I need to get out of here before that happens. I throw the bag over my shoulder, hard enough that it knocks a bit of the air out of me. I'm clearly getting too in my feelings right now. I need ice cream and then sleep.

At the very least, I can satisfy myself with the fact that other people liked the show. If I can't be happy with myself, maybe other people can.

ROS

DAD'S SITTING ON THE COUCH WHEN I GET BACK, watching some TV show I can't put a name to. Books and piles of scribbled-on papers are scattered across the coffee table and the empty seats on the couch. He turns toward me and smiles as I enter. "Hiya, kiddo. How was the play?"

"Ugh."

"That bad?"

I toss my bag down near the coatrack. "What do you expect? A high schooler wrote it."

"I'm not sure that's very fair. Plenty of young people have done amazing things. Not to mention, *you're* a high schooler."

There's a dish of now-cold lasagna on the kitchen island. I cut myself a square and plop it onto a plate, not bothering to throw it into the microwave. "Not at Northeastern, they haven't."

Dad laughs and shakes his head. "Well then, at least you've got something to write about."

He moves aside a few stacks of paper so I can join him on the couch. Dad's a relatively skinny guy, and aside from a few wrinkles coming in around his eyes, he doesn't look much older than the college students he teaches. I've been told he was a total catch when he was younger. I've also been told I don't look anything like him, which, duh. It's hard to see a family resemblance when we share absolutely no genetic material.

"How was school?" he asks.

My mouth is full of cold lasagna, so I take a second to answer. "Fine. Mr. Travers gave us a three-page paper to write over the weekend."

"On?"

"*Heart of Darkness*."

"Ah, that . . . gem." He has a hard time hiding his distaste. "Are they really still teaching that?"

"Don't look at me, Dad. Take it up with the school board."

"Fine, fine. But if you need help, I'm afraid I've completely blocked most of that book from my memory, so I won't be much use."

"It's okay," I say. "I've already read it."

The two of us fall into a comfortable silence for a few minutes. The TV keeps playing some popular reality show garbage, the kind Dad likes to turn on while he's grading papers to have something in the background. Looking around, I can see he's mostly given up on the grading for the night, and now he's just watching the show. A few of the books on the coffee table are his

18

own—textbooks about the Ottoman Empire, Genghis Khan, the rise and fall of the Romanovs, all with his name printed on the spine: *Hector Shew*.

Having a college professor for a dad hasn't really helped me out with school so far. High schools mostly focus on more "popular" subjects, like American history or the ancient Greeks. Anything that's not Dad's particular focus, he tends to forget about completely: He couldn't tell you when the Stamp Act was passed, but he could list all eleven of Süleyman the Magnificent's children. It makes him *really fun* at parties.

"The big birthday double feature is coming up in a few months," he says after a while. "Any ideas what we should do?"

"Besides the usual?"

My dad and his late husband—my biological dad, Charles—have birthdays only two days apart. It's become a tradition between the two of us to celebrate both on the same day. Usually, that means cooking a big dinner together and then watching Dad's favorite movie.

I shrug. "I'm fine with the same old thing if you are. April Thanksgiving again?"

Dad smiles. "Sounds good to me. Turkey, pie, and *Cinema Paradiso* it is."

I've seen *Cinema Paradiso* enough times by now not to roll my eyes whenever Dad mentions it. It's an old Italian movie from the eighties about a boy who befriends a cinema projectionist. It's sentimental garbage, but Dad loves it, so I indulge him at least once a year.

Speaking of sentimental garbage.

I wolf down the last of my dinner and then stand to take my plate to the sink. "I should get started on my review. Want to get some of my thoughts down before I fully regret the last hour of my life."

Dad laughs again. "Have fun, kiddo. Do you have support group tomorrow?"

"Yeah, same time as usual."

"All right, then. Good night."

"Night, Dad."

I leave him to his papers and his reality show and head upstairs. My room has started to collect some serious clutter over the course of the school week.

That'll probably be one of my jobs tomorrow: clean my room before I have to go to the support group for surrogacy kids—people carried by someone who wasn't their biological parent. There aren't many of us, at least not in the Worcester area, but I've been going since I was a kid. At this point, it's more a habit than anything else. That, and I guess it's good to know I'm not the only one.

Pulling my hair back in a scrunchie to get it out of my face, I sit down in front of my laptop and boot it up. It's an older model, so it takes a good few minutes to actually get going. That's okay, though, because it gives me time to pull out my notebook and sort through my thoughts about the performance. I give another quick glance over the program tucked into my notebook: *So Long, Toledo!* A one-act play by Sam Dickson. The title makes it sound like it should be a classic musical, like *Carousel* or something, but the final result was definitely less entertaining than that. And less well written, too. God, that ending line . . .

With the computer finally up and running, I open a Word document and start writing a basic introduction for the piece:

> This Friday, January 4, at seven PM, Flannery's Coffee Shop was the site of a student-produced and -run one-act play titled *So Long, Toledo!* About fifty people were in attendance, including yours truly. The play claimed to be an autobiographical work of one Sam Dickson, fellow student at Northeastern High School.

I have to snort at that one. *Autobiographical.* I'd say that's about as real as the show on TV downstairs: everything working out just a little too well to be a coincidence, always tied up in a neat bow by the end of a thirty- or sixty-minute block. I did some background research on Sam before going to the show tonight, and it turns out her mom is a fairly successful actress living in LA. That checks out, I guess—it's hard to remember what real life is like when you're surrounded by actors. Based on the performance of Sam herself, I'd say she's not far behind her mom. Talented, definitely, and pretty driven to be able to put together a whole show by herself. The play might have actually been good if it hadn't done its best to be so completely predictable.

That's the first thing I'll mention, I decide. The predictability. I've never met a person whose life worked out in such convenient ways. Ask anyone, and I'm sure they'd tell you that things rarely ever go the way you expect them to. Charles Marlow in *Heart of Darkness* never planned on his trip down the Congo taking him where it did. I don't think my dad expected to lose *his* Charles three years after starting a family with him. I certainly never anticipated I'd be sitting in my room on a Friday night, writing a review of a bad student play. Unless Sam Dickson is the luckiest person in the entire world, I highly doubt things happen for her the way she claims.

I've seen Sam around school a few times. She's in the drama club, obviously, but she also runs track in the spring and served on the prom committee as a sophomore, before she was even allowed to go to the dance without an upperclassman as her date. I've never seen her without someone tagging along behind— either this week's most eligible bachelor or some group of girls desperate to make a powerful friend. Always made up within an inch of her life, and always wearing something that looks ripped straight from a fashion magazine. She never gets dress-coded, either, which is just another testament to how charismatic she can be.

A girl like that always knows the right thing to say to get people on her side. She knows what makes people tick, how to make them feel however she wants them to feel. Some would call that magnetism, but personally, I think it leans more toward manipulation than anything else. If I'm going to talk to someone, I want to know I'm talking to the *real* them, not the person they put on because they think it'll make people like them more.

Still, there's a power to being that socially savvy. It's how she's gotten as popular as she has. Networking's a good skill in any business. Maybe I could learn something from someone like her.

I shake my head, blinking hard so that the computer screen comes back into focus. I'm not writing an article on Sam. I'm writing a review of her terrible play. I roll my shoulders, getting ready to rip her saccharine little story to pieces. Maybe my opinion will be unpopular. But I've never once apologized for speaking my mind, and I don't plan to start now. She may have the rest of Northeastern wrapped around her little finger, but she won't get to me.

4

CHRISTIAN

MOM MAKES IT BACK TO THE HOUSE BEFORE I do, and her car is already in the driveway by the time I pull up. Dad's black BMW is there, too, sleek and shiny under the streetlight, exactly where it's been since around five PM today. Dad didn't go to the show, but I knew he wouldn't. Theater isn't his thing. Not that I blame him: Theater isn't really *my* thing, either.

As soon as I get through the front door, I'm attacked by two blurs of motion. One wraps itself around my torso, squealing, and the other jumps up to lick my face. I have to stumble back against the door to keep from falling over.

"Yankee, *down!*" I shout at eighty pounds of golden retriever, and then softer, "Hi, Aimee."

My kid sister grins up at me. She lost another tooth a few days ago, so the usual smile is a little lopsided. "Hi, Chris."

Yankee wags his tail at me until I give him some well-earned attention, and after a minute or so, Mom shows up to observe the chaos.

"There's the star of the show," she says with a grin. "Good job, hon."

I shrug, a little embarrassed. I could mention the line I messed up, but she probably didn't notice and I don't really feel like talking about it. "It was all Sam, Mom, I swear. She just needed somebody on the stage to talk at."

I hear Dad's voice from the living room. "And how's that different from any other day of the week?"

I kick off my shoes and fight past the welcoming party to get to the rest of the house. Dad is in the living room, with his feet up on the coffee table as he watches TV. He's out of his work clothes and wearing jeans and an old sweatshirt I recognize from when I was a little kid.

He nods at me. "How did you do?"

I shrug. "All right, I guess."

"He was fantastic," Mom pipes up from across the room, near the entrance to the kitchen. "Don't let him lie to you."

"Of course he was. He wouldn't be Christian if he was anything less than excellent." A grin from Dad, but he's clearly distracted as he keeps one eye on the TV. "Does Sam have plans to drag you into anything else, or are you allowed to focus on your other activities for a while?"

Dad never really liked Sam. He always thought she was too overbearing, too "much" for every room she was in. If I ever talked about her around him, he'd make a whip-cracking sound effect and laugh at his own joke like it was the funniest thing he'd ever heard. I see where he's coming from: Sam definitely isn't for everyone. He still thinks it's weird that we're friends now, but for the most part he tolerates it.

"She asked me to be in the play because it would look good on my college applications," I remind him.

He snorts. "Babson doesn't care about school plays. You'll be fine."

Babson University is Dad's alma mater. He insists that outside of Harvard, it produces some of the best students on the East Coast. He's dead set on my going there, too.

"But it never hurts to diversify," Mom says, rounding the corner from the kitchen. She frowns at Dad. "Bill, hon, get your feet off the coffee table."

"Why? I've been at work all day; haven't I earned it?"

I shake my head at both of them. "I'm going to start on some homework and then go to bed," I say. "Coach is hosting some workouts early tomorrow morning, and I said I'd go."

"No dinner?" Mom says with concern. "I saved some for you."

"I ate on the way back. Thanks, though."

She frowns. "Tell me that next time."

Dad waves a hand at me. "Go on and get to your homework. Don't forget to ask Coach tomorrow about those recommendation letters for the Babson scholarships. And you should look into some independent ones as well."

"I will, Dad. G'night."

Great. *More* homework. Both of my parents can be pretty demanding when they want to be. They have good reason, though. My older brother, Will, used to fight with them a lot, back when he still lived with us. That was four years ago, though, and none of us has heard from him since. I think they're trying to make sure I don't end up like him. Whatever that means.

Mom hugs me good night, and then Yankee follows me up the stairs. On the second-floor landing, Aimee stands with her hands on her hips. I stop a few steps down, mimicking her pose. "What's that face for?"

She pouts. "I wanted to go to your show, but Mom and Dad said I couldn't."

"You would've hated it, Mee-mee. There was no singing or dancing, just a bunch of talking."

"Still! I wanted to see you be a big star!" She leans forward and cups her hands around her mouth, whispering. "Did you and Sam have to kiss?"

I roll my eyes. Aimee's only seven, and unlike my dad, she *loves* Sam. She swears that Sam's the coolest girl she's ever met, and she might not be wrong. "No, we didn't. Can you move now?"

She pouts again but steps aside and lets me climb the rest of the stairs. "I still think you should ask her to be your girlfriend again!" she shouts after me, and I ignore her until the door to my room is closed behind me. Yankee managed to sneak in along with me, and he immediately plops his big golden retriever body onto my bed, taking up the space I was about to sit down on.

I head to my desk instead, where my backpack is already sitting from earlier in the day. I wasn't lying—I do have homework due Monday, and I probably should get started on it sooner rather than later—but that isn't the main reason I wanted to get upstairs. My head isn't in the right place for trig assignments right now, anyway. What I'd *rather* think about is the girl at Flannery's. Who was she? I know she looked familiar, definitely someone from school, but I can't quite figure out who. One of the band or theater kids, maybe? She seemed like the artsy type. If she is a theater kid, maybe Sam knows her. I almost pull out my phone to text her, but then I remember she might still be mad at me for screwing up my line. Probably not the best idea to talk to her right now.

Something in the pocket of my jeans is digging into my leg. I reach in and fish out my lucky piece. Most of the time, I forget it's there, because I always have it in my pocket. It's small, white, and perfectly round—a relic from an old game of Go—and weighs practically nothing, so it's kind of a miracle that I haven't lost it or thrown it in with my laundry any time over the last four years or so. Maybe that's what makes it lucky. That, or I'm really sentimental. Either way, I keep it with me at all times, especially when I feel like I need extra help: soccer games, big tests, you name it. I made sure I had it with me tonight, since I was already so far out of my depth with the whole acting thing. I turn the little token over and over in my hand. Technically speaking, I did still kind of screw up the play, even though I had this with me. But maybe that's not what the luck was for. Maybe the lucky part was getting to see *her*.

My face flushes. Jesus. I haven't felt like this since Sam and I first started dating, nearly a year ago now, all nervous and awkward and sweaty. I feel like a socially anxious twelve-year-old trying to ask a girl to a middle school dance. What *was* it about her? The lights were dim in Flannery's. And the ones that were on were shining right in my face, so it's not like I got a very good look at her. I remember long brown hair, a thick black sweater, big eyes. Other than that, she's mostly a blur. I didn't see her leave after the play, either, so if I don't find out any more, I might never see her again. Just the thought makes my stomach sink a little.

You fall for people way too easy, Christian.

I set my lucky piece down on the desk and cover it with my hand for a second. "Thanks for the help," I mutter to myself, feeling stupid. "But I think I'm gonna need a little more luck to find her again."

There's no response, because of course there isn't. I sigh, shaking my head at myself, then stand up and move toward my dresser.

"Enjoy hogging the bed while it lasts," I call to Yankee over my shoulder, "because you snore, and I am not about to let you steal all the covers again."

He wags his tail at me, wearing a big doofy dog grin, and I can already tell that he doesn't believe me, either.

SAM

MONDAYS SEEM TO BE THE DAYS WHEN I FEEL THE
most productive. Maybe it's something about the start of a new
school week, but I tend not to question the motivation when
it hits.

I wake up earlier than usual and put on coffee for Nana—she
only drinks decaf, so I don't share, but I try to start the coffee
for her whenever I can. Then I do some yoga to get myself moving. In the name of being extra about it, I change into my nicest sports bra and film a time-lapse video of me going through
some poses, too. That'll be something to keep for Instagram on
a day when I'm out of other ideas.

Next, before I head to school, it's working on some extra-credit
assignments I begged from a few of my teachers. I don't technically need extra credit, since I've got a strong B-plus average in

all my classes. Still, the extra bump never hurts. I might never be valedictorian, but nobody gets to be the next Emma Watson without a decent GPA and some honest-to-God hard work.

I feel like I'm misunderstood a lot when I say I want to be like Emma Watson. Most people only ever think about the acting, especially the whole Harry Potter thing. And sure, I'd love an acting career big enough to make my mom jealous, but it's so much more than that. People forget that she got a degree from Brown University in English literature, all while still doing movies and modeling for huge companies. She's a Women's Goodwill Ambassador for the United Nations, for crying out loud. *That's* what I mean when I say I want to be her. Not just the fame, not the fact that she's undeniably gorgeous, but because she doesn't limit herself. She does whatever she wants, and she does it all well. She looks, acts, and is completely unstoppable.

About halfway through a worksheet packet for chemistry, I get distracted by one of my favorite hobbies. A little *ding* sounds from my phone, and I reach for it right away. Another dating app notification. Looks like my latest victim is still on the hook after all.

I open the app and read the message. It's some corny, slightly thirsty "good morning" crap that I barely skim over before shooting back a reply. This guy, Salam, mentioned in his bio that he hated it when girls took forever to respond, so the girl I'm pretending to be is a model conversationalist. I'm pretty sure she's also an actual model, too. I flick back through my bio just to make sure. Fake name, fake pictures, fake description. Every week or so, I make up a new persona and then scroll through dating sites, trying to pick up the exact types of guys I think would be into this imaginary girl. It's like a game: Every time I get a guy to give me his number, I score a "point." Once the number's been given, the game pretty much ends there. I ghost them, block them, and then make up somebody new.

At first, it was something to do when I was bored, but over the past year or so, I've almost got it down to a science. You can usually tell from the types of pictures a guy puts on his profile, as well as his description (if he bothers to write one), exactly what kind of girl he's looking for. They don't even have to explicitly state it—after so long experimenting and testing, I just sort of *know*. I'm basically a teenage anthropologist, at this point.

I use all the evidence to form my first impression, and then, based on the girl I'm pretending to be, I reinvent myself to be exactly what they're looking for. Once we match, the game really begins. I study the way they talk—how much they have to say, whether they use "hahaha" or "lol," use of emojis, and so on—and mirror it back to them, keep them coming back for more until they finally crack, and then it's another point for Team Sam.

Part of me thinks I should feel a little bad for being a serial catfish. Aside from the occasional creep, most of the guys I talk to aren't actually that bad. Here they are, thinking they've made a genuine connection, and then suddenly the girl of their dreams vanishes without a trace. But really, it's not like I'm doing any lasting damage. They'll forget about that girl eventually and move on to bigger and better things. Maybe I'm even doing them a favor: Next time they come across a person who seems too good to be true, they might be a little more suspicious and save themselves the trouble of getting hurt for real.

On my way out of the house, I pass Nana sitting at the kitchen table, sipping her coffee.

"Morning, sweet pea," she says, lifting her mug to me in thanks.

"Morning, Nana."

"What's on the agenda today?"

"To be determined. I don't have rehearsals for the show anymore, but I might see if somebody wants to hang after school."

"You can always invite them over here if you want," she says.

I avoid meeting her eyes. "That's all right. I might go to the library, get a few projects done ahead of time. I'll let you know."

"You got it, sweet pea."

I'm not ashamed of where I live. I'm *not*. We don't exactly live in the nicest area, but it's what Nana can afford, and she works hard to keep it looking good. I'm proud of her for it. It's just that some of my friends might not see it the same way. They'd look at the peeling paint on the house next door or the ratty roof tiles Nana hasn't been able to replace yet, and they'd assume things. I'd rather not deal with that if I don't have to.

I grab an apple off the kitchen counter. "I'm gonna head out so I'm not late for school," I tell her. I swoop in to kiss her on the cheek as I move past, and she gives me a quick, one-armed hug back, and then I'm gone. It's freezing outside, and I didn't think to bring a warmer jacket. But I've already committed to leaving, so I just sit in my car and shiver for a couple of minutes until the heat melts the frost on the windshield. Overall, not my most productive start to a week. I might have to play catch-up for the rest of the day, but at least I've got some more time on my hands now, thanks to play rehearsals being over. The car's a little too cold, but I push away the discomfort and put it in reverse, pulling out onto the faded asphalt.

Traffic is light, and I end up with more time than I thought to get to school. So I take the long way and swing by Flannery's for a coffee. It's packed, but my favorite barista, Andrew, sees me walk in and waves. "Same thing as usual?"

"You know it."

"I'll get it started, then. Should be ready by the time you make it to the register."

I give him a grin. I'd never tell him, but I matched with him on a dating app once, as a hipster-looking girl named "Kadyn." We only talked for maybe an hour or so until he gave me his number. He might have a real wholesome, friendly barista vibe, but the guy's got a dirty mouth like you wouldn't believe.

As the line starts to inch closer to the register, I notice the magazine rack in front of the pastry display. It's got the local newspaper, the university paper, and, right on the top shelf, a few thin copies of *Art Pulse*. My mind instantly goes back to Ros, the girl Christian was staring at during the show. I think she writes for *Art Pulse*. It's been a few days since the show—did they publish her review of my play?

A buzz of excitement starts in my gut, like the moment right before the stage lights go up. I've never had anything I've done *reviewed* before. High school shows don't count. This project was entirely mine, and somebody may have written about it in a magazine. Other people are going to read it, people I've never met, and they're going to know about me and what I do.

I swipe a copy off the top of the stack. The line moves forward a bit, and I shuffle absently with it, already thumbing past the cover page. Sure enough, in the table of contents, I see a page for a review of *So Long, Toledo!* I almost can't flip to it fast enough. There at the top is some basic headline for the piece, followed by the author's name, Rosalyn Shew. The first paragraph or so is introductory stuff, giving background on the show, where it was, and who was in it. I skip to the middle, looking for the juicy stuff.

> Despite the fact that the play is, for the most part, fairly well written, it can't be ignored that the primary plot is lacking in authenticity. The emotion seems manufactured, inserted only because the playwright expected to get a reaction from the audience. Things happen exactly as they should to produce the "right" ending.

Well, *that's* not a good start.

> For all that the play's premise ensured us—a hard-hitting, emotionally complicated story about two young people at odds with each other—I personally

struggled to find anything "complicated" about it.
The main character, played by Northeastern High
junior Sam Dickson, was painfully two-dimensional
in her ambition, and rather than root for her, I almost
found myself hoping that her plans for the future
would fail—if only for the chance to see some actual
emotional growth from her.

My stomach hits the floor. She hated it?

Dickson's costar, fellow Northeastern junior Christian
Powell, was fairly charming in his role as the main
character's romantic partner, and yet he was
presented as a roadblock to her success. Dickson's
character was flat, uninteresting, and overly perfect
to the point where her only flaw could be considered
being "too" driven. Overall, I found the characters
uninteresting, the plot stale, and the premise of the
play too basic to produce any real drama.

The words on the page start to blur together in front of me.
Jesus, she *really* hated it. Suddenly, the thought of someone else
seeing this review makes me feel sick. They're going to think
these things she said are true. They won't even know me, but
they'll know that some girl from an arts magazine thinks I'm
a complete hack. And since she's the one writing the article, it
must be true. They'll hate me before they've ever even met me.
"Sam?"

I jump. The line in front of me has evaporated, and Andrew is standing at the register, staring at me like I'm growing another head. I remember I'm in public and suddenly realize that my throat is starting to close up.

Not here, Dickson.

I straighten my shoulders. My eyes still feel a little watery, but I ignore it. Draw attention to it and other people will notice, too. Instead, I give Andrew a winning smile.

"Sorry! Got distracted."

I step up to the register and pull out my card. Andrew's posture relaxes, and I can tell he believes me.

"No worries," he says. "Just the coffee for you today?"

I glance down at the magazine in my hand. Part of me knows I should put it back on the stand, forget about one bad review, and move on with more important things. But right now, it feels like it's glued to my hand. The panicked feeling is still there, rising as I look down at Ros's name under the article, but the longer I stare, the longer I focus on the name and let her words fade into the background, the more I think I can replace it with another emotion. Something less painful, more productive. Why not get *angry*?

I set the magazine on the counter next to my coffee. "I'll take this, too," I say coolly. "In case I need a coaster."

The girl behind me in line snorts, and I feel a rush of vindication. *See, Ros? I made a stranger laugh. Not so two-dimensional after all.*

I pay for my drink and the magazine and get out of Flannery's as fast as I can, coffee burning my throat and *Art Pulse* crushed in my fist.

6

CHRISTIAN

GOD, I HATE TRIG.

I have trouble concentrating in this class most days, but today, it's basically impossible. Between the beginnings of a headache and my nonstop thinking about the girl from Friday night, I have a feeling I'll be asking Monty for his notes later.

I can't get her out of my head. I swear I've seen her around before, but where? I've never seen her hanging around the soccer team. I don't have any classes with her, either.

My phone buzzes in my pocket. I pull it out and squint at it under the desk.

SAM: 👀 👀 I'm waiting
CHRISTIAN: waiting for what?

SAM: Oh my god

SAM: You are so hopeless

I hate it when Sam gets like this. I know why she's mad at me, but I'm not sure what she wants me to say.

CHRISTIAN: are you looking for an apology??

SAM: YES, genius!!!

CHRISTIAN: fine, i'm sorry. i swear i didn't mean to screw up the end of the play. i was just distracted

SAM: Yeah, I could tell

CHRISTIAN: to be fair, you call me dum-dum all the time. it's not totally my fault

SAM: DUMB, yes. DUM-DUM?? Come on

"Christian?"

I almost jump out of my chair. Mr. Hernandez is staring at me, and so is the rest of the class. How long has he been calling my name?

I swallow. "Yes, sir?"

"Are you still with us?"

"Yes, sir."

He frowns at me, and I can tell he's debating whether to make me answer a question as punishment for being distracted. I have no clue where we are, and that definitely won't end well. I try to give him my most sincere expression.

I think it works, because he looks at me for a few more seconds before turning back to the projector. Relieved, I settle back in my seat but put my phone away in my bag. Sam is going to keep texting me, but it'll be the same thing over and over again. I've got more important things to think about right now.

In the halls between classes, I scan every face. I even consider taking the long route to my next class, just in case I catch a glimpse of Mystery Girl somewhere along the way, but that makes me feel like a creep. So I decide against it. As it turns out, the detour wasn't necessary. Just as I reach the door to US History, I see a flash of long brown hair from two doors down.

I turn around so fast my bag nearly flies off my shoulder. There—she's got her back to me. I see her for only a second as she walks through the door, but I know it's her. She's wearing a loose plaid button-up and dark jeans, and her head is down.

Without thinking, I drop my stuff on the floor of the hallway and make my way over to the classroom. It's AP British Lit—a class I've never taken and probably never will. Mystery Girl moves to sit near the front, already pulling out some books.

I grab the arm of another kid as he pushes past me into the room. "Who's that?"

He yanks out of my grip, looking offended. "Who?"

"That girl. Brown hair, two rows back."

The kid glances from her to me, frowning. "You mean Ros?"

And just like that, I know who she is. That's Rosalyn Shew. Without another word, I duck out of the doorway and retrieve

40

my backpack before heading into US History, managing to make it to my seat seconds before the bell rings.

Ros is easily one of the smartest kids at Northeastern. She's got a crazy-high GPA, and she's on the debate team, writes for a local magazine, and takes more AP classes in one semester than I've taken in my entire high school career. I'm pretty sure her dad's a teacher at a nearby college, too. Maybe that's where she gets it from. I've never actually had a conversation with her, and until now, I wouldn't have been able to even put a face to her name. But from what I've heard, she can be pretty cold. I've never seen her hanging out with any other guys (or *girls*, either, because if there's anything I've learned from Sam, it's that girls who like girls always wear plaid), and I don't think she's ever dated anyone at Northeastern. Does that make my chances better or worse?

I fish my phone out of my backpack again. Surprisingly, there are no new text messages from Sam. Maybe she's decided to give me the silent treatment for the rest of the day. I pull up Instagram and try searching Ros's name to see if anything comes up. I get nothing. I try her full name, then a combination of "Ros" and "Shew," and even "Shrew," in case the nickname I've heard tossed around about her is actually something she goes by. Still nothing. Maybe she doesn't even have an account. Is she on Facebook?

I actually have to go so far as to redownload the Facebook app and then log back in, but once I do, I don't find any results there, either. When it comes to the internet, this girl pretty much doesn't exist. I flip back to my messages.

CHRISTIAN: hey sam

CHRISTIAN: hypothetically, if i said i had a crush on someone who's completely out of my league, what would i have to do to get her to like me?

Sam responds almost immediately.

SAM: Please tell me you're not talking about the lollipop girl from the other night

CHRISTIAN: maybe i am. so what?

SAM: 🚫🚫 No way. NOT HAPPENING.

CHRISTIAN: seriously? i said i was sorry!!

She doesn't answer for a while, and I decide she's not going to, throwing my phone back into my bag with a sigh.

For the rest of class, I do my best to focus. History is actually one of my better subjects, and unlike most teachers, this one does her best to make it interesting. We're starting to cover the 1940s now, but it's hard to focus on a lecture about the Zoot Suit Riots when my mind is floating somewhere two doors down the hall.

Jesus, Ros Shew. Of all the girls I could have fallen for. And after just a few seconds! That's a record, even for me.

How do you talk to smart girls?

My first instinct is to try all the stuff that used to work on Sam, like the usual flirting and complimenting her outfit, but somehow I don't think that would go over well. Sam is really smart—witty, practical, always thinking three steps ahead, and good with people in general. She *likes* talking about little things like that. Ros seems like she'd be more into deep conversations, and based on what I've heard about her, she's not easy to talk to. I'd have to be on her level, and brainwise, she is completely out of my league. How do I even compete with that?

Catch up to her after class. Ask her what books she's reading. Maybe it's something we've covered in English, too? If it's anything other than *The Great Gatsby*, I'm pretty sure I'm screwed.

Jesus. Why am I so useless at stuff like this?

To be honest, it's not like I've had that much experience. Sam was my first real girlfriend. Anything before that was just the usual middle school crush thing—sure, you called it "dating," but it didn't really count.

I've never felt like this about *any* girl before. Not even Sam. I thought she was cute and everything, but it wasn't until she started flirting with *me* that I actually started catching feelings. After that, I let her take the lead, happy to follow wherever she went, until eventually she told me she didn't want me following her around anymore. But even then, Sam knew how to break up without making me feel bad about it. It's the reason we're still good friends almost seven months later.

What's bothering me the most, though, is why these feelings came on so suddenly. Like I said, I've seen Ros around before, even if I didn't know who she was. Sure, she's cute, but why wouldn't I have noticed that earlier? Maybe it was something about the stage fright that messed with me. Sam's told me about "showmances" before: when you get feelings for a character mixed up with the actor who's playing them, and then suddenly you've got a crush on your costar. But Ros wasn't my costar: She was just some girl in the audience who happened to eat a piece of candy at the exact right time to make me completely lose my cool.

The bell for the end of class takes me by surprise. As everyone else starts to pack up their stuff, I throw my notebook into my bag and make a beeline for the door. If I want to catch Ros before she leaves, I need to be out there early.

I'm one of the first into the hall. As other students start to file past me, I keep my eyes fixed on the door to AP British Lit.

Somebody bumps into me from behind, and I nearly trip. "Watch out, Powell!"

It's Adam, one of the midfielders on the soccer team. I shoot him a distracted smile. "Sorry, man."

"What are you doing just standing in the middle of the hall?"

"Nothing. Just waiting for somebody."

He seems like he wants to push it, but he apparently decides otherwise and shakes his head before leaving me alone. Relieved, I turn back to face the door—and I see her.

Ros is standing in the doorway of AP British Lit, digging around for something in her backpack. Her eyebrows are creased together in a frown, and she bites her lip slightly, like she's trying to concentrate. My feet are frozen to the linoleum.

Then she looks up, and my heart actually skips a beat. I didn't think it could do that outside of movies. But I don't give it much more thought than that, because I've finally realized something. Her eyes. *That's* why I fell for her so fast. The times I've seen her in the past, she was always walking around with her head stuck in a book, or with her hair hiding most of her face. She doesn't seem like the type to make eye contact much. We've never had a reason to interact before now, so why would she look at me?

But on Friday, at Flannery's, I was the sole focus of her attention. I finally noticed that her eyes are a sharp grayish blue, which makes her dark hair even more striking. There are slight shadows underneath them, like maybe she stays up too late reading or working on assignments. Every single point in her freakishly high IQ is visible in those eyes. I never really got to see them before, never got to really study the depth of them. But that's all changed, because I've seen it now. Now I know what it feels like when she looks at me.

And it's right then, after a good fifteen solid seconds of staring, that I realize she's staring right back.

ROS

THE LAST THING I WANT ON MY WAY OUT OF AP
British Lit is to be stared at by one of the school's soccer stars. I
kind of knew it was coming after Darius came into class earlier
and asked me, "What's up with you and Powell?"

I looked at him like he was out of his mind, so he continued,
"Christian! You know, the soccer player. He just asked me who
you were. Grabbed my arm and everything."

I have no idea why Christian would ask about me. From the
way Darius described it, their conversation was kind of hostile,
so to be honest, I'm expecting some stereotypical jock bully routine. As he starts making his way across the hall toward me, I
wonder for a second if it might be because of the play. Did he
read my review? Is he pissed about what I wrote?

But instead of pushing me into a locker or something, he gets within a few feet of me and stops, staring again. He almost looks nervous. "Hi," he says.

"Hi," I echo.

"I saw you at the play the other night." He jerks his head to the side, like "the other night" is standing just to his left. "What did you think?"

So he hasn't read the review. I feel a little relieved. This isn't going to be the confrontation I thought it would be. But then, what *does* he want?

"It was . . . well produced," I say carefully. "You guys clearly put a lot of work into it."

He grins. "Thanks. Yeah, Sam worked really hard." He almost flinches, like he said something he didn't mean to, and I realize it's because he mentioned his ex-girlfriend. "But, uhh . . . no. That's not what I wanted to talk about. I've seen you around school before, but I realized we never got a chance to talk before this. Um—"

I glance down at my phone. My next class is all the way across the school, and if I don't leave this conversation soon, I'm going to be late.

"Sorry, but is this going somewhere?"

That pulls him up short. "What?"

"Are you trying to ask me something, or are you just making conversation, because I have a class to get to, and—"

"No!" He puts out a hand, like he's going to physically stop me from leaving. "Sorry. I'm—I saw you at the play and thought you looked familiar but realized I didn't know anything about you, and I was thinking, maybe—"

Whatever else he's saying dissolves into white noise as I realize what's going on.

Oh God.

He's trying to ask me out.

I'm not bragging when I say this has happened several times before. I guess quiet, smart girls are some people's "type," and since that's my title at Northeastern, more than a few people have done the same thing this guy is attempting right now. It's awkward and uncomfortable every single time, mostly because these people come at me with an opinion about the kind of person they *think* I am. They see quiet, they see smart, they see bookish, and that's about it. No attempts to dig further than that before trying to relate to me, like maybe the fact that they read half of *Jane Eyre* one time is supposed to impress me.

I hate it.

This guy seems more genuine than the others, but it doesn't change the fact that the approach is the same. Besides, he's the school sweetheart: athletic, popular, loved by everyone. He could get any girl he wanted. He dated Sam Dickson, for God's sake. He doesn't actually want me. He wants the *idea* of me, and that's not something I'm willing to be. Not for him. Not for anyone.

Calmly, I take one step forward and look him in the eye. He seems a little taken aback by my change in attitude, and I use that to my advantage.

"What's my name?"

"Huh?"

"My full name."

"R-Rosalyn Shew?"

"Okay. And my favorite movie?"

"I—"

"How about what kind of music I like to listen to? How about my favorite book?"

This guy couldn't look more surprised if I'd slapped him across the face. He stares at me, mouth open, blinking over and over and looking like a fish. I don't think he has any comebacks prepared, so instead, I plow on. "No offense, Christian, but you don't actually know anything about me. You know my name, you know I was at the play, and that's pretty much it. You might be able to start friendships like that, but I can't. Sorry."

He still doesn't say anything, and to avoid having to make more conversation, I adjust my bag on my shoulders and walk away as fast as I can. It's not until I'm around the corner and out of sight that I let my posture relax some and realize that my heart is pounding.

Why? I didn't *want* him to ask me out. I've never felt the urge to date anybody, much less had the time for it. That hasn't changed. It's the nervousness, I decide. I thought he was going to harass me about the play at first. I guess the adrenaline of that is starting to wear off.

The warning bell rings, and I quicken my steps. This isn't worth thinking about. Not right now. If there's one thing I promised myself I'd never do, it was let thoughts of a boy distract me from more important things. I've kept that promise my whole life so far, and today is most definitely not the day to break it.

8

SAM

"YOU *HAVE* TO HELP ME," CHRISTIAN SAYS.

There's a reason he's the golden boy at Northeastern: As Nana would say, he's about as all-American as apple pie, with a great smile and killer jawline just to make things worse. He's never been great with words, but he doesn't need to be. One flash of that blinding smile and everyone falls in love with him. Right now, he's employing his second-most-convincing tactic—big kicked-puppy eyes and a desperate look on his face.

I'm chatting at my locker with a girl from one of my classes when he walks up. I glare at him for a second before I turn back to her, saying, "Talk to you later, Hannah. Sounds like this is important."

She gives me a nod and a wave as she heads off, and then I'm left with Christian and his problems.

"I don't actually *have* to help you with anything, Christian," I say, avoiding eye contact as I slam my locker door shut. "Remember how I gave you a part in my play because I thought it would look good on your college applications?"

"But I figured out who that girl was," he insists. "That girl at the show, the one I—"

"I know who it was. Ros Shew. She writes for the arts magazine."

Christian stops short, looking surprised. "Yeah. That's the one. You know her?"

I can't help laughing. "No, but she knows me." The magazine is open on top of one of my binders, the page already dogeared, so I thrust it at him. "Or she thinks she does."

He gawks at the article for a second, not even reading it, before he registers what it is. Then his eyes go wide. "Oh."

"Yeah, *oh*." I shove the rest of the books into my bag. "She didn't have anything bad to say about your performance, if that's what you're worried about. Even called you 'fairly charming' once."

"Really?"

"Christian!"

"Sorry, I know, not the point." He looks down at the article, shaking his head. "I didn't know she was a critic, Sam, I swear. But I've been trying to figure out who she was all weekend, and—"

"I'm not blind, Christian. I saw you making goo-goo eyes at her when you were supposed to be saying the lines *I* wrote. I dated you for five months—I know what your 'I've fallen and I can't get up' face looks like."

He blushes to the roots of his hair. "I blew it, Sam. I tried to talk to her just now, and I completely froze up. She was pissed. How do I fix it?"

"You don't. She's not worth the effort."

"But you're so good at talking to people. There's gotta be something—"

"There are literally a hundred other girls who would gladly jump on you *right now*, and you want to flirt with The Shrew? She's the ultimate ice queen. There's no getting on her good side, I promise you."

He flashes me the kicked-puppy look again. "I know, but I can't help it. You've *seen* her, right?"

I have. Tall, willowy, long brown hair with the perfect amount of wave in it, big gray-blue eyes, perfect eyebrows that I *know* are natural, which somehow makes it worse. The kind of girl who manages to look beautiful and intimidating without having to try. She could probably date anybody at this school if she wanted to, but the vibe she gives off is that none of us are even close to being worthy. She'd never give Christian the time of day.

Above us, the warning bell rings. I shake my head. "Forget it, Christian. I'm not helping you flirt with the girl that just canned my play. Give yourself some time to cool off. You'll get over her."

"I've had all weekend to cool off, and it hasn't worked so far. Please, Sam?"

He *really* needs to stop looking so pitiful. When he gets like this, there's almost nothing I can do to convince him otherwise, and picking this fight now will make both of us late to class. I sling my bag over one shoulder. "I will *think* about it," I say sternly, trying to ignore the way his face lights up when I do. "That's all I can promise."

"You're my hero." He slaps me on the back like I'm one of his soccer buddies. "I owe you a milkshake."

"If I even consider doing this, you're gonna owe me more than one, Christian Powell."

I get another one of his all-star grins before he bounds off down the hallway, looking like he won the lottery. I shake my head and stuff the rolled-up magazine into my back pocket, navigating back into the crowd of latecomers heading for class, and feeling that by admitting I'd think about it, I've already promised too much.

The library is always quiet during last period. I like it better that way: The lack of activity makes it easier to focus, and God knows I need that. Choosing Latin for my foreign-language credit was obviously a mistake. I just wanted to take something that sounded interesting, but now it's my second semester and already too late to turn back. It's either stick it out or admit defeat and take another two semesters of French or something and risk not graduating on time. That's not in the plan. I have things to do with my life other than summer school. As Julius Caesar probably said at some point, *semper ad meliora*—always toward better things.

I hope that's what that means. I don't remember doing very well on the last test.

Since this school doesn't have the budget or the space for an actual Latin class, I take my course online in the library's computer lab. Only a few other students are in there when I show up, and I choose a computer off to the side, hoping for some privacy. I am *not* in the mood to talk to anyone right now. I resist the urge to pull the article back out and read it again. All the important parts are burned into my memory now, anyway. I try to force them into the background as I log on to the computer and boot up the next lesson. Present perfect tense. I don't know what makes it *perfect*, but I'm pretty sure I'm not going to enjoy it either way.

True to my earlier suspicion, present perfect tense is a slog. I spend most of the period staring at the screen, underlining the same notes over and over in the hopes that they'll actually start making sense. I get distracted by Instagram a couple of times, and in the end, I make it maybe halfway through the lesson before the bell is about to ring. Angrily, I start to put my notes away. Did Ros write that review *knowing* I'd see it? That seems like the kind of thing she'd do. Why else would she be so needlessly critical?

> The ideals of the main character are overly romanticized, almost to the point of being saccharine. Moments meant to be dramatic or woo the audience ultimately fell flat, simply because we could see the beats coming from a mile away. For a self-proclaimed autobiographical work, I find it hard to believe that parts of *So Long, Toledo!* aren't at least a little bit fake.

The magazine is burning a hole in my backpack. What does Ros "The Shrew" Shew, ice queen extraordinaire, know about romanticism? For that matter, what does she know about my *life*?

I will never, ever admit it, but Ros intimidates me a little. She's pretty, smart, and talented enough to be really well liked, if she wanted. I know at least three guys and one or two girls who have fallen hard for her over the last three years, not counting Christian, but she never even gave them a chance. Come to think of it, I don't think I've ever heard of her dating *anyone*. She'd rather sit in a corner reading instead of talk to people. Does she care about any of this? The idea of someone being so oblivious about how other people see them—it kind of creeps me out.

A loud beep goes off as the intercom crackles to life. The voice of Mrs. Reagan, the vice principal, rasps through the old speakers.

"Good afternoon, Northeastern! I know you're all eager to get home, but before the final bell rings, we have just a few quick announcements. First up, tickets for the underclassmen's Winter Formal will go on sale this Friday during lunch. If you're looking to go, swing by the ticket table outside the cafeteria."

I roll my eyes. Nobody goes to the Winter Formal. I tried it freshman year, but there were maybe twenty other students. And the DJ didn't play anything that came out later than 2006. I'll save my money for junior prom.

"Second, after reviewing your entries, the faculty has selected a student keynote speaker for this year's Bellerose Assembly."

That gets my attention. The Bellerose Assembly is an event named after an old, prestigious donor to Northeastern from about ten years ago. Apparently, some alum got so rich they decided they wanted us to have an assembly named after them. It gets us out of class early for a day in late April right after spring break. There's a school-wide assembly and invited speakers, and we all welcome the brief break from actual schoolwork as things ramp up before finals. The most important part to me, though, is the position of student keynote speaker. Overachievers like me submit a proposal for speaker, suggesting an act or presentation to be performed at the Bellerose Assembly under whatever theme the faculty has decided on. This year, the theme was "What does 'love' mean to you?" It's a surprisingly complicated process, involving a video submission where you talk about the prompt and your plans for the presentation. More than a few people duke it out for the position every year—mostly because it looks good on college applications—but for some of us, it's also another method of creative expression. There's no better way to make a statement or form a reputation than by making the entire school watch you put on an act. I worked on my submission for weeks. It's meant to be a speech about the different kinds of love and their examples in media, but it reads like a monologue. A one-woman show about love and how universal it is in the human experience. Not going to lie, I'm really proud of it.

"We had a lot of really fantastic entries this year," Mrs. Reagan continues. "And I want to congratulate all of you on your hard work. However, there can only be one winner, and this year the honor of student keynote speaker at the Bellerose Assembly goes to . . . Rosalyn Shew!"

I think my jaw might have actually hit the floor.

Ros?

She was in the running for Bellerose speaker? Miss "overly romanticized, saccharine" Shew? There's no way.

Mrs. Reagan is still talking. "I know I speak for the rest of the faculty when I say that we can't wait to see her final presentation, and we hope you'll give her all your support in the days leading up to it. That's all the announcements we have for this afternoon. Make it a great day, and we'll see you back here first thing tomorrow!"

The bell rings, and the few other students still in the computer lab start making for the exit. I'm glued to my chair, staring into space as I process what just happened. Ros beat me. Beat *me*. What could she possibly have shown the faculty that made them think she was the right person for the job?

No. She doesn't get to win. She tore apart my play, called it sentimental and fake, and now she gets the Bellerose speaker position over me? To make a speech about *love*? Not if I can help it. I may not be able to change the faculty's decision, but there is still something I can do.

My phone is in my hand as I walk out the front entrance, already deep in conversation with Christian.

SAM: Still want my help with ice queen?
CHRISTIAN: yes!! i seriously owe you one, sam 🤜
SAM: Thank me later. Call me once you're done with practice today. We've got a LOT of planning to do

My mind is already spinning, running through different tactics and game plans that might give Christian a chance. To date, I've convinced over thirty guys that I'm the girl of their dreams without ever once seeing them in person. I snagged every eligible bachelor in this school and left them in my dust. I am *that* good at persuading people to fall in love with me. I know what it looks like, sounds like, when somebody is so head-over-heels for you that they can't think straight. I'm practically an authority at this point. As far as I know, Ros has never been on a date with *anyone* before—at least, not at Northeastern. But no, she called the romance in my play "fake," and now she gets the chance to prove that she knows better than me.

Well, I'm nothing if not competitive.

Christian wants Ros so bad? Fine. I'll make him irresistible. I'll make him the man of her *Pride and Prejudice* dreams. I'll play her like every guy I've collected numbers from online. She might think she's above it all, that she's better than the rest of us for whatever reason, but I know she isn't.

I'll prove it.

ROS

I WANT TO START WORKING ON MY BELLEROSE project as soon as I get home. There's no real reason to, at least not this early—I've got a little over three months before the actual assembly, and it's not that complicated—but I'm feeling inspired, and I need to take advantage of that whenever it appears. That, and I can't get Christian's disappointed face out of my head.

Some mail is scattered on the entryway floor in front of the mail slot, so I scoop it up and look through it as I make my way to my room. A newsletter from Dad's school, junk mail for some car dealership, and a postcard from Aunt Rhetta. Looks like she's in Portugal this time. I don't get to see her very often, not since she moved across the country to Seattle, but she still likes to send Dad and me little letters every now and then, especially when she leaves on one of her adventures.

Technically speaking, Rhetta isn't actually my aunt. We're not even blood-related. But she was Dad and Charles's surrogate, and she gave birth to me after my dads got the other half of my DNA from an anonymous donor. She's an old-school hippie, born slightly too late for the actual Flower Power decade. She was also the only person who agreed to be a surrogate for two gay men in the early 2000s in Worcester, so she and Dad have been friends ever since.

I set the mail down on the kitchen counter and head up the stairs to my room. It's been a while since I practiced my violin, and the strings are, understandably, pretty out of tune. For a second, I consider leaving it that way. Wouldn't the dissonance of playing a song a little off-key be more jarring than intentionally playing wrong notes? But in the end, I decide against it. That would just sound like I'm a bad violinist, and "bad" is definitely not what I'm going for.

This year's prompt for the Bellerose presentation was "What does 'love' mean to you?" The first things that came to mind were all the stuff I'm used to hearing about, in books or plays or movies: Romeo seeing Juliet across a crowded ballroom, Lancelot and Guinevere meeting in secret, Elizabeth and Mr. Darcy admitting their feelings. Problem is, that kind of view of love makes me want to throw up. Real life doesn't work like that. Romantic love shouldn't be the be-all, end-all of everyone's existence, but so many people seem to think it is.

The story I included in my proposal was the real-life story

of Charles and Hector Shew, also known as my dads. Charles has been dead since I was three years old, but as far as dads go, Hector is pretty great. His and Charles's relationship definitely wasn't the storybook kind, but at least they were in love when it ended. That's more than I can say for a lot of people.

I've been thinking about that a lot lately, especially since my support group meeting this weekend. My situation might not exactly be ideal, but it's better than some of the other stories I've heard—like one kid whose parents used an American surrogate before taking him to live in France. Apparently, it caused problems with his citizenship, and now it means he might not be able to go to college here. The stress of it even caused his parents to get divorced. How am I supposed to share after something like *that* when my own story sounds so selfish in comparison: *Hi, my name's Ros, and I still have one really great dad, but sometimes I'm sad because I don't look like him?*

In her office, after I found out I won the speaker position today, Mrs. Reagan gushed over how "romantic" the story was, how she cried at her desk on a Thursday morning thanks to my "brilliantly moving" story. Thing is, that wasn't the point. The point was to show that sometimes love is the worst thing that can happen to a person, that the happily ever after you see on-screen is never the real end. It isn't the end until both people involved are dead, and usually, it isn't under very happy circumstances. Call me a downer, but it's the truth. I don't need to look any further than the people in my own life to see it.

Once the violin is tuned, I pick up the bow and start going through some basic warm-ups. The strings squeak a little, and my dexterity isn't as good as it used to be. Still, if I start practicing now, it should be perfect by the time I actually have to present.

My plan for the presentation is to interview my dad, have him tell his story in his own words while I film it. On the day of the presentation, I'll stand onstage next to the projector and, while the interview plays, I'll accompany it on my violin. I'll take a bunch of traditionally romantic songs and tweak them just slightly so that every so often, you're struck by the wrongness of it all. Maybe some notes don't resolve quite like they should. Maybe the song slips into a minor key. Maybe it plays a little too fast. Either way, I don't want people to be sentimental when they watch my presentation. I want them to be sad or angry. I want them to see the unfairness of it all.

As I start to play, my mind wanders to this past weekend—to the show, writing my review, and then the support group meeting on Saturday. The lady who runs the meetings, a painfully chipper twentysomething named May, led a discussion about "community" and what that means to kids like us with a less-than-typical relationship to our biological families. "You have the unique opportunity," she said, "to really examine what it means to be a family. In the same way your parents chose how to have you, you have the chance to make your own community by *choice*, instead of just being connected by blood."

I almost laughed out loud at that. What was the point of *choosing* more people to let in? You don't always get to keep the ones you were born with. Why take that chance with anybody else?

Again, I see Christian's disappointed face, the shock on it as I walked away. My fingers slip on the strings, and the violin lets out an off-key squeak that makes me cringe. It takes a lot of self-control not to throw the violin to the side. I need this guy out of my head. I refuse to feel bad for him. He came up to me with some half-baked idea of who he thought I was and just expected me to fall for him like everybody else. Talk about "finding a community." Christian Powell makes himself a community wherever he goes. He's universally loved, without even trying. He never has to feel alone.

Oh God, am I *jealous* of him?

Maybe I am. It's all well and good to talk about finding a community, but that requires meeting people you can relate to. People who share your culture, your interests, your values. And to find people with those same things, you have to actually know what your own culture, interests, and values are.

Dad is half Dominican. You can see it in his warm skin, his brown eyes. Charles came from a long line of Jewish New Yorkers and was an only child. Aunt Rhetta traces her Dutch heritage all the way back to the 1800s. The woman who donated the egg that made me must have had blue eyes, and unless something completely insane happens, that's probably the only thing I'll ever know about her. Dad has always worked really hard to make me feel included at family dinners and events, and all the relatives on his side love me to death, but that doesn't change the fact that despite all of it, I still feel like I'm out of place.

I don't speak Spanish. I've never been to temple or had a bat mitzvah. I have no idea if I'm Dutch—my blue eyes could be Swedish, or English, or German. What am I, other than just . . . Ros? Some days, that feels like it should be enough.

Other days, like today, I'm not so sure.

I put the violin under my chin again, ignoring the fact that my hands suddenly feel shaky. *Do what you've always done, Ros. Focus. Focus on something else. Maybe this time it'll stick.*

I play the songs again, over and over, and the notes feel all wrong and shaky, but not in the way I want them to.

10

CHRISTIAN

I'M DEFINITELY NOT BRINGING MY BEST GAME TO practice today.

Coach has us running drills on the indoor field while the weather is still cold. Northeastern has a football team, too, but it hasn't been a contender in years. The soccer team is another story, though. We're one of the best teams in the state, and so the school district always makes sure a little more money comes our way. Even though it's technically the off-season, Coach Branson likes to make sure we stay sharp with regular practices and workouts. He's been coaching the team to victory for almost a decade, and he's not about to let us slip under his watch.

Which is maybe why I end up running a couple of extra laps as punishment for being distracted. Monty notices it, too; he keeps shooting me weird looks while we run drills or whenever I flub a pass that should have gone straight to him. Eventually, when Coach stops us for a break, Monty makes his way over to me and bumps me in the shoulder. "Where's your head today, man?"

Monty and I have been friends since elementary school. He's seen all my awkward phases and probably knows me better than anybody. As the other team forward, he's had my back for years, and off the field is no different. He was there for the middle school not-quite-girlfriends, for the bad days after Will left, for the breakup with Sam. I was also one of the first people he came out to, apart from his dad. I won't say I was a perfect ally right away, and even though he didn't change his pronouns, the concept of someone being nonbinary took some explaining. But in the end, Monty was still Monty, and nothing about the two of us had to change. And if any of the guys on the soccer team act weird about it, well—he knows I've got his back, too.

I shake my head at him, plopping down on the Astroturf with my water bottle. "Sorry, Monty. Just somewhere else."

"Yeah? Well, Adam doesn't need any more excuses to steal your spot, so maybe focus before he starts trying to convince Coach you're losing your edge."

I glance across the field. Adam is the team's best midfielder, but it's common knowledge that he wants one of the forward spots. We compete for it each year at tryouts, and I get the position every time. He must see us as rivals, but honestly, I couldn't care less.

I grumble as much under my breath, and Monty sits down

and bumps me again. "You're such a pushover, Chris. Would it kill you to fight for anything once in a while?"

"I'm working on it."

"Oh?" Monty cocks his head at me, curly black hair flopping to one side. "Do tell."

I self-consciously rub at the back of my neck, where I can feel myself starting to blush. "I met this girl the other day, at Sam's play. I tried talking to her today, but I think I blew it."

"Who was it?"

"Do you know Ros Shew?"

"*Ros?*" Monty actually leans back, staring at me in shock. "Oh, you are so far out of your depth, man."

"What? Why?"

"She's just a loner, that's it. Doesn't really talk much, and anyone who tries hitting on her gets completely shut down."

"Yeah, I figured that last part out, actually," I say with as much sarcasm as I can.

"But you're not giving up?" Monty prompts me.

"No. Sam said she has a plan or something to help me out."

Monty puts a hand over his face. "Oh my God. You asked Sam for help?"

"Why wouldn't I? She's smart, and she knows how to make people talk to her. If anyone could give me advice on this kind of thing, it's her."

"And you don't think it's a little weird to ask for dating help from your ex?"

I bite my lip. "Honestly? I don't. We work better as friends anyway, and she agreed to this."

"I'll say it again: You are so far out of your depth."

Now it's my turn to shove him. "Shut up."

Monty just laughs. "So what is this amazing master plan Sam's cooking up?"

"I don't know yet. She said we should talk after practice to start getting some ideas. Knowing her, it'll be way more involved than I want it to be."

"Yeah, but you asked her for help, so now you have to deal with it. Who knows? Maybe she actually *can* help you melt Northeastern's ice queen."

Coach Branson blows his whistle, and everybody jumps to their feet. "Do you really think someone like Ros wouldn't be into me?" I ask as we make our way back onto the field.

"I don't think there's anyone in the world who wouldn't be into you once they got to know you, Chris." Monty picks up one of the practice soccer balls and balances it on the instep of his shoe before kicking it toward me. I have to catch it quick, before it completely brains me. "Just make sure it's still *you* Ros is talking to by the time Sam's had her fun."

SAM

PHASE ONE OF MY PLAN IS GOING TO INVOLVE some heavy-duty research. Christian said he couldn't find any evidence of Ros online, but he's an amateur-level internet stalker. To find someone *this* elusive, you need the work of an expert.

Back home, at my desk with a fresh cup of Nana's decaf coffee, I plug my phone in to charge and begin the difficult task of locating Rosalyn Shew. Like Christian said, she's nowhere on Facebook. Not that I expected her to be there anyway: Someone as private as her doesn't seem like the type to put personal life updates on social media.

Instead, I focus my search on Twitter and Instagram. People can use any sort of username they want on either site, so it becomes a lot harder to identify people, but I'm not an expert for nothing. When searches for her full name come up empty, I try a couple of test usernames I think might suit her; "tamingoftheshew" is my personal favorite, but that doesn't turn up anything. Even a generic Google search brings up little information. Either I'm incredibly unlucky or this girl is so hipster that she avoids social media altogether. That could kill this little plan before it even starts.

I switch tactics and look for things she might be involved in. I know she's on the debate team, and the school-run Twitter posts about those tournaments every so often, but they don't go as far as tagging their own students, because of course they don't. Just like in real life, it doesn't look like I can rely on Northeastern for very much help in this virtual quest.

Ironically enough, *Art Pulse* is the thing that finally gives me a break. It has a Twitter and an Instagram, and both are fairly active. The Twitter account seems mostly made up of links to articles or rants about how gentrification is killing graffiti culture (which is true, but why does everything have to be in all caps?), but as I scroll my way back through old Instagram posts, I strike gold—a sepia-toned photo of an empty theater, lit only by one dim spotlight that casts long shadows along the rows of seats. The description is some quote from a famous playwright about the nature of theater, but underneath that is a photo credit and link: *@rosshewphotography*.

My heart is hammering. *Yes!* That has to be her. What are the chances that another person with the name Ros Shew also works for *Art Pulse*? This person doesn't have an especially big following, but if it's who I think it is, then eight hundred followers isn't bad.

Not as good as my 15K, but still.

I scroll through the photos to see if I can get a better idea of the person running the account. It's got some of the usual "photography" stuff—landscape shots, close-ups of autumn leaves, an artistically styled picture of a latte—but some of the stuff on here is actually surprising. There are candids of people in real, heartwarming moments, like a public proposal with the guy already down on one knee. Even the typical stuff is shot from an odd angle or an interesting point of focus, almost like the photographer wants you to look at this random thing in a completely different light, like maybe there's something important about it that you've missed, and they're determined to show it to you.

I feel a smile start to creep across my face. That's *definitely* Ros.

I quickly shoot off a text message to Christian.

SAM: What's your insta password?
CHRISTIAN: why?
SAM: Just give it, dummy 😤

He responds a couple of minutes later, and once I've logged in under his account, I take a second to scroll through his profile. Just as I remembered, it is . . . comically bad. It's mostly awkward selfies, blurry stills of soccer fields, or pictures of his dog with way too many filters slapped over them. It's very "Christian," but it isn't interesting. Not interesting enough to make a hard-core, intellectual photographer type want to talk to him. This needs to change.

SAM: Your account is NASTY 😖

CHRISTIAN: at least there aren't half naked pictures of me all over the place, like some people

SAM: That was a sports bra, you chauvinist

SAM: We're hanging out tomorrow after school. You need an online makeover

CHRISTIAN: does that mean you found her??

SAM: You're welcome 😏

CHRISTIAN: you're a wizard, sam

SAM: A half-naked wizard, yes

CHRISTIAN: sorry about that . . .

SAM: Shut up. Just take a half-decent picture of yourself tonight and all will be forgiven. I can't be expected to do ALL the work myself

CHRISTIAN: 👍 you got it

I put the phone down, taking a sip of my now-lukewarm decaf. This project is shaping up to be one of the most complicated plans ever. But if it works? Christian will be thrilled, and I'll know once and for all that I'm better than that review. Besides, Ros would have to be the coldest person on Planet Earth not to be interested in a guy like Christian.

And more important, she'd have to be a robot to ignore the kind of flirting I'll be throwing her way. With Christian's all-American charm and my perfect catfishing record, Rosalyn Shew doesn't stand a chance.

12

CHRISTIAN

"IF YOU MOVE AGAIN, I'M ACTUALLY GOING TO kill you," Sam growls.

I shoot her a nasty look. "I'm *exhausted*, Sam. Can we at least take a break?"

"Fine, ten minutes."

Relieved, I take a few steps backward and collapse onto my bed. The sheets are so tightly stretched after Sam took it upon herself to straighten up my room that I bounce a little more than I was expecting.

Sam scoffs. "So dramatic."

"It's been hours!"

It really has. I didn't have practice after school today, so Sam insisted on meeting up with me after class for a "social media makeover." She explained how she found Ros's Instagram and how we'd have to make my profile interesting enough for Ros to talk to me after the disaster of a first impression I made. It started with deleting some of my older posts, like pictures of me with random girls or other things Sam deemed too bad to keep ("We get it, you play soccer!"), and now we're on the makeover part. So far, I've changed shirts at least six times, to make it look like all these photos were taken on different days. It's almost five PM, and I've spent every spare minute since getting out of class being lectured about using natural lighting, the most flattering angles, and smiling like I actually mean it.

My cheeks hurt. Smiling is the *last* thing I want to do right now.

Yankee jumps up onto the bed next to me and licks my face. "We've got to have enough pictures by now," I say as I fight him off.

Sam shakes her head. "Not yet. I need some more variety to work with. This has to look like a natural transition, not like you suddenly got good at Instagram. That would be too suspicious."

"You're putting way too much thought into this."

"I'm not, Christian! People actually notice these things. Trust me here. I'm making changes for the better."

Yankee is determined to suffocate me, so I sit up a bit. "But none of this feels like me, you know? I don't normally put this much work into stuff like pictures or the way I look. I'm not that kind of person. If I spend time with Ros, she'll figure that out."

"That's why I'm being smart about it." Sam sits on the other side of the bed, distracting Yankee for a moment. She scratches his head, her eyes glued to the phone in her other hand as she scrolls through the photos we've taken. "I'm not going to try to make you into a completely different person, I promise. If you want this thing to last, then it has to still be familiar. I'm taking the pieces that are great about you and making them pop. All this is still you. Only better."

"Good to know that I'm the garbage version."

Now it's Sam's turn to shoot me a dirty look. "I can leave, Powell."

I grin at her. "You wouldn't. You're too invested now."

She flops down on the bed, too, letting the phone bounce away. "I hate that you know that."

I stare at her for a second, fighting with a question that's been bugging me for the past couple of days. "Sam?"

"Hmm."

"Why *did* you agree to help me? You were so pissed off when I asked you at first, but now you're treating this like some test you need to pass. What changed your mind?"

Sam stills, biting her lip. I can see something working behind her eyes, something I've seen in her before but she's never admitted to.

"The Bellerose Assembly announcement," she says finally. "Ros got the spot as the student keynote speaker. After all the things she said about my play being too sweet and unrealistic, she gets to be the one to make some sort of statement about what love is really like, as if she actually knows anything. It's not fair."

"So, what? You're trying to get her to date me as revenge?"

She sits up quickly. "No! I have no idea what you see in her,

Christian, because personally, I think she's awful. But I care about you. You asked for help, and that's what I'm here to do. We look out for each other, right?"

She holds out her fist, and after a second or two, I reach out and bump it with my own. That's not exactly an answer, but it's probably the closest thing I'm going to get. "Yeah, we do."

Off to my right, I hear the door creak open. A pair of big blue eyes and a gap-toothed grin peek in at us through the crack. I sigh. "What do you want, Aimee?"

Aimee pushes the door open, hands on her hips, and loudly announces, "Mom sent me up here to make sure you were being *appropriate*!"

I bury my face in one of my pillows with a groan as she and Sam both laugh. "Go away, you pest."

"No, this is perfect." Sam jumps off the bed and crosses the room. Everything goes quiet, and I look up from under the pillow to see her whispering something in my sister's ear. Aimee's eyes flash with little-kid joy, and suddenly she's launching herself at me with a shriek.

I barely have time to throw up my hands in self-defense before she's on me, tiny fingers digging into my ribs and high-pitched laughter ringing in my ears. I jackknife to try to get away, but for a seven-year-old, she's shockingly strong. I'm powerless to resist, and it forces laughter out of me in a shotgun blast.

Yankee decides it's a party and jumps back onto the bed to join in. Now there's nasty dog breath in my face, I'm my sister's tickle hostage, I might be suffocating, and literally nothing about this is funny, but I'm laughing anyway. And if someone asked me right now if I wanted to get away, the answer would definitely be no.

I hear giggling from the doorway. Sam's still standing there, holding up her phone to record this as I suffer. "Help me, you sadist," I wheeze helplessly.

"Absolutely not." She's grinning wider than I've seen in a long time: not her school smile, not the one she puts on to look good in photos, but the real one, the *real* Sam. Even I don't get to see this side of her too often. It's nice. It reminds me what I saw in her in the first place. She shakes her head, leaning against the doorframe and holding her phone out farther. "This is the best footage I've gotten all day."

SAM

WE'RE OFFICIALLY THREE DAYS INTO OPERATION Get Chris His Weird Girlfriend, and I think it's time to attempt first contact. I've been posting the pictures we took on Tuesday steadily over the last few days, and the transition from Christian's painfully plain content to my thirst-trap pics is fairly seamless, if I do say so myself. With any luck, it should make a good enough second impression for Ros to be willing to give him another chance.

> **SAM:** I think it's time, dude
>
> **CHRISTIAN:** wait seriously?? are you sure?
>
> **SAM:** Of course I'm sure. Are you free to chat if I
>   manage to get her number?
>
> **CHRISTIAN:** yeah, i think so

CHRISTIAN: jesus, i'm so nervous

SAM: Don't be. I'll be starting off the conversation, so with any luck, the hardest part will already be out of the way. You've just gotta relax and do everything I tell you

CHRISTIAN: okay

SAM: I'll keep you posted 💋

I've had the script for "Christian's" first interaction with Ros saved since yesterday afternoon, after a stroke of romantic genius hit me during fifth period. All I've got to do is copy and paste that into Instagram, and then everything moves on from there.

I realize my hands are shaking a bit as I open Ros's account to start a private message. Why am *I* nervous? This isn't my first catfishing adventure, and it definitely isn't my first time asking someone out, either. The stakes in this feel different somehow, though. Maybe because I'm not the only one being affected.

Taking a deep breath, I press the SEND button and then put my phone down to keep myself from staring at the message until I start second-guessing myself. My approach is perfect: not too humble, but not too cocky, and perfectly like Christian. He's lucky I know him so well. It's out of my hands now. Either she responds or she doesn't, and no matter what, I can say I've done my best work here.

I don't know much about chess, but I'm pretty sure the side that makes the first move usually has a bigger advantage. I've set my pawn in motion, and now I just have to wait for my opponent to engage.

Here's hoping Ros isn't better at chess than me.

ROS

I don't usually look at my phone while I'm doing homework, but I'm in the middle of an essay for history and I can't remember one of the dates I need. Googling is always faster than trying to look it up in the textbook, so I grab my phone. But once I do, I notice the little notification bubble over the Instagram icon. That's pretty unusual. My notifications are on, but I don't get a lot of hits, and it's usually someone who found my photography account and wants to ask for my rates or something.

Figuring this could be a chance to earn some extra money, I open the app and click on the little speech bubble in the corner. Just like I thought, it's a DM request from an account I don't recognize, but the message isn't the one I was expecting.

> **chrispow2002:** hey! it's Christian, from school. this is Ros, right?

Oh God. First the asking me out on Monday, and now this. Is this happening? Quickly, I type a response.

rosshewphotography: Yes, it is. How did you find this account?

The answer comes a few minutes later.

chrispow2002: i follow art pulse's instagram. saw this account credited for one of their photos, and once i saw the other pictures on here i figured out it must be you

I'm about to respond again, but I notice the little "typing" notification under his name and realize he's got more to say. My heart starts racing. Is he about to chew me out or something? Some guys really don't take well to getting rejected. Maybe I should block him.

Instead of doing that, though, I just stare at the screen until the second message pops up.

chrispow2002: listen, i wanted to say sorry for the other day. i wasn't thinking straight and i kind of cornered you at a weird time between classes. didn't mean to make such an awkward first impression, haha

Oh. I feel some of the tension go out of my shoulders.

chrispow2002: but . . .

And then it ratchets right back up again.

chrispow2002: no offense, but how am i supposed to
know all that stuff you asked if you don't tell me first?
you're not on facebook, and i had to get lucky just to
find this account. plus it doesn't seem like you really
talk to people at school much. was i supposed to
snoop around to find all that stuff out just in case you
asked me? i'm pretty sure i read somewhere that girls
don't like stalkers. what gives?

He's right about a couple of things: He *did* corner me at an
awkward time, and his overall approach wasn't a good one. But
on the other hand, he's also right that I set him up for failure
with those questions. There isn't an easy answer for *why* I did it,
though, because even I'm not sure.

rosshewphotography: Apology accepted. And yeah,
maybe I was a bit unfair. But you caught me off
guard, what was I supposed to do?
chrispow2002: give a guy a chance? i promise i wasn't
trying to catch you off guard on purpose. i just got
nervous

Nervous? Christian Powell doesn't strike me as the kind of
guy who gets nervous. Everything I've ever heard about him says
that he's everybody's favorite person.

rosshewphotography: Why were you nervous?

chrispow2002: do i really have to answer that??

rosshewphotography: You're the one offering apologies here, so yes.

chrispow2002: fine, fine. because I think you're cool

rosshewphotography: . . . I think you've got the wrong person.

chrispow2002: i really don't

rosshewphotography: In what parallel universe does someone like you think I'm cool?

chrispow2002: idk, you just give off a vibe. like you're so smart and put together that nothing ever bothers you

I want to bang my head against a wall. That "vibe" is the exact thing that's gotten me in this situation before. People always assume things about me without bothering to find out if it's true or not. I'm about to tell Christian that exact thing, but I guess he's faster at typing than me, because he beats me to it.

chrispow2002: you're right, okay? i don't actually know you. but i kind of want to. i figured i'd try talking to you to see if you wanted to get to know me too, but i screwed up the first try. i at least wanted to talk to you again just to say sorry, and see if maybe you'd let me have a do-over. if not, i completely get it. just wanted to ask

I stare at my phone screen for a few minutes. This is nowhere close to the way I expected this conversation to go. Maybe I was unnecessarily harsh at first, but is it worth it to give this guy a second chance? Do I even *want* to?

Stalling for anything else to do, I back out of the conversation and take a look at Christian's Instagram page. It seems fairly basic: His bio lists only his name, where he goes to school, and the name of Northeastern's soccer team, the Deacons. The pictures seem to be pretty regular fare, nothing that I'd be shocked to find on a seventeen-year-old guy's profile. The most recent picture is a regular selfie—Christian in a bright red T-shirt, smiling directly at the camera. There's some sort of filter over it that makes his blue eyes pop.

I'm not completely detached from high school reality. There's a reason Christian is so popular. He gets along with everybody, even the teachers, and that he looks like he got ripped straight out of the pages of a sports magazine doesn't hurt, either. He's gorgeous. Which is why this whole thing makes so little sense. What is it about me that would attract somebody like Christian? What does he think he sees in me that could match up with him?

The next picture is a shot of Northeastern's outdoor soccer field in the late evening. The shadows are long, and the golden-hour light makes the colors pop. It's not a bad shot, if I do say so myself. The caption underneath it says, "missing my second home."

God, this isn't one of those stereotypical jock-falls-for-the-bookish-girl-type things, is it? I think I might actually throw up. That's another one of those clichés that drive me crazy but everyone else seems to eat up.

But the post after the soccer field surprises me a little bit. This one's a video. Any of the professional polish from the previous two is gone: It's blurry, and at first, it's hard to tell that it's of Christian at all. He's sprawled on his bed, nearly hidden under the bodies of a golden retriever and a little girl; based on the hair and eye color, I assume it's his sister. It looks like she's tickling him, and Christian's mouth is wide open in a laugh I can almost hear even with the video muted. He looks so unabashedly happy. In the back of my head, a little voice I don't often hear whispers, *maybe he's different.*

I open the message thread again.

rosshewphotography: Technically, the play was your first impression. This would be your third.

chrispow2002: is that a yes?

rosshewphotography: It's a "we'll see."

chrispow2002: i can live with "we'll see"

chrispow2002: now, because i know i'll get chewed out if i don't find this out asap: favorite book?

That makes me laugh a little. Interesting. He's actually going to try.

rosshewphotography: I don't have one. I like the classics, but I also read some fantasy and sci-fi when I'm in the mood for something different.

chrispow2002: so you gave me that question before just to trick me?? that's not very fair 😂

chrispow2002: what about favorite movie?

It feels like a cop-out to say I don't have a favorite there, either. Movies aren't really my thing, but if I say that, Christian might start to think I'm just screwing with him. My mind goes to Dad and our yearly tradition on Charles's birthday.

rosshewphotography: Cinema Paradiso. Do you know it?

chrispow2002: do i lose points if i say no?

rosshewphotography: Not this time. It's an old Italian movie. It's not very common, so I wouldn't blame you for not knowing it. What about you?

chrispow2002: the godfather. call me cliche, but i grew up on that movie and i stand by it being amazing

rosshewphotography: I've actually never seen The Godfather.

chrispow2002: what??

chrispow2002: you have no idea what you're missing, i'm serious. you've gotta watch it

rosshewphotography: You're definitely not the first person to tell me that. I guess peer pressure will finally convince me to see it one of these days.

chrispow2002: and if that's the only thing that comes from this conversation, i'll be happy

chrispow2002: also no offense, but it feels a little weird to be talking about favorite movies and stuff like that on your professional photo account. is there some other way we could talk?

I bite my lip. This feels like a crossroads. If I stop him here, this stays at a stage I'm familiar with. Giving a guy my number feels . . . so final. Like I've committed to this being a thing, when I'm still not sure this is a *thing* I want in the first place.

But that video of Christian with his sister keeps nagging at me. Something about the way he was smiling, how carefree it was. Guys who want things from girls like me aren't usually secure enough to post pictures of them with their little sisters on their Instagram. I always assumed Christian's affable, friendly personality was an act, but I'm starting to realize that might not be true. I'm on the edge of a decision here, and the answer isn't the one I was expecting.

May said we should look for our "community" in life. I haven't done much to find mine so far. Who knows? Maybe this is a chance.

rosshewphotography: My number is 774-555-6129. I'm begging you not to make this weird.

chrispow2002: i won't if you won't. deal?

rosshewphotography: Deal.

SAM

I stare down at my screen, grinning so wide my cheeks hurt. What was I so worried about? Turns out Ros Shew is mortal, just like the rest of us.

> **SAM:** Ready for your turn?
> **CHRISTIAN:** does that mean it worked??

I send him screenshots of the whole conversation, including the phone number at the end. Suddenly, I'm not so concerned about how the rest of this is going to go. If I can crack Ros's thick shell in under twenty minutes, then getting her to like Christian is going to be a cakewalk.

> **SAM:** Follow my lead, Chris. As long as you do that,
>   you'll be fine
> **SAM:** Checkmate, baby ♟

14

CHRISTIAN

ALL THINGS CONSIDERED, THE FIRST CONVERSA-
tion doesn't actually go that badly. I read the messages between
Ros and Sam over and over, making sure I don't miss an important detail they might have already talked about. When I finally
get the courage to send the first text (it takes ten minutes, and
Sam laughs at me over text the entire time), Ros responds pretty
quickly. I keep things light, making sure to stick to topics I
already know she likes or easy small talk, and it works. She
seems a little distant, but she isn't completely trying to shoot
the conversation down, either, and that gives me a tiny spark
of hope.

The whole time, I'm sending screenshots of everything back
to Sam. She tells me how to respond, which questions to ask
next, and sometimes what a certain thing Ros said might mean.

CHRISTIAN: she doesn't use emojis and puts periods at the ends of all her sentences. i'm so out of my element here

SAM: It's just the way she types. She cares about grammar and stuff like that. Try typing better and see how she responds

CHRISTIAN: okay, now you're assuming i actually know good grammar 🙈

SAM: Fair point, I've read your English essays

I honestly don't know what I'd do without Sam's advice. When we were dating, she was always the one in charge. She asked me out first, she initiated the first date, the first kiss, and always knew what to do in any situation. And I was fine with that: I'd go along with whatever she wanted, and it seemed to work out. Having that same intuition on my side in this conversation is a complete lifesaver.

SAM: You haven't sent me a screenshot for a while. Status report???

CHRISTIAN: nothing much happening. i think she just made a joke?

SAM: Then laugh at it, genius

CHRISTIAN: i did!

SAM: How though

SAM: Like with just a lol or 😂 or what

CHRISTIAN: i said hahaha

SAM: Just like that?

CHRISTIAN: . . .

CHRISTIAN: i might have accidentally done it in all caps

SAM: Jesus christ

Because of the way the last conversation was going, Sam and I agree it's a good idea to keep asking basic questions to get to know Ros. Sam already figured out her favorite movie, but now our texts get into more interesting stuff, like favorite music and what she does for fun when she's not at school or writing for *Art Pulse*. As I predicted, most of Ros's interests are way over my head. She likes classic books and foreign directors, all her favorite musicians are people I've definitely never heard of, and her favorite things to do for fun are read and practice her violin. I'm starting to worry, but Sam reassures me there has to be something we've got in common.

ROS: What do you do when you're not at school?

CHRISTIAN: idk, soccer kind of eats up most of my life.
  if it's not that then i'm usually either hanging out with
  my family or my buddy Monty

ROS: Is that your sister on your Instagram?

CHRISTIAN: yeah, that's her

ROS: She's adorable! Definitely looks a lot like you,
  too. Does she make you play dress-up?

CHRISTIAN: sometimes, hahaha. mostly she just likes
  to pretend that she's wonder woman and i'm lex
  luthor or somebody. that or playing about a million
  games of candyland

ROS: Ha! There are worse board games to play, I
  guess.

CHRISTIAN: do you have a favorite board game?

ROS: I haven't played one in years, honestly. I used to
  play Go a lot with my dad, though. That's one of his
  favorites.

I feel a weird swooping sensation in my gut. Here I was hoping we'd have something in common, and it had to be this. I can't tell if I'm happy about it or not.

CHRISTIAN: i used to play that game all the time! it's a
  little more complicated than candyland though, lol

I'm fidgeting with my lucky token without even noticing it. I stuff it back into my pocket and try to focus, but for the rest of the conversation, a part of my mind is somewhere else, in a place I usually don't go if I can help it.

Will's favorite board game is Go.

Don't ask me why. A million other games are more fun or interesting, but he had some special attachment to Go. Maybe it's because he was good at it; he taught me how to play when I was eight, and ever since then it was our favorite thing to do on nights when both of us were bored and couldn't decide on something else to do. Being born four years apart means that it was hard to find stuff to agree on. I was always just a little too young for Will, and Will just a little too old for me.

That changed, though, once Aimee came along. Suddenly I wasn't the youngest anymore, and Will had to deal with the fact that he was now a teenager with a newborn sister. We got closer after that, after Aimee started taking up all of Mom's and Dad's time. We looked out for each other, entertained ourselves when they were too busy, and formed a kind of united front against the new-baby invasion.

Maybe that was why he taught me to play Go. He wanted us to have something that was *ours*, something we could relate to each other with. I remember asking him once if he'd ever teach Aimee to play when she was old enough.

He wrinkled his nose. "Maybe," he said. "But only if she asks. I still want this to be our thing for a while."

I agreed with him then, and we went back to playing like the conversation never happened. He beat me. He always beat me, but it never stopped me from trying.

Aimee's going to be eight in a couple of months. We don't have that old Go set anymore, but maybe I'll get one, just to teach her. It would have to be a secret, though—Mom and Dad don't like anything that reminds them of Will. Dad gets angry, and Mom gets quiet, and then everyone in the house is in a bad mood for the rest of the day. Mostly, we just don't talk about it. I think we've agreed that it's better that way.

Maybe teaching Aimee would be a bad idea. The game has weird associations in our family now. How would I explain it to my parents if they found out? How would I tell them that I miss playing and that I miss having that connection I did with Will? They wouldn't get it, and it's not worth the trouble it would cause. Besides, Aimee was barely three when Will left.

At this point, I don't know if she even remembers she had another brother at all.

15

SAM

THE CURSOR BLINKING ON MY COMPUTER SCREEN
is starting to freak me out. Instead of staring at it more, I mini-
mize my internet tab and go back to the Word document for *So
Long, Toledo!* In between school and helping Christian with Ros,
I've spent the last few days looking over the script and tweaking
parts to see if it makes a difference. In hindsight, a couple of
the lines are a little cliché, and I'm immediately embarrassed by
them. No wonder Ros thought parts of the show were "overly
romanticized." It's not like I can go back and change the performance, though, so there's no point to making edits. Unless . . .

I open up the internet again. The banner at the top of the
page reads: "Greater New England Young Playwrights Competition." Below that is a submission form that I've partially
filled out. The Young Playwrights Competition is something

I've heard about before but never really looked into. I think my drama teacher, Mr. Campbell, encouraged me to submit something when he first found out I was interested in playwriting.

The more I read about this competition, the more I realize that it's kind of a big deal. First prize is $2,000 and a staged reading of your play by a professional theater company. I'm always after different opportunities to show off my work, and winning this competition would be a huge validation.

More than one thing is stopping me from pressing the SUB-MIT button, though. Words from Ros's review are on repeat in the back of my head, and it's getting harder to ignore them, because instead of hearing them in Ros's voice, they're starting to take on the voice of somebody else.

There's a road map tacked to the wall in the corner of my room. It's nothing special—the kind you'd pick up at a gas station somewhere, old and faded and almost falling apart. Mom and I took a trip to LA when I was a kid, and I insisted we pick up a map because it made it feel more like an adventure. I was maybe in first grade, still learning to read, and so I sat in the back seat trying to sound out the city names. At the bottom of the map, nearly hidden in the corner, was one tiny dot with the name LOREDO written next to it in gray letters. I remember liking that name for some reason, and I asked Mom if we could visit there.

She frowned at me. "What in the world is there to see in *Loredo*? I've never heard of it before."

I showed her the dot on the map, and she laughed. "Oh, that's nowhere, baby," she said. "Probably just a Podunk town where hippies raise chickens."

And because I was seven and prone to obsessing over things, Loredo was the only thing I talked about for the entire trip. We saw the stars on the Hollywood Walk of Fame, watched a movie at the El Capitan, and ate dinner at a restaurant on the top floor of a skyscraper, but all I cared about was this random little desert town on my road map. I kept asking Mom if we could feed the hippies' chickens. Finally, she got annoyed with me and snapped, "Nobody important lives in Loredo, Sammy. We're in Los Angeles! Stop being ungrateful and start paying attention to a city where things actually happen."

I stopped talking about Loredo after that. I still wanted to go, but it made Mom mad. And if she thought there wasn't anything worth our time there, then she must be right. I thought I threw away the map, too, but years later, when I was digging through old photos and stuff to make a collage for my wall, I found it at the bottom of a box. A big, clumsy circle was drawn around Loredo in black Magic Marker, and next to that, in my sloppy first-grade handwriting, was an arrow and the words *Let's go!!*

Loredo was something Mom loved to make fun of me for, growing up. It became a weird inside joke. Whenever either of us complained about how nothing ever happened in Worcester, the other would always shrug and say, "At least it's not Loredo, right?" If I refused to do my homework, she would threaten to pull me out of school altogether, and then I'd have no choice but to move to Loredo and live with the hippie chickens. It was her version of the old "You'll be an unemployed loser living in your mom's basement" line, I guess. That town became a synonym for the word *nowhere*—a place where people went when they couldn't make anything of their lives. If you were there, then you'd given up.

Six years later, when she finally decided to move to LA for good—and happened to mention that I wouldn't be going with her—the arguments went on for weeks. She said she felt like she was trapped in Worcester, and if she didn't leave now, when would she ever get the chance? She already had friends and connections on the West Coast, and a brand-new life was stretching out in front of her—a life that she didn't think she could live with me there. An actress starting her career as "late" as she was had an image to worry about.

Throughout all this, she insisted she wasn't abandoning me. We would talk. She'd still be my mother. In a way, I guess she kept that promise. I get a card on my birthday and a phone call every year at Christmas. Any gifts she sends are mostly cash. She wouldn't know what to get me anyway, so I don't mind that so much. For my sixteenth birthday, she sent Nana—her mom—the money to buy me my first car. It was a really nice gesture, but I can't help but see a little bit of irony in it. In a sort of poetic way, she gave me the gift of freedom. I can get in the car and just drive, get away from Worcester and go anywhere I want. I could even join her in LA if I wanted. Or I could always give up and drive to Loredo. I still know how to get there, after all.

I'm glad I hung on to the map. Now I keep it on the wall

above my bed, held up by old, tarnished thumbtacks, Magic Marker and crappy handwriting still visible. Nana thinks I'm being sentimental, but really, it's the opposite. That map is a cautionary tale, a warning of what might happen if I don't push myself hard enough. Nobody gets what they want in life unless they're lucky or hardworking, and I've seen enough already to know that I'm not one of the lucky ones. I have to be the best at everything I do, otherwise what's the point? Every time I feel like giving up or taking a break, I look over at my wall, and the urge dies. Loredo isn't the place important people go. It's the place you see a road sign for on the way to better things and then keep on driving past.

I grit my teeth, then turn my attention back to the Greater New England Young Playwrights Competition submission page. Nerves aren't going to get me anywhere. Winning this contest would be proof that the play is good—that *I'm* good—and honestly, I need that kind of confidence booster after Ros's absolute dumpster fire of a review. Without giving myself time to think anymore, I click the SUBMIT button and then shut my laptop, letting out the breath I've been holding for the past thirty seconds. There. Now it's out of my hands, and I can stop thinking about it until the results are in. A *ding* from my phone shows me another message from my current Tinder victim, and I'm more than happy to distract myself. Here, at least, is something I *know* I'm good at.

16

ROS

VICE PRINCIPAL REAGAN IS EXPECTING A PROG-ress report from me by the end of the week, so I decide that now is as good a time as any to record the interview with Dad. To get an idea of what the final project will look like, I have to have something to set the music to, otherwise the pacing will be off. Besides, it's better to get one of the biggest parts of the project out of the way now so that I can stop worrying about it and focus on the performance itself.

After dinner, I corral Dad into the living room and start setting up a filming space. Thanks to my photography skills, I have enough knowledge about getting the right lighting for certain shots, so all it takes is a bunch of household lamps and a few extension cords to get the right amount of exposure. My camera shoots decent video, too. I set it up on its tripod in front of the couch while Dad fidgets with the top button on his shirt, watching me.

"You're putting an awful lot of effort into this," he says.

"Yeah, well." I gesture at him to sit up straight so I can line up the shot, then fiddle with a few more buttons on the camera. "The whole school's going to see this. I want to make sure it's my best work."

"I know they'll be impressed, kiddo. You always do great work."

I bite my lip and pretend to adjust the white balance some more. The truth is, I've been stressing about this project more than I thought I would. After the disaster of a violin practice the other day, I can't help but feel like I've gotten off to a bad start. As if to emphasize the point, my phone buzzes in my pocket. It's probably Christian.

We've been talking steadily for a few days now. As it turns out, my first impression of him was off the mark. He's actually a nice guy. A little awkward maybe, but not bad to talk to. He's definitely better at carrying a conversation than some people, and he at least acts like he's interested in getting to know me. Still, it's weird. I know what he wants out of this, and I'm still not sure if that's something I want, too. If it turns out that I don't, and I've been stringing him along all this time, how's he going to react?

I try to force the thought out of my head. I don't have time to think about my own semi-romantic train wreck right now. *I'm* not the one getting interviewed. "Ready?" I ask.

Dad nods, fidgeting in his seat a little more. "I guess so." He laughs quietly. "It's odd. I've never had to tell the story like this before."

I smile back at him. Even as a professor who teaches in some pretty big lecture halls, Dad still gets nervous talking in front of people.

"Just pretend you're telling it to me again."

I watch him visibly relax as he turns his attention away from the camera and on to me. I've heard this story more times than I can count now—Dad always gets sentimental around this time of year, as it gets closer and closer to Charles's birthday. And even though I can't remember my other dad very well, he wants to make sure I have something of him to hold on to. It's sweet, even though I'd much rather have the real thing. But we don't always get what we want in life. That's kind of the whole point of my project.

Without breaking eye contact, I reach up and press a button on the side of the camera, and a little red light flicks on.

"Start from the beginning."

Dad met Charles in New York City at the tail end of his undergrad. Charles was studying to be a botanist, and so their first apartment together overflowed with little plants, ferns blocking the sunlight from the tiny windows, and succulents resting on stacks of books about Genghis Khan and the Romanovs.

They moved to Massachusetts when Dad was offered a job at a university here, and this is where he's been ever since. They were together through the height of the AIDS crisis, through *Lawrence v. Texas*, and through everything that came after. They always knew they wanted kids, but that kind of thing just didn't happen for two gay men in the nineties. It took them six years, thousands of dollars, a whole army of lawyers, and one "miracle" of a surrogate in Aunt Rhetta to get it to work out.

"We just wanted you so badly," Dad used to say, smiling at me.

By the time I was born, Charles was my only legally recognized father. Dad and Charles weren't even allowed to get married. They finally did, two years later, once state officials finally got their act together and legalized it. They were lucky: Massachusetts was the first state in the US to start handing out marriage licenses to gay couples. They had a quick, completely informal ceremony at the local courthouse, with Aunt Rhetta holding me in the front row. Apparently, I cried through most of it.

Then, a couple of months later, Charles got the diagnosis. Bone cancer, stage three and getting worse by the day. Suddenly, Dad was swept up in a tornado of doctor's appointments, chemo, and radiation therapy, raising a two-year-old girl, and having to come to grips with the fact that the man he'd been with for almost twelve years, the man he'd barely been allowed to call "husband," might not be around for very much longer.

The worst part of it, he says, was not knowing what would happen to me. Hector wasn't my biological or legal father: It was Charles's DNA and Charles's name on my birth certificate. Charles's family didn't approve of their relationship, and my dads worried that after Charles died, they might make a bid to be my legal guardians. They threatened as much when he told them about the diagnosis. If that happened, they almost certainly would have cut Hector off altogether, and he never would have seen me again. So on top of the constant hospital visits and health scares, the enormous bills, and working full-time, Dad took on the incredibly complicated and scary task of adopting a kid who was already his.

Even through this, though, neither of them showed me how much they were hurting. I was too young to remember much at the time, but the memories I do have are good ones: Dad reading a book to me every single night, Charles singing and dancing with me in the living room. When Charles was admitted to the hospital, they were both all smiles every time I came for a visit. I don't remember Dad explaining to me that Charles might not be around forever. That's not to say he didn't, of course, just that it didn't stick with me for very long. Maybe that's for the best.

Charles died six months after being diagnosed, about three weeks after my third birthday. The adoption still hadn't become official. There was one last hearing to go to, and Charles's relatives decided to make an appearance to plead their side.

Dad says he prayed that day for the first time in almost fifteen years, and whatever higher power there was out there must have listened. The judge took his side, and finally, *finally*, the Commonwealth of Massachusetts legally recognized what Dad knew all along—that I was his, and nothing could ever change that. He still sends that judge a Christmas card every single year.

We're both choked up by the time he finishes telling the story. I stop the recording, and Dad lets out a long, heavy sigh. It feels like the atmosphere in the room lightens a bit. "I don't suppose you can Photoshop out the tears, can you?" he asks with a laugh.

I laugh, too, relieved. "Don't think so."

"It was worth a shot." He stands up, clapping his hands together. "Is that everything? Do you need more, or can I get a start on grading some work?"

"I think I have everything. Thanks, Dad."

"No problem, kiddo. I'm excited to see how it turns out."

While he starts on the grading, I run through a bit of the footage. The lighting definitely isn't as good as it could be, and I'm worried the audio could be too quiet. But it's too late to fix it now. Besides, I don't want to make Dad go through telling that story again. He puts on another crappy reality show for background noise, and as I try to tune out the billionaire housewives arguing on the TV, my mind wanders.

When I submitted my proposal for the Bellerose Assembly project, I included a short written summary of Dad's story to show what would be the focus of my presentation. Vice Principal Reagan said she cried when she read it, so moved by my dad's "beautifully tragic" story. I can only imagine how much more she'll cry when she hears the full version. I can't blame her for feeling that way, either, since every famous love story in history is full of drama and adversity—Romeo and Juliet, Lancelot and Guinevere, *Titanic*, *The Notebook*. The only problem is, none of those have what you'd call "happy endings." Romeo and Juliet both kill themselves. Lancelot and Guinevere are together behind King Arthur's back. Jack dies in Rose's arms. Allie forgets Noah when they get older. Why are *those* the greatest love stories in history, when nobody actually gets their happily ever after?

Overall, I guess Dad's story is pretty inspiring. He smiles when he tells it, and the tears are followed just as quickly by laughter when he recalls something funny Charles used to say. He's told me over and over that it was worth it, because in the end, he got to have me. But somehow, I can't help but feel like that's a pretty terrible consolation prize. Sure, my dad was brave to fight to keep the things he loved, but why should he have had to fight at all? Why was that work rewarded by heartbreak? It's not fair.

On the coffee table in front of me, my phone lights up with a text from Christian.

CHRISTIAN: so do you only read classic books? or do you like more modern stuff too?

I frown at my phone screen.

ROS: I'll read anything that has a compelling story, but I prefer the classics, yes. Why?
CHRISTIAN: i was just hoping that reading pride and prejudice 2 years ago was gonna pay off someday
ROS: You've read Pride and Prejudice? What for?
CHRISTIAN: because someone dared me i wouldn't
ROS: Why am I not surprised?

I think Dad notices my conflicted mood, because after a minute or two, he leans over and nudges my arm. "You okay, kiddo?"

I nod absently. "Yeah. Just thinking."

"Penny for your thoughts?"

"It's nothing, I promise."

My phone buzzes again. He looks down at it, then back up at me. "Is that anyone I should know about?"

I can already feel my face heating up. Dad and I don't normally talk about this kind of stuff. We've never *had* to before. "Some guy from school."

One eyebrow goes up. "And . . . is this the part where I have to pretend I own a shotgun?"

"*No*, Dad. God."

"Well, I have to ask."

"It's not like that, I promise. We're just talking." But I know he can hear the caginess in my voice, and the fact that my face is on fire right now probably doesn't help much, either.

Still, he doesn't push it. "Okay, kiddo. I believe you. But you know, if that changes, he's always welcome over for dinner."

I honestly don't think my face could get any hotter right now. "Good to know," I mutter, standing and snatching up my phone and camera. "I'm going to go to my room now and pretend we didn't have this conversation."

Dad's laugh follows me all the way up the stairs.

17

SAM

ENSURING THAT THE PLAN TO MAKE ROS FALL for Christian goes off without a hitch means having to do a little homework. Thanks to the information we've gathered over the last few days of text conversations, I now know enough about Ros to start getting a sense of who she is. It's mostly surface-level stuff—favorite things, the fact that she's an only child, and so on—but that can tell you a surprising amount about a person. Only problem is, I've never heard of some of her favorite things, especially that movie she mentioned.

So that's how I find myself sitting on my bed on Sunday night, laptop in front of me and Christian hogging most of the room, as we both watch an obscure, subtitled Italian movie that practically screams "I watched this before it was cool."

Based on what I've seen so far, *Cinema Paradiso* is about a kid who grows up to be a famous director and his childhood in a tiny Italian village where he learned how to be a projectionist. There's a romantic subplot (surprising, considering how much Ros supposedly hates romance), but for the most part the movie focuses on the friendship between the kid and the old cinema projectionist. It's not a bad movie, I guess.

Next to me, Christian won't stop fidgeting. I elbow him in the ribs. "Are you even paying attention?"

He lets out a dramatic sigh. "When you said 'movie night,' I was hoping for Michael Bay or something."

"O ye of little taste."

"I don't watch movies to *read*, Sam. I looked away for one second and missed half the plot!"

"That's your own fault. Besides, we're researching. You want to get to know Ros? You've gotta watch her favorite movie."

Christian lets his head fall back against the wall with a *thunk*. "Please kill me."

I pick up a decorative pillow and throw it over his face. "That can be arranged, Christian Powell. Now shut up and watch."

We both go silent again for a few minutes as the movie keeps playing, and I watch as the teenage guy who grows up to be the director writes letters to his girlfriend.

All things considered, I guess the story for this movie isn't bad. I agree with Christian—watching a foreign-language movie makes it harder to focus—but the friendship between the kid and the projectionist is kind of sweet. I guess I was expecting some kind of completely esoteric, art house type movie, coming from Ros. Does that mean she likes more mainstream stuff, too?

Could be worth asking, since it would make my and Christian's job easier.

I ask him to text her something, and a few minutes later his phone beeps with the response:

ROS: I'll read anything that has a compelling story, but I prefer the classics, yes. Why?

"Tell her you read *Pride and Prejudice*," I say.

Christian frowns. "But I didn't. What if she tries to ask me about it?"

"Oh, come here." I grab the phone out of his hands and type the message myself, sending it before he has a chance to protest. "Guess who's got more homework to do this week?"

"I have to read a whole book now?!"

"Aw, poor baby."

He shoots me a death glare. "Remind me why we're still friends."

"Because you'd be completely lost without me and you know it." I grin and watch Christian's face as he tries to keep from smiling back. After a minute, he rolls his eyes and turns back to the computer screen, mumbling something about trying to focus on the movie. He's not actually mad, though; he's hiding a laugh, and when I lean into his shoulder, he doesn't pull away.

I've always made it a point not to be friends with my exes. I've dated plenty during my time at Northeastern—boys, girls, and other—but it usually doesn't last long, and once it's over, we don't talk. What's the point in forming a lasting relationship in high school? Once I graduate, I want to get out of Worcester as fast as I possibly can. I don't need people holding me back.

Christian was always a little different, though. We've been in each other's orbit for years, ever since grade school, but I didn't even think about dating him until last year. I was interested in him because of his status as star forward on the soccer team and how easily he seemed to get along with everybody. He was a chance to raise my status, maybe form connections with some of the social groups I wasn't part of yet. But once we started dating, I realized Christian wasn't nearly as ambitious as I first thought. He wasn't playing soccer to go pro, and the friendliness wasn't an act. He really was that nice. A little tongue-tied sometimes, sure, but nice. I stayed with him for a few months longer than I normally would because I hated the idea of upsetting him. That niceness was infectious. It made you *want* to be around him. What I had to work so hard to achieve, he managed to do without even trying. I'd rather die than admit it, but I was a little jealous of that at first.

I'm used to people asking to stay friends when we break up, but Christian is the first one I ever actually agreed with. I think it was the first time I ever saw him stand up for himself. I was proud. That's when it hit me, too: I liked this guy. Not as a boyfriend or anything, but just as a person. I would miss hanging out, talking every day, going over to see his sister and his dog. Come to think of it, Christian's also the only person from Northeastern I've ever let into my house. The fact that he's sitting here, on my bed, watching a movie and stealing all my pillows—it means something. It means I got closer to him than I ever meant to, and now I think I'm stuck with him.

His phone dings again, and he looks down at the message and smiles. "She thought what you said was funny. Time for me to SparkNotes the plot of the book, I guess."

"Cheater."

"We don't have six months for me to finish reading it, Sam."

"Fine. But I expect a three-page essay on the plot. Single-spaced, MLA format. And if it sounds like you plagiarized anything, I'm going to flunk you."

Now it's his turn to throw a pillow at me, and I shriek as it hits me in the face. He laughs, loud and ridiculous, and I can't help but join in. The two of us completely give up on watching the movie as, on the screen, the wannabe director leaves his tiny town without looking back.

18

ROS

EITHER THE HEAT IN MRS. REAGAN'S OFFICE DOESN'T
work as well as the rest of the school, or she sets it to be colder
intentionally to make people uncomfortable. I shiver and adjust
my jacket over my legs, trying to trap some warmth while I wait
for her to figure out how to plug my USB drive into her sleek
little computer.

She wanted to see progress on my Bellerose project, and that's
what she's getting. I managed to pull together the rough footage
of Dad's story, as well as a recording of the music I'm planning
to play, and put them together to make a sort of presentation.
It's nowhere close to the kind of polish I want on the final prod-
uct, but all in all, I'm proud of what I've got to show so far. The
footage turned out really well, and the music is just unsettling
enough to give the right effect.

Mrs. Reagan gives me a quick smile. "I've been looking forward to seeing your progress all week," she says. "Your proposal was so moving; I can't imagine what hearing the full story will be like."

Once she manages to pull up the file and start playing it, though, she goes quiet. I can't see her screen, but I hear the violin and my dad talking. As her eyebrows furrow, I feel sweat start to prickle at the back of my neck.

Something's wrong. Is the video quality not good enough? Is it my playing? I knew I should have practiced more, or even brought my violin to play it in person. You really can't get enough of the emotion from a crappy recording I took on my old phone. A bit of panic starts to settle in, and it takes a lot of my self-control to keep sitting still.

Mrs. Reagan doesn't even watch the whole video. She pauses about halfway through, and as she opens her mouth, I blurt out, "That's not the final cut, obviously. I still have some things to clean up in the video, and I don't have good sound-recording equipment at home, so the music is a little—"

"The music is actually what I wanted to talk about." She's frowning, her earlier excitement about the project gone. "Don't you think that it's . . . I don't know . . . unsettling for a Bellerose Assembly project?"

I shake my head. "That's what I was going for. Something to contrast the story a bit, make the viewer think."

Clearly, that's not what she wanted me to say, because she sits back in her chair, pursing her lips. "I understand that your fathers' story has its sad moments, and it's certainly worth addressing the hardships gay couples have suffered in the past"—*It was barely fourteen years ago*, I think but decide against saying out loud—"but I don't know if a school-organized assembly is the best place to make that statement, Miss Shew."

"If not there, then where? Sure, love is great or whatever, but so many people take it for granted. I said that was something I wanted to address in my original proposal."

"Yes, but I didn't think you'd take quite this approach to it," Mrs. Reagan says, pinching the bridge of her nose between her fingers. "As it stands now, I can't approve this version of the project for presentation."

I stare at her. "All because the music isn't *happy* enough?"

"The music is *unsettling*, Rosalyn. It doesn't fit the tone of the rest of the assembly or the day at large. It would be out of place to include it the way it is now."

"So, what, I'm just supposed to scrap everything and start over?"

I don't think I've ever been this up-front with a teacher before, but I can't help it. I told Mrs. Reagan what I wanted to do in my proposal, and she agreed to it. But now—because she assumed I would ham everything up and make it sweet and easily digestible for people—I have to lose my hard work?

She shakes her head, giving me a tired smile. "The footage is good. Nothing about that has to change. Just . . . change the music a little. It can be sad at times, but from what I read of your proposal, your fathers' story ends on a hopeful note. The music should probably do the same."

She says "probably" as if it's optional, but I know it isn't.

Without a word, I take back my USB drive and leave her office, my head in a fog.

She doesn't get it. No one *ever* does. They swallow tragic, doomed love stories every day, as long as they're presented in a way that makes it seem "worth it," rather than actually understand the loss involved. I'm trying to present something complicated, something nuanced and above the level of thought normally shown by high schoolers, and nobody wants to hear it. Or at least, the ones who do won't get to because idealists like Mrs. Reagan can't handle any story that doesn't come with a "happily ever after."

It dawns on me, the farther I walk away from her office, that I'm angry. I don't get angry often—a caring dad and years of support group ever since I was old enough to know what feelings were have made me pretty good at handling negativity—but in situations like this, it's the only emotion that makes sense to feel. If I follow Mrs. Reagan's guidelines, I lose my creative vision, but if I stick to my guns, then it's more than likely I won't get to present my project at all.

I pull out my phone to text my dad—something unrelated, something to take my mind off how mad this is making me—and instead I see a text from Christian.

CHRISTIAN: hey! sorry this is short notice, but i was wondering if you wanted to grab a coffee or something at flannery's? i'm free the rest of the afternoon and thought i'd ask

I'm torn between laughing and screaming at Christian's perfect, horrendous timing. It's almost as if he *knew* when the worst time to ask me out again would be and then waited until that exact moment. I'm tempted to shoot him down right away, but as I open the message thread, something stops me.

Why not consider it more of an experience? I'll be the first to admit that I don't know anything about how high school dating is supposed to work. I've avoided everything to do with it, even in the books I read or movies I watch. I've never dated anyone before, nor have I ever really wanted to. Is there something I'm missing here, something that might help me understand what Mrs. Reagan wants from this project? Maybe going on this date will give me some kind of insight into what I'm apparently getting so wrong.

If nothing else, maybe it will help take my mind off how pissed I am right now.

> **ROS:** Okay, sure. I'll be there in ten, that okay?
> **CHRISTIAN:** sounds good! see you then 👍

I shove my phone back into my pocket and head for my car, shaking my head at myself as I go. Going on a date with somebody as research for a project? Maybe this is a little too far. But I already said yes, and honestly, what could it hurt? This way, I can do my stupid research while I figure out if I actually like Christian at the same time. Two birds, one stone.

I throw my backpack into the passenger seat and start the car, whispering a silent prayer as I put it in gear and start to peel out of the student parking lot, ignoring the thrill of nerves starting to build in my stomach. This is normal. This is what normal teenagers do with their lives on weekday afternoons.

For once in your life, Ros, pretend to be normal. Even if it's just for an hour.

19

CHRISTIAN

EVERYTHING ABOUT THIS DATE IS A MISTAKE.

Sam set the whole thing up. I think she got tired of my constant procrastinating and insisted that if I didn't do something soon, Ros would lose interest. She decided the best place for us to meet would be Flannery's, since it's where the two of us first locked eyes with each other and we'd both be on common ground. She told me exactly what to text Ros, and when she agreed to it, I was shocked. I think even Sam was surprised. The nerves before Ros got here were so bad I almost bailed. But now she's here, sitting across from me at a tiny table in the corner, and it's so much worse, because I'm remembering that I *hate* coffee dates.

Here's the problem with them, and the reason I've never been good at them: Coffee shops aren't active dates. There's not much to look at and nothing to do except sit there, sip mochas, and talk. All you can do is talk. It makes these sorts of places perfect for people like Sam, but I'm not Sam. I don't know how to just . . . talk. So Ros sits across from me with a mug of some kind of herbal tea, staring at me like she expects me to say something, and I feel like if I even attempt to open my mouth, I'll throw up.

I wonder if Ros can see the shake in my hands as I point at her mug. "What kind of tea is that?"

She looks down at it, like she has to remember what she ordered. "Lavender and honey."

"Oh. Are you sick?"

She frowns at me. "What?"

"Oh, I assumed—my mom, when she's sick, that's what she drinks."

"No, I just like the taste."

"Oh."

Stop saying oh!

My phone buzzes on the table, and I'm more than happy to distract myself by looking at it.

SAM: How's it going??
CHRISTIAN: NOT GOOD
SAM: What? Why??

She should know why. *I'm* the problem here. Without her constantly looking over my shoulder, I'm useless in the conversation. This is such a disaster.

CHRISTIAN: i have no idea what to say! and she's not talking either so we're both sitting here not talking

SAM: What was all that research we did for?? Ask her about something she likes!

Something she likes. Yeah. She doesn't have a favorite book, but she's read a lot of the classics. I don't read books. I read a summary of *Pride and Prejudice* in case she asked about that, but now in my panic I'm forgetting most of it. What about that movie she likes, the Italian one? With the kid who makes friends with a projectionist? What was the name of that movie? I just watched it. I should remember this.

I look up to see Ros staring at me and realize I've been engrossed in my phone for the last minute. This can't look good.

"Sorry," I say. "It's . . . my sister is texting me about a homework assignment. She'll blow up my phone even worse if I don't answer her."

Ros nods. "That's okay."

Starting off the date with a lie. Good going, Christian.

I suddenly remember what Sam told me to ask about, so I blurt out, maybe a little loudly, "I watched that movie you liked."

Ros looks startled. "I—the movie?"

"Yeah, the one with the kid and the projectionist guy named . . . well, I can't remember their names, but it was good."

"Oh, you mean *Cinema Paradiso*?"

"Yeah, that was it."

"The projectionist's name is Alfredo."

"Yeah, I wanted to say something about pasta, but—"

121

"And the kid's name is Salvatore."

"Sure, yeah."

She frowns again. "You watched it because I said it was my favorite?"

Uh-oh. Is that a creepy thing to do?

"W-well, yeah," I stammer, starting to consider how fast I could run out of this building and all the way home. "I just, I'd never heard of it before, you know? And if it was something you liked, I mean, I thought it must be really good. And I did like it."

Stop talking, stop talking, stop talking!

Ros still looks a little uneasy, but she nods. "Well, I'm glad you liked it. It's kind of a nostalgic movie for me. My dad and I watch it every year."

"Oh! It's like your tradition?"

She smiles, and for a second, I think I'm getting somewhere. "Yeah."

"That's great. Does your mom like it, too?"

And then the smile drops. "I don't have a mom."

"Wha—oh, I'm sorr—"

"We watch it every year on my other dad's birthday. He's been dead since I was three, so—"

"No, I get it; that makes sense."

That. Makes. SENSE? That's it. I have to get out of here before either Ros kills me for being a jerk or I die from embarrassment right here and now.

Both of us go back to being silent, Ros staring down into her tea, and I reach for my phone again.

CHRISTIAN: ABORT MISSION

SAM: Calm down, you've got this

CHRISTIAN: no, i really don't

CHRISTIAN: i tried to ask about her favorite movie
and somehow it turned into a conversation about her
dead gay dad

SAM: You WHAT

CHRISTIAN: please help me

SAM: Look, change the subject. NOW. And stop
looking at your phone, it makes you look distracted

I set the phone on the table facedown, keeping my hand on it in case Sam decides to give me any more advice, but it doesn't buzz again. So instead, I sit there, glancing sidelong at Ros as she avoids eye contact and wishing with every fiber of my being that my lucky token, sitting uselessly in my right pocket, could suddenly become sentient, jump down my throat, and choke me.

ROS

Maybe this was a mistake.

I realized as soon as I saw Christian standing in front of the counter at Flannery's that I hadn't actually agreed to the date because I wanted to spend time with him. I'd wanted a distraction. But now I'm here, and it's too late to back out.

I think Christian might be realizing something's off, too, because he's acting . . . different. The guy I've been texting has been nice, maybe a little dorky, but overall easy to talk to. In person, it's a completely different story. He's nervous, almost twitchy, and any time he tries to start a conversation, it sounds like he regrets it before he's even finished.

Maybe I should help him out. After all, he did watch *Cinema Paradiso* just because I said I liked it, and that's kind of sweet. I'm not exactly making it easier for the guy by giving him short answers and not offering up any topics of conversation myself, but what am I supposed to say? We have barely anything in common. I know basically nothing about soccer, and aside from the few things I've learned about him in our text conversations—did he say his favorite movie is *The Godfather*?—this guy is kind of a mystery.

I watch him flounder for something to say for a few more minutes before I decide to take pity on him.

After a sip of my cooling tea for courage, I say, "So when does soccer season start?"

I watch his eyes light up. The relief on his face is almost enough to make me laugh. Finally, it seems, we've landed on a topic he feels comfortable with.

"It's usually more of a summer and fall thing," he says. "But Coach has us doing drills and scrimmages and stuff in the off-season to keep us all in form."

"I didn't know high school sports were that intense."

"Yeah. We're the best high school team in the state, so that means we're under a lot more pressure to stay on top." He grins, and I can tell he's proud of that fact. "Not that I mind. It keeps me busy."

"Are you going to try to get a scholarship for it?" I ask.

He shrugs. "Probably. Babson's got a pretty decent soccer team, but they're not as competitive as some other schools, so I might be able to get a small scholarship for soccer."

I raise my eyebrows. I've looked at Babson as a possibility for college, but it seemed more focused on business and marketing—not really my area. I didn't think it was Christian's area, either.

"So you're trying to be a soccer player professionally, or are you applying there for other reasons?"

"Oh, I don't think I could do professional soccer. I'm pretty good, but not that good. Nah, Babson was my dad's alma mater, and he's pretty set on my going there, too."

"Do *you* want to go there, though?"

He shifts in his chair. "He thinks it would be a good fit for me."

Ah. So he's one of *those* guys. A carbon copy of his dad, whose only ambition in life is to do the same thing the guy who raised him has already done. I can't say I'm surprised.

I think he senses my cooling attitude, because he quickly clams up. He starts chugging his coffee (which must be almost cold by now) and then immediately goes back to fidgeting with his phone. *Again* with the phone. This is the third time he's texted somebody in the past fifteen minutes or so. Is he actually talking to his sister? Does he even *want* to be here, or did he ask me out expecting me to say no?

The worst part is, I'm almost rooting for him. *Come on, Christian. Ask me where I'm applying to college. It's an easy conversation topic. Come ON.*

But he doesn't. He just keeps typing away, so thoroughly not looking at me that I'm sure he's doing it on purpose, and any goodwill he might have gained from the conversation a few minutes before has vanished. It was a bad idea to come here. I'm remembering now that I barely know this guy, that we come from completely different circles, that there's nothing about the two of us that could work, and I don't even think I *want* it to work anyway. Maybe I should go home.

And it's right about then, as if he senses my thoughts, that Christian looks up from his phone and blurts out, like he's just thought of it and he's desperate not to lose me, "You want to get out of here?"

SAM

I've definitely made a mistake.

Sending Christian in on his own this early in the game was a calculated risk, and clearly, it's not paying off. He's been frantically texting me every few minutes, recounting parts of their train wreck of a conversation and begging for my help. I can only do so much from a distance, though, and I know that the more he looks down at his phone, the more it looks to Ros like he doesn't want to be there. It's a catch-22, and if I'd thought this through a little more, I would have seen that.

Northeastern's library is basically deserted after classes let out. No club meetings get held there, and usually people don't want to stick around here any longer than they have to on a Friday. Normally, I'd be right there with them, but Flannery's is an easy walk from campus, and I wanted to be close by in case something went wrong on Christian and Ros's date. Clearly, my instincts were correct.

Trying to fool somebody in real life is so much harder than over message. At the end of the day, Christian still has to be the one Ros talks to. I can't very well substitute for Chris, or go as him myself. But really, I think the worst of my nerves comes from the fact that if Christian fails here, I fail, too.

I should be used to my success relying on other people by now. It's one of the biggest parts of acting—you learn your own part, do your own work, and all you can do after that is trust that the other actors are going to do the same. My recent adventures in directing and producing were a refreshing change because suddenly, I could be in charge of everything like I wanted and still have something creative to show for it. Now, though, I'm feeling more helpless than ever. I can give Christian all the direction in the world, but whether he follows it is up to him, and even if he does, Ros may still want nothing to do with him. I can put in the work, and this could still fail.

I'm not going to think about why that makes me feel so nervous.

Christian is texting me.

CHRISTIAN: she went quiet again. i thought we were
having a pretty good conversation but i think i said
something wrong
SAM: Did you mention her dead dad again?
CHRISTIAN: i'm not an idiot, sam
SAM: Could've fooled me, dude. Look, clearly this isn't
working out. Maybe you should bail before things get
any worse
CHRISTIAN: no! i want this to work
SAM: Yeah, but it ISN'T. If you keep this up, you're
gonna scare her away
CHRISTIAN: there has to be something you can do to
save this

Me? *I'm* doing everything I can to make this work, but it's hard when the person the job depends on can't follow my instructions!

Maybe he needs a different environment. Christian's never been a coffee shop kind of guy, and I only told him to invite Ros to Flannery's because I thought it might be her kind of scene. He's out of his depth, and that's partly my fault.

SAM: What were you having a good conversation
about earlier?
CHRISTIAN: huh??

SAM: You said you were talking about something good before she went quiet. What was it

CHRISTIAN: just soccer stuff. why?

I roll my eyes. Christian's one strength in any conversation, and it has to be a thing I'm sure Ros couldn't care less about. Still, the change in scenery might not be such a bad idea.

Someone across the library calls my name: Vicki, one of the girls from my algebra class last year who's trying to be my new best friend. I give her a big fake smile and gesture to my phone, mouthing, "Sorry, gotta go." To really sell the idea, I stand up and start putting all my stuff together.

She looks disappointed but backs off, and I turn my attention back to my phone.

SAM: Ask her if she wants to walk to Northeastern's soccer field with you

CHRISTIAN: what for?

SAM: Just do it! If she agrees, then maybe this isn't a complete loss. Maybe you can get her to listen to you talk about soccer some more on the way

CHRISTIAN: you'd better be right about this, sam

SAM: When am I ever wrong?

He doesn't respond, so I assume he's following my advice. If they're headed to the soccer field, then I need to be there, too. Hiding, obviously, but still. I feel like I can keep a better eye on the situation if I'm actually there. If nothing else, I can at least *watch* this date fall to pieces instead of just hearing about it secondhand.

I grab my bag and hurry out, nodding to the librarian as I go and offering up a quick prayer to whatever will listen that leveling the playing field will be enough to save both my reputation and this disaster of a first date.

20

SAM

ROS AND CHRISTIAN ARE EN ROUTE TO THE SOCCER field. This is such a gamble on my part, but what else am I supposed to do? It was a mistake to leave Christian on his own this early. And on a *coffee date*? The only thing you can do on dates like that is talk to each other, and that was the exact thing he needed my help with. It was a mistake, but maybe I can still save this.

It's a few minutes' walk to the soccer field from Flannery's, so I have some time to think about what to do. Obviously, Christian's nervous, and he could use a boost. Hopefully, being on the field will make him feel more at ease, maybe loosen him up. There's only so many talking points I can give him over text.

The one variable I'm most worried about, though, is the one

I can't control. Ros doesn't have a reputation as the forgiving type, especially not with guys. If Christian screws this up, who knows if she'll give him another chance? There's only so much magic I can work here.

My phone buzzes.

CHRISTIAN: she's just stopped talking. i don't know what to say!!!
SAM: Does she look angry?
CHRISTIAN: maybe? it's really hard to tell

I bite my lip. *Not* a good start. If she's pissed, then this thing might already be over.

SAM: You're heading to the soccer field, right? Ask her if she played any sports as a kid
CHRISTIAN: just did. she said no
SAM: And what did you say back?
CHRISTIAN: what am i supposed to say to "no"????

I peek around the side of the bleachers and see two figures walking through the gate on the far side. I can't read body language from here, but there's a decent amount of distance between Christian and Ros. I swear under my breath. The more I text Christian, the more it looks like he's ignoring her to talk to someone else, but if I don't say anything, they're going to walk the track in complete silence. Either way, we're doomed.

This is ridiculous. I refuse to let a stupid coffee date with the school ice queen be the thing that defeats me. If I have to step in myself to save this, then that's what I'm going to do.

One of the biggest lessons you learn in acting classes is the concept of "acting as if." You put yourself in the place of the character, and even before they come onstage, you have to come up with a reason for why they're entering the scene. Then it's your job to act "as if" they've been there the whole time. Who says I can't do that in real life?

Quickly, I take off my sweater and stuff it into my backpack, so I'm just wearing my leggings and sports bra. I always keep sneakers in my bag, so I swap those out, too. Then I stuff everything else under the bleachers, and with phone and earbuds in hand, I step out of hiding and start casually jogging along the track that surrounds the soccer field. I've been here the whole time. I came to school to run the track and just happened to run into Chris and Ros there. What's unusual about that?

Christian notices me first. He does a double take when he realizes that it's me, and before he can gesture at me to leave, Ros turns her head and sees me, too. I watch her recognize me, eyes widening as she looks me up and down, and feel a little rush of victory. *There's* the reaction I was hoping for. With any luck, my showing up should put her on the defensive. If she doesn't already hate Christian, maybe she'll feel like she has to protect herself from the Evil Ex-Girlfriend. That's exactly what I want.

"Hey," I call out as soon as I'm close enough, stopping my jog and adding a little extra breathlessness to my voice to help sell it. "What are you guys doing out here?"

"Just walking," Ros says warily, not taking her eyes off me.

I flash Christian a smile, and it takes all my self-control not to wink. "Hey, Chris."

He's staring at me, mouth hanging open in shock. He looks at Ros, then me, then back to Ros again, like he can't quite wrap his head around the two of us standing within ten feet of each other. "What are *you* doing here?" he says finally.

I gesture to my shoes. "Track season is coming up again soon. I want to make sure I'm still in good condition for tryouts."

Then I turn my attention to Ros, making sure to give her the same up-and-down look she was just giving me. "You're Ros, right?"

Her eyes narrow. "Yeah. And you're Sam."

"My reputation precedes me." It's off topic, but I can't help adding in the little jab of, "You were at my play, right? I think I remember seeing you there. What did you think?"

Ros stiffens, eyes darting between Christian and me. After a second, she says, "I . . . it was well written. A little predictable for me, but I see why other people would like it. You two had good chemistry."

Christian winces like he just got slapped. The chemistry between the two of us should *not* be what she's focusing on right now, so instead, I decide to latch on to the other part of the review. "Never heard anyone call my life 'predictable' before."

"That's right. I remember reading in the program that it was based on a true story." Ros frowns.

"I submitted my play to a young playwrights competition," I say, starting to feel smug. "So I can use the win as a talking point on my college applications."

One perfect eyebrow goes up. "*If* you win."

Okay. So *this* is how we're playing it. If Ros thinks she can outdo me, she's got another think coming.

I pretend to be unfazed and shrug. "Everyone who watched the play seemed to love it. Why wouldn't I win?"

This is the part where I expect Ros to get angry. It takes a whole lot less than what I said to start a fight between most people. But instead, I watch her give me that same up-and-down look again. There's no anger in her expression. It looks more like she's trying to study me, trying to figure out what makes me tick so she can take me apart. It's a challenge, and one that I'm more than happy to match. *Game on.*

"You've got a lot of confidence, I'll give you that," she says. "And it's pretty impressive to have an acceptance letter from a university before junior year is over. Which school was it?"

I shift from foot to foot. "Well . . . that's artistic license. Obviously, I can't start applying until next fall, but that's not far off. I'm thinking probably Tisch, NYU, Juilliard if I want to get a more classical-arts education—"

"So it's not real, then."

"Hmm?"

"Your play. It's fake."

She's got a look on her face like she's caught me in a lie. I give my voice a sharper edge. "Again, it's creative license. You're in AP English, right? You know what that is? Besides, I said it was *based* on true events. Obviously, parts of it aren't real."

"Right." The look doesn't leave her face. "I wonder which parts."

I think Christian can see I'm getting angry. To defuse the situation, maybe win himself a couple of points in Ros's book, he says, "The city it's based on is called Loredo, not Toledo. Sam told me she thought it would be better if the town name was somewhere people recognized."

The look I give Christian could almost set his hair on fire. Aside from me, my mom, and Nana, he's the only other person in my life who knows about Loredo. I don't tell anybody my weird obsession with that town for a reason—because it's personal. I should be the only person who gets to decide what people know about me, but here's Christian deciding to spill it to impress *her*. He sees my look and shrinks, shoulders hunching in self-defense.

Ros spares him a quick glance before locking eyes with me again. "Is that right?"

". . . Yeah. I've never been there, though. Some random hick town in Southern California. A place where nobodies live." I try to keep my voice even, keep it from betraying how personal a detail Christian just gave away for free. "I figured I might win more points from the audience if I didn't call the town Worcester, at least."

She frowns. "Worcester's pretty far from a hick town. We're the second-biggest city in Massachusetts."

I can't help laughing. "Yeah. Big and empty. Believe it or not, there isn't a lot of show business in this area."

"So you hate it here?"

"Don't *you*?"

"Not really, no."

"Well, good for you."

Christian is looking back and forth at us like he's watching a life-or-death game of tennis. The tension in the air is growing by the second, and I'm not even sure if Ros and I are fighting or not. Ros's expression hasn't changed. She looks completely unfazed by the whole conversation, which makes me the only one showing any kind of weakness here, and I hate it.

I'm expecting her to take advantage of that, use this new information to tear me a new one, but instead, Ros takes a step back. "I should get back home," she says easily, turning to Christian. "I had fun. Thanks for the tea." I can tell she's lying, and when she looks over at me, a tiny bit of that venom I'd been waiting for slips out, though not in the way I'd hoped. "Have a good day, Sam."

She leaves without another word, not looking back at either of us as she goes. Her dark hair catches some reflections from the late-afternoon sun, and she walks calmly all the way to the other side of the track, across the soccer field, and through the gate at the other end.

As soon as Ros is out of earshot, Christian rounds on me. "What the *hell*, Sam?"

"She started it," I say defensively. "I was trying to help you out, and she turned it into a competition."

"Help me out? You were supposed to help me from a distance, not show up and take everything over!"

"You told her about *Loredo*! Was that your solution, selling me out so you'd make yourself look better?"

"I was trying to change the subject! You were turning it into an argument! What do you think it looked like when my ex-girlfriend shows up at the same place I am while I'm out with someone else, tries to start a fight, and the whole time you're not even *wearing a shirt*?"

I roll my eyes. "I was trying to make her jealous. Usually that works for most other girls."

"Yeah, well, I think we've established that Ros is different from a lot of other girls." Christian runs a hand through his hair, chewing at his bottom lip. He looks pissed, and it's right about then that I start to feel bad. Christian doesn't get angry easily, so if he's mad now, I might have really screwed this up. He doesn't deserve to lose his chance with Ros because I couldn't resist a fight.

I heave a deep sigh. "Okay. I'm sorry. I didn't mean for it to go as far as it did, but I promise I was trying to help. I can fix this."

Christian shoots me a look. "*Can* you?"

"Have you met me? Of course I can. I'll apologize to Ros myself if I have to. Just give me a few days, and I'll get everything worked out."

He doesn't look like he believes me, but after a long moment, he sighs and looks away. "Fine."

I feel an odd rush of relief. "Thanks, Christian. I promise I actually will fix it."

"Yeah, okay. Are you gonna let me in on your brilliant fix-it plan?"

"I will once I figure that part out. For now"—I reach out and put a hand on his arm—"go home and ice your ego. We'll regroup tomorrow."

Christian looks down at me with a reluctant smile, then quickly up at the sky. "Please go put your shirt back on."

"Dude, you've literally seen so much worse than this from me—"

"Shut up. I will *pay* you to shut up."

"Okay, fine. But don't expect me to start acting different around you." I give him a wink. "You're the one we're trying to make look perfect here. I think we both agree I'm already perfect exactly the way I am."

21

CHRISTIAN

THE ANXIETY OF WAITING TO SEE HOW SAM plans to fix things with me and Ros is starting to become unbearable. Every time I catch a glimpse of Ros in the hallway, it feels like something in my chest is about to explode. I texted her a few hours after the date (on Sam's instructions, of course), but she never answered. It's been eating away at my nerves ever since. Sam told me not to worry, that silence doesn't necessarily mean that it's over, but how am I supposed to be calm when everything about this is still so uncertain?

I don't even notice that I've been staring at the same trig equation for ten minutes until Aimee comes bursting into my room, making me drop my pencil at the loud noise of the door banging against the wall. "I'm bored," she whines, draping herself over the back of my chair. Yankee comes loping in behind her, grinning and panting.

"So you decided to have a party in my room?" I say.

Her eyes light up. "We *could* have a party! I'll play some music, and you can make Yankee dance."

"I'm doing homework, Mee-mee. I can't. Maybe later."

"But you've been doing homework for *hours*!"

"Yeah, well, I'm still not done, so you'll have to—"

A loud voice booms from down the stairs. "Aimee! Are you interrupting your brother?"

Aimee freezes, eyes wide. "No, Dad."

"Leave him alone, Aimee. He can play once he's done with his work."

We both know better than to argue with him. I give Aimee an apologetic shrug. "It's almost your bedtime, anyway. Maybe tomorrow?"

She pouts but leaves my room without any more argument. I watch her go, struck by a weird sense of déjà vu, and turn back to the homework that is most definitely not getting done tonight, reminded that even though things look different in the house these days, not a whole lot has actually changed.

I'm sitting on the floor of Will's room, the Go board set out in front of us, and I'm losing by a mile. Will is sitting propped up on a pile of unfolded laundry, face screwed up in concentration as he tries to work out his next move. He always plays with the white pieces, and right now his white tokens way outnumber my black ones. He's sixteen at the time, which would make me twelve, and I'm trying to distract him from his next move by talking about someone from school.

"Why do girls always stay in big groups? It makes it so hard to try to talk to one of them on their own."

He laughs, placing one of his Go pieces at an intersection and capturing another one of mine. "You're asking the wrong person, Chris."

"Aren't older brothers supposed to have all the answers?"

"Not this older brother." He shoots me a sideways glance. "Why are you trying to talk to random girls anyway? I don't remember you being friends with any girls from elementary school."

"I'm not. But if I wanted to be, I wouldn't be able to talk to one of them without her friends staring and whispering about me."

"It's a defense mechanism to keep away the creeps. Are you acting like a creep?"

"No!"

"Then you're fine." He gestures at the board. "Your turn."

I sigh, moving another piece without much thought. I'm pretty sure I can't win at this point, and the game is really just an excuse to talk anyway. "Middle school sucks."

"Yes, it does. High school isn't much better, either, so don't get your hopes up."

"That's not what you're supposed to say! What happened to 'it gets better'?"

Will laughs and shakes his head. "If it does get better, then it only happens once you're finally out of school. You've just gotta survive until then, Chris."

"I don't think I like your advice anymore."

He grins. "Then stop asking for it."

We go back to playing for a few more minutes in silence, until I can't resist anymore and ask, "Have you ever had a girlfriend, Will?"

He freezes up, hand halfway to the board.

"I won't tell Mom and Dad."

That makes him relax a little. Telling our parents *anything* is a touchy subject with Will. He takes his turn and says casually, not looking at me, "Sure."

"Really? When?"

"Last year. It wasn't serious or anything, only for a few weeks."

"Do I know her?"

He smirks. "You definitely don't."

"How did you ask her out?"

"What's with all the girl questions, Chris? Are you trying to hint at something?"

I feel my face heat up and avoid making eye contact. "No."

"Liar."

"Am not!"

"Liiaaaarrr."

"Fine!" If I get any hotter, my hair might catch on fire. "There's a girl I like in my homeroom, but I don't have any classes with her, and she's always with her other friends."

"Have you ever talked to her before?"

"No, I just said she's always with her friends."

"Do you know her *name*, even?"

I fiddle with one of my captured Go pieces. "It starts with an A, I think."

Will just laughs. "You fall for people way too easy, Christian."

"Do not."

"Do too. It's who you are. You *care* so much about everything. Remember three years ago when I told you how I dissected a frog in biology class, and you cried for an hour?"

"It was *not* an hour!"

"Pretty sure it was. I counted it."

I'm about to yell at him, start a real sibling fight, but before I get the chance, the door to Will's room opens, and Mom is standing there. She's got Aimee on her hip, and she takes in the two of us and the Go board with wide eyes.

"William," she says, and I can hear the warning in her voice. "Did you finish your homework before you started playing a game?"

I watch Will's shoulders tense. "Yes."

"Did Christian finish his homework?"

He shoots me a sideways look. "I . . . I didn't ask."

"Christian, did you?"

Sensing the beginning of an argument, I look at the floor and mutter something too quiet to hear.

Mom looks at Will again. "Put the game away, now. You're distracting Christian when he should be getting work done."

Will's eyes flare. "That's not my fault! He wanted to play, and he didn't tell me that—"

"Do *not* raise your voice at me. You're the eldest, so it should be your responsibility to ask. Dad's going to be home in ten minutes. Do you want him to hear about this?"

He definitely has more to say, but the threat of getting Dad involved is enough to shut him down. So instead, he balls his fists and stares at the ground, eyes burning and shiny. "No."

"Okay. Then clean up the game and let your brother go back to work. And for God's sake, fold that laundry instead of sitting on it. I'm not going to iron it again."

She leaves the room, and as soon as she's gone, Will starts scraping the Go pieces off the board and tossing them into the box, letting them bounce and scatter in his frustration.

I don't understand why he's so angry. He and my parents have been arguing more and more lately, but usually I play music or bury my head in my pillows so I don't have to hear what they're saying. I know teenagers are supposed to be extra moody, though. Maybe it's that.

I start to leave the room, but as I reach the door, I turn back and say, "You were gonna win anyway."

Will pauses, about to slam the Go board back into the box. He looks over his shoulder at me and smiles weakly. His eyes look a little red, but he's my big brother, so I pretend I don't notice. "I know. Now get out of here."

I give him a big gap-toothed smile in return and leave. It's not like I'd rather be doing my homework than playing a game. But if I don't start now, it'll turn into another fight, and I'm not the kid who starts fights in the family. Besides, I don't want to make anyone more upset than they already are.

SAM

CHRISTIAN'S STILL MAD AT ME FOR WHAT HAP-
pened at the track the other day. I'll admit, it was a risk—picking
a fight to try to make Ros jealous—but I was hoping he'd understand that sometimes risks pay off. He texted me afterward, like
it took him a while to put together what he wanted to say to me.

> **CHRISTIAN:** you have to run ideas like that by me,
> sam. i'm involved in this too
> **SAM:** I didn't exactly have time to ask for your
> approval, did I?
> **CHRISTIAN:** then don't do it! you come up with
> something else that doesn't involve you completely
> taking over

SAM: I thought we were doing this because you WANTED me to take over

CHRISTIAN: i want you to HELP. i might not be the best at talking to people, but at the end of the day, it's not you trying to date ros. it's me. you've gotta let me have at least a little say in what's going on

I wanted to tell him that beggars can't be choosers, but I didn't think he'd take that very well.

Regardless, I can agree that my intervention didn't go the way it was supposed to. The stilted, awkward conversation between Ros and Christian at Flannery's was a bad start, and my trying to make Ros jealous only made it worse. A stupid mistake, really. I should have known Ros wasn't the type to fall for the usual tactics.

Still, I was surprised she didn't seem more angry at the time. Maybe she's good at hiding her feelings, but it seemed more like she was . . . testing me. Blocking all my attempts to make her angry, turning them back on me and waiting to see how I'd respond. Whatever the test was supposed to be, I'm not sure if I passed or not, and that bothers me.

Ros isn't supposed to be the one with the upper hand here. If she is, then my texting her without telling Christian probably isn't the best idea. But the way it stands now, it's going to take more than a weak apology from Christian to turn this around. I'm going to have to do some good old-fashioned groveling.

Plus, a tiny part of me wonders what she'll act like when she learns it's *me* she's talking to, without Christian's influence anywhere. If she talks to me at all, that is.

Whatever the next test of hers is, it's one I'm determined to pass.

ROS

When my phone goes off, I'm expecting another text from Christian. He sent me one after the disastrous first date, then went silent after that; if nothing else, he at least knows how to give a girl some space. Instead of Christian, though, when I open my messages, I see a number I don't recognize.

UNKNOWN: Hey, Ros? This is Sam Dickson

My heart thuds in my chest. I should have known this was coming. This girl is ballsy, I'll give her that. Especially showing up in her sports bra, like that was supposed to intimidate me or something. Sure, she can talk a good game, and she actually seems smarter than I first thought, but none of that's good when it's paired with jealousy and also directed right at you. If I'm about to get thrown into some fight over a guy, then none of this is worth it. I don't have the patience or the energy.

I can see that she's typing, though, so I try to cut her off with a quick message.

ROS: Sam, I don't know how you got my number, but if
this is about Christian, then you can forget it. He's all
yours.

The typing bubble vanishes. For a moment, I think I might
have actually averted disaster. But then it pops up again, and a
few seconds later, the message comes through.

SAM: Actually, Chris gave me your number. I wanted
to apologize for the way the other day went. I swear I
wasn't trying to be weird or possessive or something.
I was jogging and saw you both and just wanted to
say hi. Then you tapped into my competitive instincts
and . . . yeah. So I'm sorry. I didn't mean to ruin your
date (?) and I don't want to mess up anything you
guys have going on

Huh. Girls like Sam are usually so protective of their exes,
even if they were the ones who broke it off. I've heard of fights
started over less. Nothing I've seen so far has told me Sam would
be any different. And yet, this weird little apology is the last thing
I expected from her.

It takes a few minutes before I think of a way to reply.

ROS: I appreciate the apology. I do think there was
some miscommunication that happened the other
day. I wouldn't call what we were doing a "date,"

> though. Christian's sweet, but I don't think we have
> very much in common.
>
> **SAM:** Really? You guys looked like you were hitting it
> off

I have to laugh at that. Clearly, Sam wasn't there for the whole of that train wreck. Christian may have given her a different story about what actually happened.

> **ROS:** Not to be argumentative, but why do you care?
> You're not dating him anymore.
>
> **SAM:** Maybe not, but he's still my friend
>
> **ROS:** Friend, huh? Are you sure?

The answer comes instantly.

> **SAM:** VERY sure. He's like my brother at this point. I
> like to look out for him, but we didn't make a good
> couple
>
> **SAM:** Can I be honest about something, though?
>
> **ROS:** Sure.
>
> **SAM:** Talking to you has made Christian really happy

I stare at my phone for a second, taken aback by the message. I was expecting a fight, some territorial crap about stealing somebody's man, maybe a threat to ruin my life. But is Sam actually encouraging me to go out with Christian?

My phone pings with another message.

SAM: He's been gushing about you for over a week now. When you agreed to talk to him, he was thrilled. You have no idea how pissed he was at me for crashing your date the other day. I swear I wasn't trying to screw anything up, and I don't want you to think I'm standing in the way of the two of you hanging out. I care about him, and that means I want him to be happy

SAM: If this is TMI then feel free to ignore all of it. Maybe you don't feel that way about Christian, and if so that's fine. I would just hate myself a little bit if you didn't give him a shot because of me

Where is all this coming from? If Sam is lying, then she's doing a very good job of it. One thing's for sure, though: In some way, she *cares* about Christian, whether it's platonic or not, and you can really tell in the way she talks about him. It's a level of depth that I didn't expect from her, and now that I've seen it, I'm not sure how to react.

ROS: That's . . . really nice of you to do, Sam. I definitely don't know many ex-girlfriends who would be so accepting.

SAM: I pride myself on doing things most people don't expect 😬

SAM: So . . . apology accepted?

I realize that I'm smiling. I'd like to think that I'm above getting charmed by smooth talkers, but Sam is an odd case.

The malicious intent I always assumed was behind her motives just . . . isn't there. I still don't know how I feel about Christian, and I don't think there's anything she could say to change that, but at least for the moment, she's persuaded me not to give the whole thing up as a lost cause.

> **ROS:** Apology accepted. I'll have to talk to Christian about this at some point, but you and I are okay.
> **SAM:** Oh, he'll talk to you, don't worry. I'll make sure of it
> **SAM:** Also, does this mean I don't immediately have to lose this number?

I smirk, leaning back in my chair.

> **ROS:** I guess not.
> **SAM:** Okay good. Because if you're still gonna be hanging around with Christian then we're going to see each other more often, and it would be really awkward to keep pretending we don't know each other or whatever
> **ROS:** From what I've heard, you know everyone at Northeastern, Sam. I don't think that was ever a possibility.
> **SAM:** Good point. Maybe that's why everyone says you're the smart one ✌️

I decide to ignore the jab about my reputation. She's only saying it to get a rise out of me. As I put my phone back down on my desk, though, it dawns on me how far from my comfort zone I suddenly am. I've never minded being a loner, never been bothered by a lack of temporary high school popularity, and I always thought it would stay that way.

It reminds me of the old anecdote about frogs and hot water. Try to drop a frog into a pot of boiling water, and of course it's going to jump out immediately, because it knows the heat is dangerous. But if you put it in when the water is cool and slowly raise the temperature until it boils, the frog will sit there, slowly cooking alive, because by the time it realizes the water is too hot to survive, it's already too late. I've been going about my life like always, not noticing the changes, and suddenly I've realized that I just went on a date with Northeastern's golden boy and am slowly becoming acquaintances with his ex-girlfriend. The craziest part is, I don't actually mind. I feel like I *should* mind. This isn't me, not even a little.

But then, I've never had the best grasp on who I am to begin with.

23

CHRISTIAN

SAM CORNERS ME IN THE HALLWAY ON WEDNES-day, a determined look on her face that says she's got an idea and I'm probably not going to like it. "You need to talk to her," she says.

I feel the blood drain out of my face. "Now?"

"Yes, now. Do you know where her next class is?"

"Sure, it's AP British Lit. Down the hall from my history class."

"Then you need to talk to her before or after that class."

I make a face. "Can't I just do it over text?"

"No." Sam is insistent. "An apology from you over text looks fake. I've already laid the groundwork, so she's open to talking to you, but you have to make the next move here."

"You did? Sam . . ."

"Yeah, I smoothed things over. Promised I wasn't trying to

win you back or anything. From the sound of it, she was pretty much ready to forgive you."

That eases my nerves a little. "Really?"

"Would I lie?"

A movement in my peripheral vision catches my attention. There are plenty of kids in the hallway—the warning bell hasn't rung yet—but I catch a glimpse of distinctive long brown hair vanishing around a corner. *Ros.* If what Sam said was true, then it shouldn't be that hard to talk to her. Just say sorry, and we can get back on track. Can't be that bad, right?

Except for the fact that even thinking about it is making me break out in a sweat. It's not only the fact that it's Ros, either— what if she *is* mad at me? How do I even begin to fix that?

I turn and look at Sam. "Are you going to help me?"

"What, over *text*?"

"I have no idea what to say!"

"But you can't stare at your phone again, Christian. That didn't go so well for you last time."

"Well, I can't exactly bring you with me, can I?"

She frowns. "Maybe not, but . . ." Then she trails off, pulling out her phone and typing something in. A few seconds later, my phone starts to buzz in my pocket.

I stare at her. "Are you calling me?"

"Answer it and leave it on. Keep your earbuds in while you talk to her, too."

"Wait, what are you—"

"Christian." Sam glares at me. "We both know how well that first date went. Talking to her solo doesn't work out for you.

This way, I can listen in and tell you how to respond in real time instead of constantly texting you."

I shake my head. "This is the worst idea you've ever had. It's like some kind of talk show prank! There's no way."

"Would you rather stand there with your face buried in your phone the whole time?"

"I'd *rather* be able to talk to her myself."

"Yeah, well, you're not ready for that yet. Until you can keep up with Ros on her level, you need my help. Otherwise, she's going to completely destroy you."

It hurts to hear it, but she's right. Ros is way too smart for me, and I still get nervous to be around her. Going in on my own now, especially for something like this, is only going to end in disaster. I need Sam's backup on this.

With a huge sigh, I stuff one of my earbuds into my ear and accept the second call from Sam. "Just do what I tell you," she says, the delay from the phone giving her a weird echo. "You'll be fine."

"If you make me say something stupid, we're not friends anymore," I mumble, and shuffle off in the direction I saw Ros disappear.

I manage to catch her before she walks through the door of her classroom. When I call out her name, she tenses but doesn't look too surprised to see that it's me. She waits until I catch up, then moves out of the way of the door, one hand on the strap of her backpack. "Hi, Christian."

"Hey."

She's looking up at me, and again I find myself pinned to the spot by her eyes, the same way I was when I saw her at the play. The same way I was when she turned me down cold in the hallway after trig. I start to sweat.

"Listen, uhh . . ." *Any day now would be great, Sam.*

And right on cue, I hear her voice in my ear. "*I wanted to say I'm sorry—*"

"I wanted to say I'm sorry," I repeat, keeping my eyes on Ros's face, "for the way I was acting at Flannery's the other day. I didn't really think through the whole date idea before I asked you, and I was nervous. I didn't want to screw anything up, but I think I was so worried about saying something wrong, I ended up doing it anyway."

Ros sighs, breaking eye contact. "Yeah, I wasn't exactly bringing my best self that day, either."

"*I like you a lot,*" Sam prompts.

"I like you . . . uh, a lot. I do actually want to get to know you, like you said, but I think I was too worried about impressing you. Would it be—uh, would it be too much to ask to make a better *fourth* impression the next time?"

She looks at me for a long time, and I can tell she's really, honestly considering what I—well, what *Sam*—just told her. I don't know whether to be impressed or scared that something I said made one of the smartest girls I've ever met *think*.

Then, slowly, she makes eye contact with me again, and she smiles. She smiles, and I realize with a jolt that it's the most genuine one she's given me so far. It's a really, really pretty smile. It kind of . . . lights her face up, makes her look more approachable, and suddenly it's hard to see why some people call her The Shrew.

"Okay, Christian," she says. "Fourth time's the charm. And . . . I'm sorry, too. I don't usually do this kind of thing, so it's all new to me. I don't know how I'm supposed to act."

"Yeah, well, it's not like—"

"—any of this is really *old* to me, either."

"That's comforting, I guess." She shuffles her feet for a second, then frowns. "Am I really that scary, though?"

"You seem like the kind of person who's hard to impress."

I'm worried Ros might take that as an insult, but to my relief, she laughs. "All right, that's fair. And at the very least, your ability to keep me talking to you is kind of impressive." She gives me a steady look. "No more awkward coffee dates. Deal?"

"Deal. And next time we hang out, you can pick the place."

"I said go *out, Chris, not hang out."*

Ros smiles again. "Sounds like a plan."

The warning bell rings, and both of us look up as other students start to hurry toward their classes.

"I should probably go," I say. "Have fun in class."

"I will."

"Text you later?"

"Sure."

I start to walk backward down the hallway, still keeping my eyes on her, and almost collide with someone going the other way. Ros laughs, shaking her head, and with one last glance at me, she disappears into her classroom.

I book it back up the hall to Sam, who's standing against a bank of lockers with her earbuds in, looking to anyone else like she's just loitering and listening to music. I grab her by the shoulder. "Sam, you're a genius."

"We already knew that." But she's grinning, too. "Nice work, Romeo. We're back on track."

"Remember when I said I owed you a milkshake? We're up to, like, ten of those now."

"Chris, you owe me milkshakes for the rest of my natural life. Now get to class."

24

ROS

I'M NOT GOING TO SAY I'M AN ART EXPERT, because that would be a lie. It's also not like I go to museums regularly, either. But Christian suggested we go somewhere I wanted, and I figured a place where there were things to walk around and look at might be better than that disastrous first date at Flannery's.

Date. That word still feels weird. It puts a kind of pressure on what would otherwise be a simple interaction. It's making me nervous and tongue-tied in a way I wasn't ready for. Is this how dates are supposed to go?

Regardless, I'm here now, and I promised Christian I'd give him another shot. The Worcester Art Museum is big, old, and full of interesting things to talk about. I like the photography collections, predictably, but we've spent most of our time wandering around looking at ancient sculptures and vases in relative silence.

Right now, we're walking through the Greek section, footsteps echoing on the marble floor. The museum is fairly busy, but still quiet, as people are mostly silent or talking in soft voices as they walk through the exhibits.

I glance over at Christian. He's more attentive than I thought he'd be, actually stopping to look at items and, once or twice, even taking pictures. He does that now, pausing in front of an Ancient Greek vase, wide and shallow and painted with a repeating pattern of men on horseback.

"You've got your earbuds in," I remark, and he jumps like I've startled him. One of the earbuds falls out, though whatever music he's listening to is too quiet for me to catch.

"Uh, yeah," he stammers, and for a second, I'm worried we might be back to square one. But after a moment of trying to pull his thoughts together, Christian clears his throat and smiles sheepishly. "I . . . get nervous, I guess. Music has always calmed me down before. I figured it might help. Plus, it's already so quiet in here."

I shrug. Fair enough. "Can't argue with that. I wish people would talk more in museums. Like, what are you looking for, a better conversation starter than a three-thousand-year-old piece of pottery?"

Christian smiles. "I don't really know *how* to talk about this kind of stuff."

"Well then, let's start here." I point to the vase he was just taking a picture of. "What are these people doing on their horses?"

He squints at the old ceramic. "Those little lines around them look like wheat. Maybe they're helping with some kind of harvest?"

"Could be. Then again, ancient art like this isn't usually subjective." I point to the little plaque under the display, where it describes the pictures: A SEATED DIONYSIUS AND ARIADNE SURROUNDED BY MOUNTED AND RUNNING SATYRS.

Christian looks embarrassed. "Oh. I . . . didn't read that far."

"That's okay. Most Greek art depicts something specific, like a story or moment in history. If you're looking for subjectivity, then you're better off in modern art."

He laughs a little. "Now there's an area of art that I really have trouble with." Then, after a few seconds of silence, he adds, "Couldn't ancient art be a little bit subjective, though?"

I glance over at him. "What do you mean?"

"Well, maybe it is showing a specific story or piece of history, but can't you usually tell how an artist feels about something because of the way they paint it? Like . . ." He pauses for a second, trying to collect his thoughts. "If you had a painting of Brutus stabbing Julius Caesar done by three different artists, they'd all paint basically the same thing, but you'd be able to tell whether they sided with Brutus or Caesar, and if they thought it was just an assassination, or if Brutus and the others were too violent. You'd get part of their opinion from the painting, because they'd be painting things the way *they* saw it. You know?"

Where in the world did *that* just come from? Weeks ago, I wouldn't have thought that kind of critical thinking possible from a guy like Christian. Even today, I hadn't expected much more from him than a cursory "nice vase," and I wouldn't have been disappointed. But, for the second time in less than a month, Christian Powell has managed to surprise me. And now that he has . . .

I feel a smile growing on my face. "That was . . . a really good point. Are you interested in the Ancient Romans?"

And just like that, he's back to looking sheepish. "I might have used up the only piece of Roman history I know."

I laugh, and a couple of other museumgoers turn to look at me as the sound bounces off the shiny walls and floor. "That's okay. I never really cared about the Romans, either. But now I kind of want to head to the second floor and see what kind of 'opinions' you think the Renaissance painters had. You game?"

He smiles at me, and in his eyes, I think I see a bit of a challenge. "Always."

25

CHRISTIAN

TALKING TO ROS IS GETTING EASIER EVERY DAY.
Not just in person, but over text as well. I'm starting to figure
out how she speaks, the kinds of things she finds funny, how to
tell when she means something or when she's being sarcastic. It
makes conversations so much easier, because I don't have to be
on edge, worrying about the next thing I have to say. It's almost
like talking to Sam.

Sam's still helping me out, of course. I'm not some sparkling
conversationalist all of a sudden. She'll listen in over the phone
when we're in person and give suggestions when I text her a
screenshot of whatever Ros and I are talking about. It's working,
but it's also nice not to feel completely dependent on her anymore. Honestly, it's great that Ros is more talkative now, too. I

was worried at first, when her responses were short and every sentence ended with a period (seriously, who does that over text?). It made me feel like I might never get the hang of talking to her. Now, though, she even initiates conversations, asks me questions, and seems genuinely interested in the answer. I'm not sure what changed, but I'd really like to believe that this thing—whatever it is—is working.

I've been wondering lately what makes me so bad at real conversations. Talkative genes are in my blood: Mom's a master of party small talk, Dad preaches all the time about the importance of "networking," and there's maybe only three things in the world that could get Aimee to shut up. And sure, if I'm with somebody familiar, and we get on a topic that both of us know a lot about, I could talk for hours. But as soon as the conversation goes somewhere unfamiliar, or if it seems like I might upset someone by saying the wrong thing, every neuron in the talking part of my brain shuts down.

Ros is . . . intense. She knows a lot about a lot of things and usually has pretty strong opinions. Sam's the same way, but where disagreeing with Sam might lead to getting mocked, Ros gives off the vibe that every conversation is a test and that the chances of failing are uncomfortably high.

Like right now, for example. She's texting me about something in one of her classes—her AP British Lit teacher took points off a recent test for something she said in an essay question—and from the sound of it, she's pissed. I think I'm supposed to play the supportive role, but I'm not exactly sure how. Sam always used to get mad at me when I tried to give her solutions to problems, and she reminded me as much when I asked for help with this.

> **SAM:** 90 percent of the time, people don't want to hear suggestions when they're angry, Christian. You don't have to fix anything. Just listen and tell her it sucks.

So I've been using different versions of "that sucks" for the last fifteen minutes, and even I can tell I'm repeating myself. I know Ros notices it, too.

> **ROS:** The whole point of analysis is that it's SUPPOSED to be subjective. As long as you have good examples to back you up, that should be enough to get credit.
> **CHRISTIAN:** sure
> **ROS:** But apparently I didn't get the memo that we're only supposed to parrot back exactly what this one middle-aged white guy thinks about a different middle-aged white guy. Independent thinking takes too long for him to grade, I guess.
> **CHRISTIAN:** yeah, that's definitely not fair

My palms are sweating. Even though this isn't an in-person conversation, I still have no idea how to handle angry people. It stresses me out, and my first instinct is to either calm them down and tell them what they want to hear or completely leave the conversation. If I'm being honest, I think the idea of someone being mad at me scares me. I've seen conflict tear people up, and I'd rather avoid it altogether than risk that. But I can't ghost Ros, so I'm texting Sam like crazy, asking her what I should do. I'm getting the feeling that "that sucks" isn't going to cut it for much longer. She must be doing something else, though, because she's not answering, and I'm starting to feel more and more stranded.

ROS: I might try going above his head to get my grade fixed, honestly. I tried talking to him about it and he wouldn't listen. Maybe Mrs. Reagan or the principal would.

Is this the part where I offer advice? Do I agree with her or give a different opinion? My heart is starting to beat harder. I uselessly check Sam's messages again, like she might have responded and I didn't see it, but there's nothing. Looks like I'm on my own here. With a deep breath, I go back to the conversation.

CHRISTIAN: what grade did you actually end up with? like, what was the grade overall?

ROS: It was a B plus, but it could easily have been an A if Mr. Travers would stop singling me out. Besides, it's the principle of the thing.

CHRISTIAN: but do you think he might grade you extra hard on other tests if you try to get him in trouble? he sounds like the kind of guy who would be bitter about something like that

ROS: Maybe. And I don't think it's actually going to affect my GPA that much or anything, it's . . . ugh.

ROS: Sorry, I know I'm ranting. I'm just annoyed. Thanks for listening to all of that.

CHRISTIAN: sure, no worries!

CHRISTIAN: and if it makes you feel any better, a B plus would be an improvement for me 😂

ROS: Okay, fair enough. :)

I lean back in my desk chair with a relieved sigh. I didn't screw it up. Ros isn't mad at me, and I handled it by myself. Maybe now my clenched muscles can finally relax.

A memory comes to me suddenly: Will, standing in the doorway to my room. I think I was fourteen, and he was a senior in high school and supposed to be looking into colleges and figuring his life out. I knew there had been another fight earlier—no shouting this time, but I heard Mom's and Dad's raised voices. I hadn't heard Will say anything, but now here he is, standing there like he's not sure if he's allowed in. I can tell that something's wrong, and for some reason, that scares me.

He's quiet for a long time, picking at his already bitten-short fingernails. I pretend to go back to whatever it was I was doing before he came in, waiting for him to get to the point. Almost two minutes pass like that.

"Do you ever get tired?" he says finally, voice soft and a little scratchy. "Just being around them."

"Mom and Dad?"

"Yeah."

"What do you mean?"

"I just mean . . . tired. Not physically, but like you can't keep thinking anymore. Like they sucked all the life out of you, and it's not even worth trying to have your own thoughts."

My heart starts beating faster. Why is he asking me this? Why does it feel like he wants me to pick a side? Will and I don't talk about deep stuff. We just don't. We play Go and make fun of each other like siblings are supposed to, and that's it. Will doesn't talk about many friends from school, either. I'm all he's got. I'd tell him to talk to Mom or Dad about it, but they're the ones he's fighting with. And even if he weren't, I know what they'd say. Mom would respond with some line about how things aren't actually that bad, and Dad would tell him to suck it up. I think I'm the only one he can talk to about this, and I have no idea what to say. I can't risk getting in trouble like he does.

So I blow him off.

I frown at him. "No. Why would I?"

And just like that, I watch something in his expression shut down. His jaw sets, and he breaks eye contact. Whatever chance that was, he's not going to give it to me again. I said the wrong thing.

"No reason," he says. "Forget I said anything." Then he turns and leaves.

He leaves the door to my room open, and once he's gone, I can hear Mom and Dad still talking in hushed voices.

". . . won't listen, he's too stubborn . . ."

". . . wrong with him?"

I stand up and shut my door, their voices cut off before I can hear any more. I don't want to hear it. I don't want to know.

My phone buzzes in my hand and makes me jump.

> **SAM:** Sorry, I was helping Nana with something. What did I miss??
>
> **CHRISTIAN:** no worries, disaster avoided. i managed to hold it down without you 😜
>
> **SAM:** Wait, really?

I send her the screenshots as proof, and she hearts each one. It's a weird rush of pride that I've managed to impress Sam, and I ride that high for the rest of my conversation with Ros, confident in a way I don't usually feel.

26

SAM

I SHOULDN'T TALK TO ROS ANYMORE.

I don't have to. I patched things up between us after our encounter on the track, and she and Christian are on good terms again. Job done. I can go back to working behind the scenes, our only interactions one-sided and filtered through Christian, either my texting him what to say or whispering in his ear when they meet in person. Especially with my status as Christian's exgirlfriend, it's probably better if Ros and I don't talk at all. Also, it's not like I don't have *other* people I can talk to. Aria and I haven't talked in a while, and we're long overdue for another hangout.

The thing is, though, I'm curious. While our talk after the disastrous coffee date *was* technically an argument, I wasn't as angry afterward as I thought I'd be. It's not often I meet someone who can keep up with me in a conversation. God knows I love Christian to death, but he's useless at it. When someone like Ros comes along and manages to almost (key word, *almost*) beat me in an argument—well, I bet that would make for some interesting talks.

I have to be careful not to mess up the situation with Christian, of course. I've worked too hard to destroy that for the sake of curiosity. Still, speaking through Christian can only give me so much information. There are things he wouldn't say, topics he wouldn't ask about, and that leaves a whole lot of unexplored territory. I pride myself on learning what makes people tick, and this is a special case. I've been assuming Ros was just a stuck-up faux intellectual, but if what I've seen so far is any indication, there's more to her than that. There are layers to Ros Shew, and I'm going to find all of them.

SAM: Remember how I said I wasn't going to lose your number?

ROS: Uh-oh.

SAM: Aww come on! Why should Christian get to have all the fun of talking to you?

ROS: Are you saying you're jealous of him?

My heart jumps. *I was right.* Oh, this is gonna be fun.

SAM: Does it help or hurt my chances of you responding to me if I say yes?

ROS: Jury's still out. Give me a few months to decide and I'll get back to you.

SAM: Ouch 😣

SAM: But seriously, if you really don't want to talk to me then that's fine. I'm a big girl, I can handle it

ROS: Can you, though? I didn't exactly get that impression from you the other day.

This girl does *not* beat around the bush. Anyone else might have been a bit more tactful, or even avoided saying anything at all, especially with someone they don't know that well. I kind of respect her for it, though. She's direct. Doesn't have time for small talk, would rather say what she means than keep silent. Two can play at that game.

SAM: There's a difference between being honest and being harsh just to get a rise out of me, Ros

ROS: Fine, point taken. Still, I would have expected someone like you to have a much thicker skin, especially if you want to work in entertainment.

SAM: Not JUST entertainment, thank you very much. I'm gonna go full Emma Watson—show business, activism, academia, and whatever else sounds like fun that week

ROS: Sounds ambitious.

SAM: That's me 😜

SAM: But enough about how great I am. How's your afternoon going?

ROS: Fine, I guess. Need to finish up some homework and work on my Bellerose presentation some more.

Right. That. For some reason, the mention of the assembly doesn't inspire the same rage in me that it used to.

SAM: Christian told me you guys went to the art museum the other day. How was that? Not as awkward as the last date, I hope

ROS: No, actually, it was nice. He had some pretty insightful things to say.

I'll fully admit I was fishing for an indirect compliment on that one. Christian is sweet, but insightful? Not so much. I was on call the whole time, and the Worcester Art Museum has their collections archived online. All Christian had to do was text me a picture, and one quick keyword search later, I could give you a hundred insightful comments from the comfort of my own bedroom. Still, it's a nice ego boost to hear that it worked.

SAM: Cool! Also what's your favorite pizza topping

ROS: . . . So we're just completely changing topics now?

SAM: Yeah, basically

ROS: Okay then. I like plain old pepperoni. But my dad likes ham and pineapple, so I usually don't mind sharing that with him.

SAM: Wait

SAM: Stop EVERYTHING

SAM: You actually eat pineapple on pizza?

ROS: Yeah, and?

SAM: My God. This is it

SAM: I never thought I'd actually meet an alien, but you've been peacefully living on earth this whole time. Going to my school. Dating my ex

ROS: I thought we were past the petty insults thing, Sam.

SAM: Have you MET me?

ROS: Barely.

SAM: Then you'll get used to it 😉

SAM: This is how I show people I like them

ROS: By being rude?

SAM: Pretty much

ROS: Then that either perfectly explains what happened on the track or makes the whole thing much more confusing.

SAM: I think I'll let you ponder that one on your own ✌️ have fun with homework!

ROS: Always a pleasure, Sam.

27

CHRISTIAN

"YOU'RE NOT GONNA QUIZ ME ON ANY OF THIS, are you?"

Ros laughs. "Do you want me to?"

"Please don't."

It's a little too cold to be in a park, but I think both of us are eager to believe that spring is already here. So here we are, on a chilly late February afternoon, the only ones wandering between the still-bare trees. Ros brought her camera, and she's trying to explain to me how it works, using words like *aperture* and *white balance* that mean absolutely nothing to me. It doesn't seem like she minds my ignorance, though. As usual, Sam is on call, ready to step in if I need help, but honestly, I'm starting to feel pretty good.

"I didn't think there'd be much to take pictures of before spring started," I say.

Ros shrugs. "Not much wildlife, sure. But I don't mind. I think it forces me to get creative, find other things that would make for a good picture instead."

She points up to a tree nearby. There aren't any leaves on it yet, and against the pale blue sky, the branches look almost black. "Like that," she continues. "Go stand underneath it and look up."

I do, squinting against the light. "It makes the branches look like a web."

"Exactly." She joins me, points her camera upward, and makes a few adjustments before snapping a picture. "That'll be an interesting one."

"*Tell her she should take over your Instagram,*" Sam says in my ear.

"Maybe I should just give you my Instagram password, Ros. You could handle that train wreck better than me."

Ros laughs. "From what I remember of your Instagram, it wasn't actually that bad. You've got decent photography skills as far as phones go. And also some friends who don't mind taking pictures of you, apparently."

I laugh, hyperaware of the earbuds still in my ear. "Yeah, true. Without them, there probably wouldn't be any pictures of me on there."

"Well then"—Ros turns, lightning fast, and snaps a picture of me staring at her—"there's another one for you."

"Hey! You didn't even adjust anything for that; I *know* it can't be a good picture, because you didn't mess with the aperture or whatever—"

"Oh, calm down, Christian, you've got the face of every teen movie star ever. I think the picture will be fine."

All the blood in my body rushes to my face, and in my ear, Sam whispers, *"Compliment her back, genius!"*

Before I can, though, Ros continues. "Besides, it's not like you care that much about what goes on your Instagram, right? Not like Sam."

"She's been on my Instagram?"

"You've been on Sam's Instagram?"

She shrugs. "Sure. It's nice, but it's curated. Yours is more real. Like that video of you and your sister." She smiles again. "I really like that one."

"Yeah?"

"Yeah. That was the thing that persuaded me to give you a shot when you first messaged me."

"Oh, thank God," Sam says. *"She actually noticed."*

"Oh, thank—" I start, before realizing Sam didn't mean for me to say it out loud, finishing with a lame "—uh, thanks."

Ros doesn't seem to notice the slipup, though. Instead, she says, "What's your sister's name? I don't think I've ever asked."

"Aimee. She's almost eight."

"Wow, that's a big age difference. Are you the oldest?"

"No, I'm the middle kid. I have an older brother, Will, but he doesn't live with us anymore." Absently, I toy with the lucky game piece in my pocket. And then, because she's got me

thinking about Will, and because the compliment from earlier is still scrambling my brain a bit, and because Sam doesn't
chime in with anything, I say, "You should come meet my sister
sometime."

Ros stops and turns to me. "Meet her?"

"Yeah, why not? I think you'd like her a lot. Plus, you could
meet my dog and my parents. I'm sure they'd be happy to have
you over for dinner sometime—"

Sam hisses in a harsh breath. "*Chris, shut up!*"

I look back down at Ros and realize she's staring at me, eyes
almost deer-in-the-headlights wide. It takes me a few more seconds to realize that the reason why is that I invited her to meet
my parents.

Oops.

"No pressure, though," I blurt out, not waiting for Sam to
jump in with help. I can hear her through my earbuds, leaning
away from her phone to swear loudly. "You really don't have to
if you don't want to. I just figured—"

"I don't think I want to kiss you yet, Christian."

I stop, mouth hanging open. "I . . . what?"

"*Yeah, seriously, what?*"

Ros isn't looking at me. There's color in her cheeks that could
probably be blamed on the cold weather, if it weren't for the fact
that my face also feels like it could be on fire. Where is this coming from?

"I've never kissed anybody before," she says. All the confidence
or intelligence I'm used to hearing in her voice is gone, replaced
by a slight shake. She still won't look at me. "I'm not saying I

don't like you or anything, but you're more experienced at this than me. I don't plan on doing anything before I'm actually ready to, so if you're looking for more than that, then—"

"Whoa, whoa." I wave a hand to cut her off, frowning. "Sorry, I'm . . . I'm confused. Obviously, I'm not gonna make you do anything you don't want to."

Ros looks like she's been thrown off balance. "Oh. Okay then."

"Sorry, Ros. I didn't mean to give off that impression. I forgot that asking you to meet my parents *meant* something. It was honestly just an invitation. You don't have to do it. And you don't have to . . . kiss me, either. Not unless you want to. If it wasn't already obvious, I like hanging out with you."

I've never seen Ros look so self-conscious before. She's doing her best to make it look like her usual stubbornness, but the details give her away. She runs a hand through her hair, taking a deep breath. "Yeah. Yeah, well, I like hanging out with you, too."

"And for the record, I do think you'd like my sister."

It reminds me of something Sam would say, and I think it works, because Ros laughs. "I probably would," she says. Then, "Maybe I should come over and meet her sometime."

And just like that, my heart is back in my chest where it belongs. I laugh, too, out of relief more than anything else, and the tension leaks out of us along with the clouds of our breath.

"*Good job, Christian,*" Sam says in my ear, and the rush of pride I feel at handling things on my own is stronger than I would ever admit out loud.

"Anyway," Ros says, swiping at her eyes and pulling herself

back together again. "We should probably keep walking. I'm getting cold standing here."

"Yeah, probably. You wanna explain white balance to me again?"

"Not really."

"That's fair."

We start to wander down the path again, still talking, the air between us feeling lighter somehow, and Sam is surprisingly quiet for the rest of the afternoon.

28

SAM

SOMETIMES, TRYING TO BE THE BEST AT EVERY-thing gets lonely.

Christian texted me earlier today asking to hang out, since he doesn't have any plans with Ros, and Monty was busy, but I've got lots of things to do that I've been putting off ever since we started Operation Date Ros. There's a chemistry project I have to turn in, a paper due for English, and plenty more random pieces of schoolwork and college-application padding I've been neglecting. What once was a few small, manageable jobs has turned into a mountain of work, and I'm not leaving my room until I get it all finished.

I've been at it for almost four hours now, watching a perfectly good Saturday pass by from my bedroom window, crawling my way through half a dozen assignments that should have taken a few minutes each. My head isn't in the game today. I could be anywhere else, doing *anything* else right now. I could have taken Christian up on his offer to hang out. I could be grabbing coffee or going out somewhere with Aria. A bunch of other cool people from drama club have offered to hang out, and people from my other classes. Casey's free, right? They're on the volleyball team, and they seem pretty cool. I have their number. Or what about André? He's cute, and I'm pretty sure he likes me. Might be fun to give him a try.

Ugh. The thought of trying to talk to anyone else right now makes me want to crawl out of my skin. What a waste of time. My gaze drifts to the map of Loredo on my wall, and my heart starts to beat a little faster. It's supposed to motivate me to do better, but today, it's just making things worse.

You can't end up there.

My phone buzzes where I left it facedown on my bedside table. I walk over and pick it up, hopeful for the smallest second that it might be Ros, but it isn't. Just another notification from a dating app. Staring at it, I realize I haven't played around with my favorite hobby in almost a month. I was so focused on other things, it completely slipped my mind. Maybe that's why I've been so off lately.

I decide to take a break from my work and flop down on my bed, phone held up above my face. I need to get back into my old routine, and I'll be back to normal in no time. I open the dating app and swipe through to my profile, trying to remember who I'm pretending to be at the moment. Turns out, I didn't stray too far from the beaten path with this one, because according to the bio I wrote weeks ago, my name is "Cary," and all I want out of life is to be a famous actress. The photo I used is a blandly pretty, dime-a-dozen white girl with a blinding smile. According to my notifications, Cary's got more than ninety potential matches.

I scroll through the list of possible victims until I come across what looks like an easy mark. His name actually *is* Mark, too. Maybe eighteen or nineteen, with some really cute freckles and a smile that even rivals Cary's. He seems like the genuine type, the kind who actually tries to get to know someone before getting together. It should be no problem to have him hand over his number. According to the app, he sent me a message about a week ago, so I click on it:

> Hi Cary! I saw in your profile that you really like sushi. I've never tried it and I'm pretty sure the idea of eating raw fish might make me puke, but I'm giving you a chance to change my mind. 😜

He's practically already asking me out on a date. So easy. I could probably have his number within ten minutes and then move on to the next guy, but when I try typing out a response—a generic excuse about being sorry I missed his message earlier, a lure that I couldn't resist messaging him back because he's cute, blah blah blah—something makes me hesitate. I read over his message again, the little quip about raw fish making me smile. It sounds like something Christian would say.

And then the reality of what I just thought hits me like a truck—that's absolutely something Christian would say to me. Because he knows me, knows my sense of humor, and because once you get to know him, he's really charming.

Once you get to know him.

What makes me think I know who *any* of these guys are? I read their profile, scroll through a couple of pictures, and suddenly decide I know exactly what they want? I've proved by now that that stuff can be faked, that the persona you put up online isn't necessarily honest, and that even in real life, some people need more than one chance to prove themselves.

If I'd met Christian on an app like this, our relationship would have been over before it started. I would have assumed he was an awkward disaster and never spoken to him again. I might never have gotten to see the side of him that I do, the side that makes him the closest thing I'll ever have to a brother. It took work to get there, to see that side of him and let him see sides of me most people don't normally see, and none of what I learned about him was something I could have assumed on first impressions alone.

I click away from Mark's message, and his freckles and his smile. I delete my account and then the app itself. I do the same with the other apps like it, and then, before I get a chance to think about it, I'm sending a message.

SAM: What are your college plans?

ROS: Good afternoon to you, too.

SAM: Sorry. You're not busy, are you?

ROS: Just got out of a support group meeting. Why?

SAM: I'm bored

ROS: And you texted me to fix that?

SAM: Maybe

SAM: No but seriously I want to know your college plans

ROS: I repeat, why?

SAM: Because I'm BORED

ROS: Would you believe me if I said I don't have any yet?

I sit bolt upright in bed.

SAM: Wait seriously??

ROS: Yeah. I don't know if I'm going to start applying next fall or take a gap year before I have to commit to another four years of school.

And this, right here, is the most surprising thing that Ros has ever said. I genuinely can't tell if she's messing with me.

SAM: But you're the best student in school. You're so smart, you could probably go Ivy League if you wanted. Why waste that on a gap year?

ROS: Because I still don't know what I want to do with
   my life. Maybe taking a year will help me figure it
   out.
SAM: Why do that when you could get into Harvard
   now and figure it out once you get there?
ROS: I don't need to go to Harvard. A decent school
   that doesn't cost me or my dad too much money is
   fine by me.

The idea that one of the smartest girls I've ever met doesn't
care about what college she goes to—doesn't even know what she
wants to go to college *for*—unsettles me more than I thought it
would. If somebody like Ros doesn't have her life together by
now, then what hope do the rest of us have? What would people
think if they thought I didn't know where I was going for college? God, what would my *mom* think?

SAM: You know, I really don't get you sometimes
ROS: What? Why?
SAM: You're ROS SHEW. You're like genius-level
   smart and you're so good at everything without even
   trying, but you don't have any plans for the future? It
   doesn't make sense

It takes a while for Ros to respond, and for a moment, I'm
worried I offended her. But then the typing bubble pops up and
stays for a while, which means she's either got a lot to say or she's

thinking carefully about what she's got to tell me. Eventually, the message comes through:

ROS: I don't like the idea that we're supposed to know exactly what we want to do with the rest of our lives before we even turn 18. I mean sure, I've got plans for the future. I want to own a house, travel some, maybe move out of Massachusetts, but as far as work, I don't know. And I don't feel like I NEED to know yet.

ROS: My dad's been super understanding about that, too. He started undergrad kind of late, and he said he's glad he waited. I'd rather learn a little bit about the world I'm going to be living in before I decide where I'm going to fit into it, you know?

I *don't* know. I've had my life planned out for years, ever since Mom moved out, and it hasn't changed one bit in all that time. I always assumed it would never *need* to change. My hard work is going to pay off in a year or so with a full scholarship, a good résumé, and an acting gig somewhere crowded and exciting. Maybe LA, maybe New York, maybe Chicago, but always a big city. That's where the steady work is, and nobody important ever lives in small towns. Not until they're rich and famous enough to retire early to a mansion in the woods, at least. It's either work hard now and watch it pay off later or slack off and end up raising chickens in Loredo.

Except lately, on slow or stressful days, a tiny voice in the back of my head has started whispering, *Would being unimportant really be so bad?* Ninety-nine percent of the people of the world aren't that important, and they seem to get along in life just fine. If people *weren't* happy living simple, quiet lives, then towns like Loredo wouldn't even exist. What is it that makes someone want to live a completely invisible life in a place barely big enough to show up on a tourist's road map and still feel content at the end of the day? What lesson did they miss in school that made them feel like that was the best they could hope for?

What do they know that I don't?

Would Ros call me naive for thinking like that? I don't know why I thought talking to her would make me feel better. She always finds ways to throw me off balance, whether she means to or not.

But then my phone pings again.

ROS: I admire you for having your life figured out
    already, though. That's a skill not many people have!
    You should be proud of that. :)

I don't have a way to explain the odd rush of warmth that reading those words gives me. A bit of the building anxiety melts away, and I manage to take in a deep breath.

SAM: Oooh don't worry, I am 😌
ROS: And there's that typical Sam attitude.
SAM: You know you love it!

She doesn't answer, but for the first time, I'm not worried I've upset her. In a way, I learned more about her in one conversation than I have in weeks of listening in on her and Christian. She wouldn't have told me any of that if she didn't want to, and the fact that she trusted me enough to say any of it means something.

I just . . . don't quite know what yet.

29

ROS

IT'S SAFE TO SAY THAT I'M OFFICIALLY OUT OF MY comfort zone.

This might be the first time I've ever been in a stadium. Sports were never Dad's thing, either, so it wasn't a part of my childhood, and right now, it shows.

I stick close to Christian's side as he navigates easily through the crowd, glancing down at his ticket every so often to check the section number.

"Have you been here before?" I ask.

He nods. "A couple of times. Usually, I go up to see USL games in Foxborough or Boston, but they didn't have anything on tonight, and I didn't think you'd want to drive that far."

He smiles at me, and I return it, hoping that I look like I know what "USL" means. It's pretty sweet of him to consider distance and crowd size for me. He knows this is the first live game I've ever been to, so the whole concept is a pretty overwhelming one.

"Powell!"

We turn our heads in the direction of the shout. From around the side of a large family group comes a tall, gangly figure with a shock of curly black hair. This must be the friend Christian told me about—Monty, I think.

Christian collides with Monty in a quick hug, then turns to me. "Have you guys met? I know I've told you about him."

Monty rolls his eyes. "Does having one class together a year and a half ago count?" Still, he grins at me and holds out his hand. "Monty Wells. I'm Christian's only decent friend."

I shake his hand and smile back. "Besides Sam, you mean?"

"I said what I said."

Christian laughs and punches him affectionately in the shoulder. "Come on. Our seats are over here."

He leads the way to our section, already deep in conversation about the game or the teams involved, and I fall back a step or so to watch the two of them banter back and forth.

Even I know the old dating faux pas of bringing a third wheel along, but honestly, I don't mind at all. When Christian first suggested going to a game, he mentioned that he usually went with a friend, but he'd make an exception for me. *I* was the one who insisted he invite Monty anyway—not because I need a buffer for this date or anything, though.

Okay, maybe a little of that.

But still, part of it was out of a desire to get to know Christian better. He's been making such an effort to learn about me, do activities I normally enjoy, and after basically cussing him out the first time he tried to talk to me, I feel bad for not returning the favor. I know the stuff about him that he's told me, plus whatever tidbits Sam's mentioned, but that can't be everything. I've seen Christian act differently around his soccer buddies, and I wanted to learn about that side of him, even if I don't have the first clue about how soccer works. Besides that, I've known Monty for only about a minute and a half, and I'm pretty sure I like him.

We find our seats without too much hassle. Monty and Christian are still chattering away, so I take a minute to look around at the stadium. It's bigger than I expected. I always figured football was more the sport people cared about in college, so a soccer stadium with this many seats is a little surprising. The name of the venue is printed in big letters over and over along the low divider wall separating the field from the seats. We're sitting pretty high up—I don't know what counts as good seats in sports, but if it's anything like theater, then we're closer to the nosebleeds—and from here I get a clear view of both ends of the field. I was hoping there'd be signs telling me what goal belongs to which team, but no such luck. Everything's illuminated by enormous floodlights, and the last hints of winter are starting to creep into the night air.

Christian is seated in the middle of our little group, with me on the left and Monty on his right, and just as I'm starting to feel a little ignored, he abruptly stops the conversation with Monty and turns to me, almost like he's just remembered something. "Ros, sorry! Are you cold? You can have my hoodie if you want."

Monty throws up his hands. "*There* you go! I was about to ask her myself if you didn't."

It *is* starting to get cold. I smile at him. "Thanks, but don't you need it, too?"

"Well, if we're lucky, the game will be so exciting I won't even notice." He shrugs off his thick hoodie and hands it over, and when I put it on, it's already warm and smells a little like him.

God, this is so cliché.

Monty waggles his eyebrows at me. "So, Ros! How much do you know about soccer?"

I shrug self-consciously. "Basically nothing."

Christian gives me an encouraging smile. "Don't worry. I can explain stuff if you're confused."

Monty's attention is drawn back to Christian, and he frowns. "Dude, what are you doing with your earbuds in?"

Christian pauses, looking suddenly nervous, and that's when I see it, too: the earbud sticking out of one ear while the other dangles over his shoulder. It's so common for me to see him like that, I guess I stopped noticing.

"It's just some music," Christian says defensively, but Monty reaches over and plucks the bud out of his ear.

"Are the two of us not fascinating enough for you, Powell? Besides, there's no way you'll be able to hear it once the game starts."

Christian looks weirdly upset about not having his music during the game. I remember what he told me about it being a coping mechanism when he's nervous, and I'm about to jump in and defend him, but then Christian squares his shoulders and grumbles, "Fine," before pressing something on his earbuds and stuffing them into his pocket.

A cheer goes up from the crowd around us, and I look back down at the field as the two teams emerge from somewhere under the stands. Monty and Christian immediately join in, standing to clap and cheer with the others. Startled, I stand up, too. We're too far away to see names or symbols on their jerseys, and I still don't actually know which team we're rooting for.

I lean over to Christian. "Why are two of them wearing different colored shirts? Are they like referees or something?"

"No, they're goalies."

"Why do the goalies wear different colors?"

Monty turns to stare at me with faux disbelief. "Oh my God. Christian, she's like a *baby*."

"Shut up, Monty."

"She's a soccer *virgin*!"

I can tell he's joking, so I laugh and say, "I wasn't kidding when I said I didn't know anything!"

Monty shakes his head. "We've got our work cut out for us tonight."

The game starts, and once there's an object to follow, understanding how everything works gets a little easier. Christian keeps up a running commentary, though, leaning close to my ear to explain rules or the different positions the players take. I didn't think it was much more complicated than kicking the ball from one end of the field to the other, but apparently, there's a whole slew of rules you have to follow. He rattles off names and terms—cross, offside, caution, through ball—and I'm doing my best to keep up, but I don't think my brain works the way his does. For the first time in maybe my whole life, I feel stupid.

It's somewhere between then and halftime that I realize I'm a hypocrite. I've wasted years worrying about people making assumptions about me—*smart girl, conceited, snooty, shrew*—and this whole time, I've been doing the exact same thing. I assumed Christian was just a jock, because I didn't understand his favorite sport and the passion and drive he puts into it. I assumed Sam was the typical airheaded It Girl because, before now, I'd never actually talked to her. All I've ever done is assume things about people and then turned around and complained when they did the same to me.

How many good people have I missed out on, how many experiences have I passed up, because I judged them without knowing them?

I don't share this revelation with Christian, obviously. He and Monty are completely engrossed in the game, shouting at the referees or cheering when the ball makes it closer to one side of the field. At one point, Monty starts up a song that, based on the terrible accent he puts on, I think must be for some British soccer team, and Christian just laughs and joins in. I watch, still reeling from my epiphany, and as I do, I'm struck by something else.

The Christian I'm looking at now is the most genuine version of him I've seen so far, singing and cheering and shouting because everybody around him is doing the same thing. He has a crowd to follow, and instead of disappearing into it, somehow it makes him more *him*. When it's just us, though? He's unpredictable. He's nervous and confident by turns, one minute picking at his earbuds and the next spitting out some comeback I never thought he was capable of. And over text, he sounds like a totally different person.

He turns and grins at me, teeth flashing in the overhead lights, and I grin back, feeling a weird swooping sensation in my chest. I like this version of Chris. I like it in the way I like Monty, in the way you like the lovable big brother character in a sitcom. That rare, clever version, though? There's something about it. Something that makes me want to know more, to seek it out and learn what's behind it. Maybe it's curiosity, maybe something else, but *that's* the version I'm sticking around for. It's the thing that drew me to him in the first place, after his apology. I want to find it again. I don't know what that part of him is, but once I find it, maybe I can finally figure out how I feel.

For now, though, I should probably focus on figuring out soccer.

ROS

I'M HAVING A HARD TIME FOCUSING ON MY homework, and surprisingly, it's not Christian's fault.

I promised to help him with trig, since I took it last semester and he's been struggling. We're both holed up at my dad's university library; it's been a favorite haunt of mine since I was a kid, and one of the benefits is the private, soundproofed study rooms tucked away in the corners. Normally this place puts me in the perfect mind to get focused on schoolwork, but right now, the environment isn't enough. I'm too busy thinking about my project.

I sent another draft of the accompaniment to Mrs. Reagan. I sort of did what she asked—tweaked the song to be less dissonant, made the intro sound happier—but still kept to my original vision. She didn't approve.

You're moving in the right direction, Miss Shew, but ultimately, you haven't gone quite far enough. I can't approve this version for the final presentation. May I suggest drawing inspiration from popular soundtracks to see what themes the great movie composers use in these kinds of situations?

She's implying that I don't know what I'm doing. That I'm making bad choices because I'm not experienced enough to know what works, rather than *intentionally* breaking the rules to prove a point. It's ridiculous. I'm still angry, but now, piggybacking off the anger is a fresh wave of anxiety. This is the second time she hasn't approved the project. How many more chances do I get? What if I don't get it right the next time, and she decides not to use my project at all?

I jump as Christian taps me on the shoulder. "You okay?" he asks.

"Yeah! Yeah, sorry. Just thinking about something."

"Was it this equation? Because I feel like I'm losing my mind, too." He gives me a lopsided grin.

I try to return the smile, but it doesn't feel right. My hands are clammy, heart still racing at the thought of all this work I've put in going to waste.

A thought occurs to me then: Christian is the perfect base-line for the students of Northeastern. People like him will be the majority of my audience, and he's likely to respond in the same way most people would to my presentation. He might just be the perfect test subject.

Still, that makes another spike of anxiety zing through my chest. This project has become weirdly personal, thanks to my self-composed music and the inclusion of Dad's story. Am I really ready to show something like that to him?

But the thought of Mrs. Reagan deciding to scrap my whole project makes up my mind for me. I sit up straighter in my chair. "Actually, do you mind if we pause on the homework for a bit?"

Christian frowns. "Sure. What's up?"

"I wanted to run something by you. I've been working on my project for the Bellerose Assembly for a while, but the feedback I've been getting from Mrs. Reagan isn't helping me. Could I . . . would you be willing to watch it for me? I just need to know if I'm doing the right thing."

For a second, Christian's eyes dart back and forth, and he fiddles with the earbuds dangling from his ears. "I'm . . . sure, yeah. I'd be happy to."

I'm not sure whether I'm relieved or anxious to hear him agree. "Great. I need to go grab my bag and some stuff from my dad's office, but I'll be right back."

"Okay, sure."

"See you in a second."

I stand quickly and make my way out of the room. It's a happy coincidence that I have my violin with me today: I was planning to use one of the university music rooms to practice later. Maybe, if Christian's review of the project is good, I'll still have the motivation to practice when all this is done. But first I have to get through it.

I square my shoulders, lift my head a little higher as the

building with Dad's office comes into view. I'm about to make myself look pretty vulnerable in front of Christian, and I'd rather not do the same with my dad right now, too.

SAM

As soon as Ros leaves the room to grab her computer, Christian picks up his phone again. "How am I supposed to critique this thing?" he panic-whispers.

"I don't know. Obviously, you can't have your earbuds in while she's playing it."

"*What?*"

"It'll make you look like you're not fully invested!"

"Well then, what do I do?"

"Don't hang up. I'll text you if I think of something you should definitely say. Otherwise, no matter what it is, tell her it's . . . a deep, complicated exploration of the effect our bonds with people have on us or something."

"And if that's not what the project's about?"

"It's Ros. That's definitely what the project is about."

Christian starts to answer but cuts himself off as I hear a noise in the background. Ros must have just come back into the room. His voice gets more distant as he takes the earbuds out of his ears, but I can still hear both of them easily.

"Oh," Christian says, sounding surprised. "You play violin?"

"Yeah," Ros answers. "I'm playing something as part of my

project. I had a recording to go with the video, but I had to make some changes to it, and . . . well, it just doesn't sound the same as playing live, so—"

Maybe it's the crappy quality of the microphone, but for a second, it almost sounds like Ros is nervous. Her voice doesn't have the usual surety to it, that icy little edge that says she doesn't care what you think about her. She sounds vulnerable, as if she might actually be a seventeen-year-old kid like the rest of us. I wonder, suddenly, what this project means to her.

There's a few seconds of rustling, the quiet *plink* of strings as she lifts the violin out of the case. I hear the clicks of her computer as she pulls up the video, then tests the violin's tuning. Chris shifts his weight in his seat. I realize my heart is racing. Something about Ros's nervousness is rubbing off on me. I feel like I'm on the edge of something, and I'm not sure I want to know what it is.

Ros takes a quick, shaky breath. "You ready?"

"Yeah," Christian says.

"No," I whisper.

Then Ros starts to play.

CHRISTIAN

On the computer screen in front of me is an older man with curly dark hair and glasses. He doesn't look at all like Ros, but I can tell it's her dad. I couldn't tell you why I'm so sure about it, but I am. He smiles at the camera and says, "I grew up in Long Island around the late seventies, early eighties. I was too young to hear about the Stonewall Riots and the Gay Liberation movement, but I definitely grew up in their shadow. I remember my mom sitting me down when I was five and explaining to me what a drag queen was after we ran into one on the subway." He laughs.

To my left, I hear Ros start to play, something quiet and slow and a little heavy. Her eyes are shut, and she's completely focused on the music, on timing it with this interview. I look away before she can feel me staring.

"I don't think it occurred to me that any of that would affect my life," her dad continues on-screen, "until I was a few months out of high school. I'd never really been one for parties or dating in my teens, and both I and my parents assumed I was just . . . a late bloomer when it came to girls. But high school came and went, and still nothing. My freshman-year roommate in college was the first big hint that I probably wasn't *ever* going to start liking girls. There were a few other hints after that, but I don't think it ever really 'clicked' until I met Charles."

The video keeps rolling, showing a picture of Mr. Shew with another man, lighter-skinned and grinning at the camera. This guy—Charles—is definitely related to Ros. Their eyes are the same shape, with the same heavy brows, and her hair is rich brown like his. I catch myself watching her instead of the video, trying to pick out more similarities until I can't find any more, until it's just an excuse to stare. She's frowning in concentration as the music starts to build slightly and takes on more of a hopeful note to match the smile on her dad's face as he describes how happy Charles used to make him.

I don't know how long the video actually is. It could be only a couple of minutes, but it feels like every second is much longer than usual as I sit there, listening as Mr. Shew tells the story of meeting Charles, of their decision to start a family, of their struggle to have Ros and, later, the struggle to keep her. The longer I listen, the more I realize that the music follows the timing of the story perfectly, so well fit that it could only have been written by Ros herself, specifically for this. She's not using sheet music, either, playing from memory the story of her dads and what they went through. I don't think she means to, but a little of the emotion slips into her expression. It's almost hard to watch, especially as her dad's voice gets more and more choked up, explaining what it was like to lose the man he'd fought so hard to be with.

Without really meaning to, my mind starts to wander to Monty and how nervous he was at first to tell me he was non-binary. He looks and acts like a cis guy at school, so not a lot of people know about him, but he still gets crap for it occasionally. Then there's Sam. There were rumors, before we started dating, that she'd been with some other girls from the popular crowd, and she never tried to deny it. I asked her about it once, and she just shrugged and said, "Sure, I like girls. So?" The "so" was the only crack in her confident mask, a clear challenge, daring me to say something negative about it, which, obviously, wasn't going to happen. They don't teach us about the Stonewall Riots or stuff like that in school, so I don't know much. But

I've seen enough through friends to know that just because it's easier now, it doesn't actually mean that it's easy.

I don't know where Ros stands on the sexuality spectrum. I've never asked. But I can tell that the story of her dad has affected her in a major way. Otherwise, she wouldn't have made this whole project about it. The music is weird—it seems determined to stay sad, even when Mr. Shew mentions how happy he was that he got to keep Ros after all that fighting with Charles's family. I think what Ros is trying to say is that some things, like love, get taken for granted by people. Kind of like me, when I first tried to talk to her and assumed she'd respond well. I'm not going to pretend I understand every part of this project. But Ros made it, and it means something to her, so that's good enough for me.

When the video ends and the last few notes of the song fade out, Ros stands there for a second, eyes still closed, letting the tension hang for a while. I'm unsure if I should clap or not. Finally, I clear my throat. "That was . . . that was awesome, Ros."

She smiles, almost looking relieved. "Really?"

"Yeah! Your dad's story is intense. You guys must be close."

"We are." She frowns, biting at her bottom lip. "What did you think of the music? I wrote it myself, and I've been getting some critiques from the vice principal. She says it doesn't fit the theme of the assembly enough."

This is the part where I would appreciate still having Sam to help me out. I consider putting the earbuds back in but decide it might look rude. What had she told me to say? *A complicated exploration about the effect of bonds*?

"It did feel a little . . . sad at times, I guess, when it didn't need to be. But maybe that's what you were going for."

Ros nods, perking up. "It was, actually."

"Okay then. So, like, are you trying to say that your dads' love story is a really sad one, or that it's more complicated than that? That the bonds we have with people are more complicated than just 'love,' or 'family'?"

I realize that that's not exactly what Sam wanted me to say, and I'm worried I screwed something up somehow. For a few quiet seconds, Ros looks surprised. Then her face splits into the biggest smile I've ever seen on her. "That's . . . that's exactly it, Christian. You get it."

I feel a little shock of guilt that the words that made her so happy weren't my own. I wouldn't have even thought to say what I said if it hadn't been for Sam.

"Maybe try to find a way to say that without making the music so sad, if Mrs. Reagan doesn't like it," I say. "I think Charles would probably want you to be happy that you're still with your other dad, right?"

"Yeah, I guess he would." She sighs, and I watch a weight lift from her as she does. "That's a different way to think about it, thank you. Mrs. Reagan wanted me to make it more 'romantic,' and that was getting on my nerves."

"Yeah, well, your first mistake was trying to listen to Mrs. Reagan in the first place."

"She's in charge of the assembly!" Ros says with a laugh.

"So?"

"You're ridiculous." She shakes her head, then looks back up at me with another smile. "Thanks for that. I really needed a fresh take. We can get back to the homework now. It's already dark outside, and I don't want to keep either of us too much longer."

We go back to the trig questions again, Ros acting much happier, and me feeling . . . conflicted. I don't exactly know what's bothering me, and I don't think I can figure it out just yet. Much like this math homework, I think it's too complicated for me to solve on my own. At one point, I check my phone to see if Sam is still on the call, but she's gone. I guess she didn't want to stick around for the homework chat. That's okay, though. I can talk to her about this later.

31

SAM

I END THE CALL.

I don't need to hear any more, and Christian seems to be doing just fine on his own. My hand is shaking so bad I can barely press the button. It's not the performance that's made me feel like this—or maybe it is? It's at least part of it. Hearing Ros play that violin, hearing the video of her dad telling that story, suddenly, it's like everything makes sense. Ros acts so cold and aloof because she's *scared*. Scared to lose people, scared that anyone she lets in is going to vanish. It's why I've never seen her date anyone before Christian, why she was so quick to dismiss him at first. She puts on a front of invincibility because it's easier than letting people in. God, do I ever know the feeling.

So the moments of vulnerability I've seen over the last few weeks must be the real Ros. The things she admitted to Christian while I was on the phone. The slight shake in her voice when she explained to Christian that she didn't want to kiss him, like she was afraid he'd be angry. Even now, sitting alone in my room, I can almost picture the look on her face when she finished playing her piece, biting her lip just slightly, waiting for Chris's opinion and pretending it wouldn't crush her if he hated it. Knowing, deep down, that it would.

I think I'm in over my head.

I turn my phone off and put it facedown on my desk, although I don't know how that's supposed to help with my racing mind right now. It's not going to get that conjured image out of my head. It's not going to stop the weird swooping feeling in my stomach whenever I see Ros in person or the sense of giddy victory I get when I one-up her in a conversation, that feeling I thought used to be something like victory, but now I realize it's my brain's reaction to knowing I made her laugh.

It's not going to change the fact that right now, I really, really wish I were Christian.

I need to find something to do. Something to take my mind off this. Doesn't matter what, just *something*.

I walk out of my room and into the kitchen, where Nana is pouring a glass of wine. "Did you wash the dishes yet?"

She gives me a weird look. "Not yet. Why?"

"I'll do them." I'm already halfway to the sink, grabbing a sponge and the first dirty plate I can reach on the counter.

Nana's staring at me like I've grown another arm. "Are you all right, sweet pea? You're acting a little off."

Of course I am. I'm panicking. But she doesn't have to know

that. So instead, I shrug and start acting like someone who *doesn't* desperately want to kiss the girl she's spent the last month trying to set up with her ex and smile at my grandma over my shoulder. "Nah, I'm just bored. I finished my homework, and I was feeling unproductive. Plus, you're clearly getting ready to be done for the night."

She glances down at the glass of wine, almost embarrassed. "I was going to leave the dishes until tomorrow," she admits. "But thank you for doing them, sweet pea."

"You got it, Nana."

She leaves the kitchen, and once she's gone, I let the mask drop. I turn on the faucet, as hot as I can make it, and start scrubbing at dinner plates and forks and glasses, and soon everything smells like dish soap. The sound of the water running drowns out my thoughts, and the scalding heat is almost—almost—enough to distract me.

ROS

WHEN I DO END UP TAKING CHRISTIAN'S OFFER of dinner with his parents, about two weeks after he first suggested it, I'm more nervous than I expected. It's not that I don't want to meet them—he talks about them a lot, and even more about his younger sister—but in this, as in everything dating related so far, I'm a complete amateur. I don't like being out of my depth in anything. But Christian assured me they were excited to meet me, and in the end, I didn't want to disappoint him by flaking.

To my surprise, Christian meets me outside when I pull into the driveway. There's a shiny, expensive-looking car parked near the garage, and I do my best to stay away from it, parking closer to Christian's instead. He smiles and waves at me through the windshield. He's wearing a plain (if nice) T-shirt and jeans, apparently immune to the chilly March air, and suddenly I'm anxious all over again.

"Am I overdressed?" I ask, getting out of the car.

Christian looks me over, examining the dark jeans and blouse I spent almost thirty minutes agonizing over before I left the house. "No, you look nice! You'll be fine."

"Okay." I let out a deep breath.

"Don't worry, Ros. I know they're gonna like you. Why wouldn't they?"

I could probably come up with a couple of reasons if he gave me enough time, but instead, I smile at him. "Okay. And thanks for walking me in. You didn't have to."

"Yeah, well . . ." Christian pauses before the steps to the front door. "Actually, I wanted to tell you something first. I've talked with you about my older brother before, right?"

"Yeah. Will, right?"

"That's him." Christian shuffles his feet, suddenly nervous. "Could you maybe . . . not mention him? I'm fine if we talk about him when it's just us, but my parents took it really hard when he left. They might be mad if they knew I'd told you about him."

"Oh." I don't know what I was expecting him to say, but it wasn't this. I hadn't planned on bringing it up anyway, but now that I know it's a taboo subject, I'll have to be extra careful.

"Sure," I say. "I won't mention him."

Christian visibly relaxes. "Thanks. Should we go in now?"

It's pretty dark outside, and in all my nervousness about

leaving the house, I forgot to bring a jacket, so the early spring chill is definitely setting in. I nod. "Let's go."

Christian's mom is all smiles when she meets us at the door. She's a pretty woman with brown hair and smile lines, and her blue eyes are the same shape as Christian's. She shakes my hand, then turns and looks Christian over. "Is that what you're wearing?"

He shrugs. "Yeah?"

"Ros got dressed up for you, and you're just going to wear a T-shirt? No sir. Go upstairs."

Christian sighs. "Fine. Be right back." He disappears up the hallway, and his mom turns her smile back to me.

"It's great to meet you, Ros," she says. "Take your shoes off here and then come on into the kitchen. Can I get you anything to drink?"

"Water is fine, Mrs. Powell," I say, kicking off my shoes and putting them near the door.

"You got it!" She moves off, calling upstairs as she goes. "Bill! Come downstairs! Ros is here!"

As I start to follow her, I hear footsteps on the stairs that sound too light and fast to belong to anyone called "Bill." Sure enough, a few seconds later, a little blond girl comes running around the corner, stopping dead in her tracks when she sees me. Her hair's messy, and one of her teeth is clearly loose.

"Hi," she says.

I smile at her. "Hey. Are you Aimee?"

Her eyes light up. "Did Christian tell you about me?"

"Of course he did! He talks about you all the time."

Aimee looks thrilled by the news. "Good. He should."

I laugh. "So what are we having for dinner, Aimee?"

"Mom's making a casserole." She wrinkles her nose. "And some salad."

"Not your favorite?"

"No. I wanted to order a pizza."

"Well, I'm happy your mom and dad wanted to cook for me. Maybe you guys can do pizza some other time."

Aimee shrugs. "Maybe." Then she starts to run backward up the hallway, gesturing at me to follow. "Come on, I wanna show you my room."

"All right, lead the way."

Aimee tries to sneak us both past the kitchen, but Mrs. Powell spots her. "Aimee, why haven't you brushed your hair yet? I told you to do it before Ros got here."

"I can do it before dinner!" Aimee pouts.

"That's not what I asked. Do you want Ros to think you don't brush your hair?"

"I don't care."

"*I* do. Go brush it."

"*Mom—*"

Mrs. Powell turns to me with an apologetic smile. "So sorry about her, Ros. Aimee's impossible sometimes. Give us a moment."

I can sense an argument brewing, so I do my best to give them their space. I wander into the living room, far enough that their voices fade into the background. Someone in this family must have a good job, because the furniture is nice, clearly expensive, and still fresh like it was just bought. There are pictures *everywhere*—Christian as a kid, grinning with his bright blond hair, Aimee when she was maybe two. There's a picture of Christian's parents at their wedding, too. Every available space seems to have pictures of the family set out on it, each one of them so perfect and all-American that they almost look like stock photos.

The one thing I do notice, though, is that Christian, Aimee, and their parents seem to be the only ones in the photos. There are individual shots of Christian and Aimee as kids, some of the two of them together, and one recent family photo with all four of them, but as far as my cursory glance goes, I don't see any of Christian's older brother, Will. If he hadn't told me about Will himself, I wouldn't have known there was a third Powell sibling.

Maybe Will did something terrible. Maybe there's a good reason he's not in their lives anymore. I don't know the circumstances behind what happened. Christian never told me, and I didn't think to ask. I tuck that question away for later. Something new to learn about Christian.

As if he read my mind, I hear his voice behind me. "Are you snooping?"

I turn and grin at him. "Aimee wanted to show me her room, but your mom made her go brush her hair, so I decided to entertain myself."

"Yeah, sorry about that. They're picky about appearances."

"I don't care. She's just a kid."

He laughs. "Try telling that to them. Anyway, Aimee'll probably figure out some way to give you the grand tour of the place after dinner. You're not missing much."

He joins me standing in front of the TV cabinet, looking at some of the family photos. There's a couple of seconds of silence, and in them, I scramble for something else to say. This feels different from other dates we've gone on. At the art museum, or the park, or the soccer game, there was something to talk about. Somewhere else to put our attention instead of on each other. And really, it isn't going to be just us tonight. Three completely new people are involved. As nice as he is, dealing with Christian so far has been plenty all on its own. "Meeting the folks" is not something I thought I'd have to deal with in high school.

I'm almost tempted to ask about Will, just to have something to say, but right about then I hear more footsteps, heavier this time, and Christian's dad joins us in the room. Here, I realize, is where Chris gets most of his looks. Mr. Powell is tall, blond, and sturdily built, like maybe he used to play sports when he was younger, too. From him, I can get a pretty good idea of what Christian might look like in thirty years. How does Christian feel, I wonder, being able to see that in someone every day? I have no idea what that's like.

Mr. Powell gives us a glance up and down. "Are we keeping it PG in here, Chris?"

Christian rolls his eyes. "Dad, I'm literally standing in the middle of the living room."

"I'm messing with you." He walks up and gives me a quick

smile, holding out a hand for me to shake. "Nice to meet you, Ros. Call me Bill."

"Nice to meet you, too. Thanks for having me over."

"No trouble at all." He turns and glances back toward the kitchen. "Anna should be almost done in there. You kids hungry?"

"Yeah, absolutely."

"Good. She always cooks a little too much. Luckily, that means leftovers for the rest of us."

With a sinking sensation in my gut, I start to realize that I'm in for a full evening of small talk. Should've seen that coming, really. Hopefully the food is good, because then I can get away with having my mouth too full to talk if something goes wrong.

All things considered, the dinner table conversation isn't too painful. Christian's parents seem nice, but they're very surface-level. They don't seem interested in talking about anything deeper than what classes I'm in or what I'm planning to do after college.

They seem a little surprised, actually, when I tell them I don't know yet. Mrs. Powell raises her eyebrows at me. "What year are you in?"

"I'm a junior, same as Christian," I tell her.

"Well, that time's coming up. Christian mentioned that you're on pace to be the valedictorian. Is that true?"

"It is."

"Oh, then I'm sure you could go anywhere! Any ideas about schools?"

"I've researched a few, but nothing concrete yet."

I think that was the wrong answer, because Mrs. Powell looks baffled, and Christian shifts a little in his seat. I remember the conversation I had with Sam a while ago, when she seemed shocked I didn't already know what I was going to do with my life. Apparently, that's a more common opinion than I thought.

"Well, what do your parents do?" Mr. Powell asks, like that's going to settle everything.

I pause. Christian hasn't actually told me if his parents are, well, *accepting* of people who have more than one dad. It's never come up, and I don't want now to be the time when I find out if they're homophobic. So instead, I say, "No mom, but my dad's a professor at Clark University. He teaches history."

Mrs. Powell seems embarrassed when I say I don't have a mom, but Bill barely registers it. "That's somewhere to start, then. Teaching's always a good choice."

I'm not interested in teaching. I've also learned enough about the Byzantines and Süleyman the Magnificent from Dad to last a lifetime, and I don't think I'd enjoy making any of that my job. But somehow, that doesn't feel like something I can talk about. There's almost no room in the conversation for it, like Mr. Powell's already made up his mind. I decide it's not worth bringing up.

Opposite me at the table, Aimee shifts in her seat, picking at her barely eaten dinner. "Can we let Yankee in yet?"

"No, Aimee. He stays outside until we're done with dinner."

I give Christian a questioning glance. He smiles and mouths, "*The dog.*"

"How come? We have him inside when we eat dinner all the time."

"Well, not tonight," Mrs. Powell says. "We have company over."

"Maybe Ros wants to meet him!"

"She can, but not until dinner's over."

Aimee frowns. "It's cold outside. Can he please come in?"

"You just want him here so you can feed him the vegetables you're not eating," Christian says.

"Nuh-uh!"

"Both of you behave," Mrs. Powell says with a loaded glance over at me.

"I don't like mushrooms. You know I don't like mushrooms. Can I just—"

"Aimee."

Mr. Powell doesn't raise his voice. In fact, his tone is perfectly even, and his face barely changes. But that one word is enough to shut Aimee up right away. She hunches down in her chair, cheeks going red and eyebrows knitting in frustration. Next to her, Christian works his jaw, uncomfortable. The tension is a sudden, awkward new presence at the table.

"Listen to your mother," Mr. Powell continues, like the new energy isn't there. "The faster you eat, the faster you can be done and we can let the dog in. Now, let's change the subject. Ros, Christian tells me you went to your first soccer game the other day. Has he managed to convert you yet?"

My head almost spins at the quick diversion. It takes me a few seconds to pull an answer together. "Uh . . . not yet. But it was a lot more fun that I thought it would be."

"That's the spirit! The next thing to do is introduce you to the Premier League. You'll be a Spurs fan like us in no time."

Mr. Powell's smile is wide and charming. I almost can't help but return it. Mrs. Powell smiles at me, too. Across the table, I watch Christian recover his own grin. Aimee looks a little embarrassed. The ghost of that tension is still there, but apparently, we're ignoring it. The conversation moves on to other subjects just as superficial and safe as the last, and while I'm able to keep up fairly well, I'd be lying if I said I wasn't distracted for the rest of the dinner. At one point, I manage to catch Aimee's eyes and give her an encouraging smile. She returns it, reluctantly, but I notice she glances at her parents before she does.

33

CHRISTIAN

THE REST OF THE NIGHT GOES FAIRLY SMOOTHLY.
Aimee eats her vegetables, Mom makes lots of small talk, and
Yankee does finally get let into the house—and of course, jumps
all over Ros in his excitement. After that, Aimee shows Ros
her room, which turns into almost a full house tour, and then
there's a little more socializing before Ros has to head home. All
in all, not a bad night. Aimee does get in trouble for talking back
during dinner, but honestly, that's nothing new.

The only weirdness comes later, when Ros sends me a text
after she gets home.

ROS: Can I ask a personal question?
CHRISTIAN: sure, go ahead
ROS: I know you asked me not to talk about your

brother while I was over. And that was fine, but I'm just curious: Why don't your parents talk about him anymore?

I hesitate, unsure how to answer. Sam definitely couldn't help me with this one, either, and I'm not sure I'd want her to.

CHRISTIAN: they never got along, i guess
ROS: "Never got along"? What does that mean?
CHRISTIAN: idk. they used to fight a bunch when he still lived here
ROS: Christian, there are no pictures of him in your house. I saw plenty of you and Aimee, but none of Will. Your parents never even mentioned him. You specifically told me not to bring him up. That sounds like a pretty bad fight.

I forget that Ros can be as perceptive as Sam sometimes. How am I supposed to respond to this?

CHRISTIAN: yeah, i guess it was pretty bad
ROS: Can I ask what it was about? The fighting, I mean.
CHRISTIAN: honestly, i don't remember much. i always tried to stay out of it, and Will never told me
ROS: Do you still talk to him?
CHRISTIAN: no
ROS: So you agree with your parents?

I'm about to tell her that sure, why wouldn't I, but suddenly it doesn't feel true. Maybe Will and my parents didn't get along, but I don't like that they packed away everything that ever belonged to him. I don't like that they never tried to contact him afterward.

Now that I'm thinking about it, I remember Dad telling Will that if he left, it was forever, that he'd better not hear from him again. Dad says stuff like that when he's mad sometimes. It doesn't mean he *means* it. So then, why haven't they reached out? And why hasn't Will?

> **CHRISTIAN:** it's complicated
> **CHRISTIAN:** sorry, can we talk about something else?
> **ROS:** Sure, of course. Sorry if that was crossing a line or anything. It just seems like it bothers you a little.
> **CHRISTIAN:** it's okay

Ros changes the subject after that, and I follow along as much as I can, but a part of me stays stuck on her last question. It's not an easy door to shut once it's been opened. Maybe I didn't agree with my parents—maybe I still don't—but I went along with them anyway. Isn't that the same thing as agreeing? I never questioned anything they did back then, never argued or fought back. That says a lot more about me than it does them.

Another memory surfaces, and this time it's of an emptier house. Will is gone. It happens fast, with barely a week's warning that it's final. The arguments had been going on for longer, of course—Will threatening to pack up and go, Dad ordering him not to, Mom begging—but the crazy part is, I didn't think he'd actually do it. He was such a constant of everyday life, fighting or not. But now he's gone, and it feels like something's wrong in the house. Everything's quiet, and even the usual noises sound strange. The stairs don't creak in the same way they used to. There's an echo now, like an empty room when all the furniture gets removed.

There was no real goodbye. He left early one morning while I was at school, and in the days leading up to it, we barely talked. Something was different between us after the night he came to my room after the argument, like he was drawing away from me. I hated it, but I was scared to say the wrong thing again, or else make my parents think I was choosing a side. What if they started yelling at me next? So I let him go and tried not to think about how terrible I felt.

Mom and Dad don't say a word about it. I try to ask, but Mom immediately changes the subject, and Dad gets so angry it actually scares me. He grounds me for the rest of the week, too. I don't ask again after that.

Aimee's too young to understand what's going on, but I know she feels the change, too. She's been fussier lately, and it takes longer to calm her down. Will would have been able to do it. He could make the funniest faces, and Aimee would stop whatever she was doing and laugh until her face went red. I can't make those faces. I try, but I think it only makes her cry more.

They clean out his room the day after he leaves. Anything he didn't take with him gets thrown into garbage bags, to be trashed or donated and put out of sight as soon as possible. By then I knew better than to question my parents or ask to keep something to remember him by. It would only upset them more. So instead, I watch Will's stuff get taken away and then, suddenly, it's over. Out of sight, out of mind. By the time Mom gets done vacuuming and cleaning his room, it's like I never had a brother at all.

I go in there sometimes, though, to see if the room still feels like him. It never does. Weeks go by, and Will doesn't come back. So eventually I stop hoping that he will. But one day, as I'm sitting in his room, avoiding my homework and staring out the window, I notice something stuck into the crack between the carpet and the baseboard. I dig my fingers into the crack, and after a minute or two I fish out a tiny round circle of plastic. It's old, a little scuffed, but white and almost shiny. The vacuum missed it, and neither of my parents noticed it when they were clearing everything out, but I found it.

A Go piece. The last remaining piece of my older brother left in the entire house, and I just happened to find it.

Maybe that means it was lucky.

I stuff it into my pocket, then quickly leave the room and wash up for dinner before Mom or Dad can ask me what I was doing in there. I never tell either of them about the old Go piece. They're happier that way, and what kind of terrible person would I be if I made them feel miserable?

I always feel a little better knowing the piece is in my pocket, like maybe it'll give me an extra boost of luck right when I need it the most. Whether it's actually lucky or not, I've kept it, for no other reason than it reminds me of the possibility of luck. No matter how slim the odds may be, there's still the tiniest chance things might be okay. All you have to do is look in the right place at the right time, and you'll find it. And even if you don't, maybe it'll come back and find *you* someday.

But I don't believe that one as much.

34

SAM

I WANT TO TELL HER.

I don't see her in person often—which is maybe a good thing, since I don't know how I'd react, especially to seeing her and Christian together. Even listening in to their dates now, the way they banter back and forth so easily, almost not needing my help anymore . . . well. I'd be lying if I said it didn't hurt just a little.

It's been two and a half months since first contact, and Christian and Ros are getting along better and better every day. Soon he won't need me, and their relationship will be just the two of them, without me listening in, the invisible third wheel. Christian deserves to be happy, to get the things he wants, and if what he wants is Ros, then that's what's going to happen. I don't know what Ros wants. I'm telling myself it's Christian, to make this easier on myself.

I can't stop myself from texting her, though. Not as Christian. As me. We talk fairly regularly now, random banter back and forth. It isn't always me starting the conversations, either. Once, a week ago, Ros texted me out of the blue a picture of the program for *So Long, Toledo!* It was bent in half, and a few of the corners were dog-eared, like she stuffed it in a drawer somewhere and completely forgot about it.

> **ROS:** Remind me why I kept this again?
> **SAM:** Because secretly, deep down, you actually loved the show?
> **ROS:** Don't push your luck, Dickson.

I should focus on so many things other than Ros right now. I have homework that's piling up, extra-credit assignments I begged to do and then completely forgot about. Submissions have closed for the Greater New England Young Playwrights Competition, which means the announcement can't be more than a few weeks away. I should stress out about that or use it to draw enough inspiration to write something else. I haven't posted anything on Instagram in days, and I usually post every day. I can't let this thing about Ros block *all* my energies like this. I went into this knowing that one day my job as Christian's "love coach" would be done. Either we'd royally screw it up and Ros would be a lost cause or they'd be together and happy, and either way, nothing about my situation had to change. It seems like it's shaping up to be the latter, but I can't shake the fact that my impending victory doesn't feel as sweet as it used to. I should be celebrating a job well done. Instead, I get a pit in my stomach every time I think about the two of them being happy together.

I feel like some sort of weird addict, vicariously living through Christian's attempts at flirting. I know that Ros sees the same potential in him that I did, once upon a time. They might actually be really happy together. Christian's going to realize he doesn't need my help soon. I'm on a time limit, and that time is slowly but surely running out.

So I make the most of it. I give Christian things to say, little things, things that so easily could have come from him.

"I listened to that band you recommended. They're really good! I'm glad you told me about them."

"You deserve to be valedictorian next year. You're smart without even trying to be, but you work hard, too. It's kind of inspirational."

"Did you know you frown whenever you're concentrating on something? You're adorable like that."

It gives me a thrill of secondhand excitement to hear Christian say it, to hear Ros laugh and thank him, or see the screenshot of her trying to act like the compliment didn't make her blush. I know, somewhere inside, that this is unhealthy. But I can't help it. There's a lot more I want to say—how beautiful her violin playing is, how the story about her dads made me understand so much more about her, how her laugh is rare and surprising but so rewarding to hear—and I don't have much more time to say any of it. Christian will come up with the same kind of things to tell her on his own, I'm sure. But it won't be me.

For a few days longer, I want it to be me.

35

ROS

I GO INTO MY SUPPORT GROUP MEETING THE
Saturday before spring break with a lot to think about.

For one thing, it's only another week until Dad's and Charles's
birthdays. Dad and I plan to do our usual April Thanksgiving
and watch *Cinema Paradiso* again. It's always a good time, and
we keep it lighthearted. But even still, Dad gets quieter around
this time of year.

Second, Christian has invited me to a party tonight. Monty
apparently throws a big one the weekend before spring break
every year, and he asked—"totally no pressure, obviously"—if
I wanted to go with him. I've never been to a high school party
in my life. I know the stuff about them on TV can't be accurate,
but when that's your only frame of reference, it's hard not to
be nervous about the idea. Besides, it's not exactly like I have

the same glowing reputation as Christian and Sam. I know what some people call me—The Shrew, as if the lazy twist on my last name is supposed to make me feel bad or something—so will anybody actually want me there? I don't mind being an outcast, but it's a whole other thing to intentionally put yourself into a situation where you know you won't fit in.

Speaking of not fitting in, I should probably pay attention to the meeting.

I know all the routines in these meetings because I've been going since I was eight. Dad didn't want me growing up maladjusted, I guess. We meet in a community center and sit in a circle of plastic school chairs. Because there aren't enough of us living in Worcester, Massachusetts, a few people join in on video chat to make it feel more like an actual "group." Some days there are topics, but most of the time, the leader sits back and lets people share stories or ask questions. I don't share often. I don't really feel like I *should*. Sure, I feel out of place sometimes, but how is that different from anybody else?

This particular session starts out with the usual chatter, but after a while, I start noticing a theme in the stories the others are telling. One girl talks about how much she hates the looks she gets when her white mom introduces her as her daughter. Another girl says she's considering getting a DNA test to find out the ancestry of her anonymous egg donor. A guy who's been going to this same support group for almost as long as I have (a guy whose name I still don't remember) tells a story about getting bullied by the kids in his elementary school when his mom—who looks nothing like him—came to pick him up one day.

Someone else is dealing with the fact that her surrogate mother was paid to carry her, and how it makes her feel like some sort of science experiment.

For me, it's always the little things. The fact that I don't look enough like my living dad to see myself in him, or anyone in my life, for that matter. The fact that I don't know where my blue eyes come from. These things aren't disasters or big, heavy truths I have to carry with me. They barely weigh anything on their own. But sometimes, on bad days, when I'm tired or stressed out, I realize how heavy it is trying to carry them all at once.

About this time, the group leader, May, interrupts. "Thanks for your stories, everybody. It seems like we've got the same things on our mind today. Let's move from stories into coping strategies. Microaggressions can be draining over time, but what are some ways to combat their effects? It doesn't have to be huge. Little things can have little solutions."

After a few seconds of silence, someone pipes up from the computer. "Finding things in common with your nonbiological parent?"

"That's a great one. Others?"

"Learning about your surrogate's heritage?" the second girl says.

"If that's something you want to do, yes."

The guy who told the story about his mom picking him up from school raises his hand. "Connections other than your parents. Finding people in your community you can relate to."

"A really good option, Michael."

He puts his hand down, smiling. May starts talking again, but I'm distracted now. His name is Michael. How did I not know that? We've been in this group together for years, and I never even bothered to learn his name. Does he know mine?

If there's any "community" I should have things in common with, it would be the kids in this group, and yet I barely know any of them. Not just here, though—I only became friends with Christian and Sam because they approached *me*. Otherwise, I would have happily gone on thinking we were complete opposites and never bothered trying to talk to them. I would have missed out on so much.

So is it my fault that I feel like I'm alone?

I've always sort of prided myself on being a loner, on being above the people at school, on being too smart and self-aware for drama and romance—I made a whole *project* about it. It's hard to find a community when you actively avoid joining one.

"Ros?"

I look up, startled. May is looking at me, frowning slightly. My thoughts must have been showing on my face. "You have something you need to say, hon?"

But I shake my head. I've barely figured out what these feelings are—nobody else needs to hear about them yet. "No. No, thanks, I'm good."

After group ends, I check my phone. There's a text from Christian, and, surprisingly, one from Sam. I open that one first.

> **SAM:** Christian said he invited you to Monty's party tonight! You gonna go? 👀
>
> **ROS:** Haven't decided yet.
>
> **SAM:** Haven't decided?? Girl, it's in like six hours, better hurry!!
>
> **SAM:** And no pressure or anything, but I'd love to have somebody else there to make fun of Christian with. Too much work all on my own
>
> **ROS:** Oh, I'm sure you can manage.
>
> **SAM:** Maybe, but I also know that Christian would loooove the chance to show off his cool genius of a girlfriend, so do with that what you will
>
> **ROS:** Cool? You've got the wrong person.
>
> **SAM:** I don't know, you have your moments
>
> **ROS:** Sam Dickson, are you admitting that I'm cool?
>
> **SAM:** Hey, I won't tell if you won't. Deal?

I'm about to reply with a self-deprecating comment, but something about the wording of Sam's text stops me. A little bell is ringing somewhere in my head. It feels . . . familiar, somehow. Like I've heard her say it before.

Wait. Maybe not *her*.

I scroll back through my conversations with Christian. It takes a while; there's nothing in our text history. For a second, I think

I'm going crazy, but then I remember our first conversation over Instagram. I open the app, scroll back, and there it is.

> **rosshewphotography:** My number is 774-555-6129.
> I'm begging you not to make this weird.
> **chrispow2002:** i won't if you won't. deal?

The same response, almost exactly word for word. Can that be a coincidence? The more I look at it, the more it starts to sound like Sam. I've been texting her almost as much as Christian lately, so I know her speech patterns pretty well. I think back to my first run-in with Christian, with how nervous and tongue-tied he was, then to our first date and his constant checking of his phone. How can he be so charismatic and well-spoken over messages but so awkward in person? How do I know it's even him I'm texting at all?

Maybe I'm reading too much into this. Friends talk like each other all the time, don't they? You pick up a saying of theirs, and soon you're not sure who actually started it. And maybe Sam gave him advice. I'm being ridiculous for no reason.

Still, I don't like the way it rearranges things in my head.

I like Chris. I do. I didn't expect to be the "boyfriend in high school" type, but Christian has surprised me, both in how not-cool he is for a cool kid, and how he has little bursts of wit, moments that make him sound almost like Sam.

It's those moments that made me want to date him in the first place.

I realize suddenly that I've been sitting in my car for ten

minutes without starting it, and the parking lot has emptied out. I shake my head and put the key in the ignition before turning back to my phone.

ROS: Fine, I'll ask my dad about the party. I'll keep you both posted.

SAM: Woooo!! 👊 🎉

I push the other thoughts out of my head to focus on driving and can't help but smile as I leave the parking lot. *Hey, Dad, remember how you said you wanted me to have more friends? Well, my new friends party. Careful what you wish for.*

36

CHRISTIAN

MONTY'S SPRING BREAK HOUSE PARTY IS KIND of a legend at Northeastern. It's happened every year since we were freshmen, and with each new edition it seems to grow in size and popularity. I remember the first one just being a couple of guys from the soccer team and our friends, but now, three years in, it's gained a reputation, and with good reason.

Monty's dad is one of the chillest parents I've ever heard of. Maybe it's something to do with Monty's mom not being the greatest, but now that she's not around anymore, it seems like he lets Monty do pretty much whatever he wants, as long as it's not too stupid or dangerous. He even leaves the house for the weekend, on the conditions that Monty cleans up after the rager and that the cops don't get called for any reason. So far, he's managed to stick to it.

Monty greets Ros and me with a grin and two cups. He's wearing something that's more his aesthetic but *definitely* wouldn't get past the dress code at school—a crop top and fishnets under ripped jeans, plus swipes of something glittery along his cheekbones. He hands me one of the cups, giving me a one-armed hug once his hand is free, then turns to Ros, holding out the other cup. "You drink, Ros?"

Ros looks more than a little out of place. She told me before we came that she's never been to a high school party before, which I already knew. I've been to almost all of them, so if she had, I would've seen her before. She was nervous at first, but it helped that she already knew Monty. She takes the cup, looking at it critically. "Depends what it is."

"Just Jack and Coke. And I keep a couple of plain sodas away from the rest of the mixers if alcohol isn't your thing."

Ros hands the cup back to him. "How about a really weak Jack and Coke, but I watch you make it this time?"

Monty grins. "Nice thinking." He takes the cup and drinks from it himself. "This way, kids."

He leads us into the living room, where most of the party is already happening. I spot plenty of people I recognize and get a couple of waves and shouted greetings as I cross the room.

Ros looks up at me. "I forget that you're popular, sometimes."

I smile, embarrassed. "I just get along with people, that's all."

"I can't think of a single person who *doesn't* get along with you, Christian."

"That's because there aren't any," a voice behind us says.

I turn to see Sam, who's grinning at us and dressed in

something the teachers at Northeastern also wouldn't let her get away with, but for very different reasons.

"Hey, Ros," she says.

Sam texted me before the party, asking if I was going to need any help while we were there.

CHRISTIAN: with Ros, you mean?

SAM: What else, genius?

SAM: I can bring earbuds in my bag if you need me to run interference over the phone or something

CHRISTIAN: i'll look weird with earbuds in. there's gonna be music

SAM: Hey, offer still stands!

CHRISTIAN: i think I've got it. it's not so hard to talk to her anymore

SAM: All right, fine. Go get her, Romeo

For a second, I'm almost worried about the two of them being in the same room, but Sam mentioned that she and Ros have texted back and forth a few times. As if I needed more evidence, Ros smiles back, with no trace of the awkwardness from their last face-to-face meeting months ago. "Hi, Sam."

"Did Christian get a drink for himself and not you?" Sam asks, pretending to look offended.

"Actually," Monty answers, appearing out of nowhere next to me with an empty cup, a can of soda, and a sealed airplane bottle of alcohol. "Ros here is just smarter than her boyfriend. She doesn't accept premixed drinks from spooky strangers."

He cracks open the soda and pours it into the cup, then adds a tiny splash of liquor. "That work for you, Shew?"

She takes it with a smile. "Perfect, Monty. Thanks."

Monty turns his attention to Sam. "Shouldn't you be mingling already?"

"Yeah, but maybe not this time. There are . . . an upsetting number of exes here right now." Her gaze darts to Ros for a second. "I think I'll stick with you guys."

"Yeah," I say, laughing. "Avoid your exes by hanging with your ex, your ex's new girlfriend, and your ex's best friend. Good plan."

"I am a master of strategy." Sam turns toward Monty. "I'm loving the fishnets. I thought about wearing some, too."

Monty wags a finger at her. "Ah, but you didn't. So now you just have to deal with the fact that you're never gonna look as stylish as me."

"I don't know, I think I'm doing okay." Sam sarcastically strikes a pose. She's wearing a tight velvet dress that stops at her thighs, along with a choker and a chunky black pair of Doc Martens.

"Fine, fair enough. I'll have you beat at prom, though."

"Wait, you're going to prom?" she asks.

"Not *this* year, obviously. There's no point in going to prom as a junior. I'll just save up and party extra hard senior year."

"Sounds like you're really planning ahead. It better be good."

"Oh, it will be. I'm thinking a tuxedo/dress combo, à la Billy Porter."

". . . Okay, well now that you've said that, you *have* to do it."

There's a shout of "Hey, Sam!" from across the room, and Sam's friend Aria appears out of nowhere to wrap her up in a hug. There's a loud squealing noise from both girls and then overlapping chatter as they start two conversations at once.

I can tell I've pretty much lost that side of the group, so I nudge Ros and gesture to another corner of the room. "Want me to introduce you to some people?"

She squints over to where I pointed. "Aren't those seniors?"

"Sure, but they're pretty nice. There are also a couple of games and things on the back porch usually, if that's more your style."

Ros laughs. "I don't really know what my party *style* is yet. Let's go talk to people, why not?"

"Sure. And hey"—I make eye contact with her for a second, leaning in to make sure she hears me over the music—"we can leave whenever you want. Monty's parties are pretty big, so I get that they can be overwhelming for a first-timer. We don't have to stay all night."

Ros smiles, and some tension that I hadn't noticed before eases out of her shoulders. "Good to know."

ROS

As nervous as I was beforehand, the party ends up not being that bad. A little noisy at times, sure, but there are places to go to get away from the worst of it, like the backyard, where they've got a game of beer pong set up next to a portable heat lamp. Monty's house is big, and I end up seeing him only once or twice during the whole night; he floats from room to room, calling out to people, laughing, handing out drinks. He's a magnetic host. Christian seems to have a habit of making friends with charismatic people. I wonder what went wrong when he met me.

Speaking of Christian. Over the course of the party, I watch him become a completely new person. The Christian I've been getting to know over the past several months is awkward in a conversation, shy and snarky by turns, quick to trip over his own words, and just as quick to apologize for them. That's not what I see here, though. With every new acquaintance or group he introduces me to, he seems to get more and more confident. He makes small talk easily, remembers everyone's names, recounts where he met them, and tells stories while everyone laughs and listens. Honestly, it's surprising.

Watching him, though, I realize this is another one of those "faces"—the ones people put on when they want to be something different to another person. This face is the one that makes Christian so popular. He's always smiling, pulling people in for quick hugs, laughing at jokes, eyes sparkling the whole time. He's like the best kind of politician. Not charismatic, really, and not fake, but nice. He's just *nice*.

I'm learning more and more that just because someone puts on a new face in different situations, it doesn't necessarily mean they're lying.

Despite the fun, the noise and talking eventually get to be a bit too much. I excuse myself from a conversation and wander off to a quieter part of the house. There's an entertainment room downstairs, packed with stuff Monty's dad apparently didn't want in the main living room. There's a TV and a few game systems, a shelf full of board games, and old, lumpy couches pushed up against the walls. I take a seat on one of them, breathing in deep and enjoying the drop in volume and the absence of people.

Just as I do, though, a shape darkens the doorway. Dark heavy boots, a choker, and a tiny velvet dress that makes me feel chilly just looking at it.

I tense for a second, my mind flashing back to my suspicion from earlier in the day. But then Sam grins, and somehow, I'm not as immune to it as I used to be.

"Needed a break?" she asks.

I nod, smiling back. "I'm having more fun than I thought I would, but I can only stand bad pop music for so long before my head explodes."

Sam shakes her head in mock disapproval. "Watch your mouth, Shew. I helped pick the songs for the playlist."

"Then in that case, I'm sorry you have poor taste."

She laughs, fast and loud and unexpected. "And here I thought we were getting along!" Even as she says it, she traipses into the room and takes a seat on the couch next to me, leaning against the armrest to give me space. "What do *you* listen to, then? Classical music?"

"Only when I'm studying or have to focus. But honestly, modern singers are too lazy. Most people don't even write their own songs anymore, and the ones they *do* write are garbage."

"Garbage songs aren't a new development, Ros. Everybody

worships the Beatles for 'Hey Jude' and 'Strawberry Fields,' but they wrote 'Octopus's Garden,' too."

Now it's my turn to shake my head. "I never said the Beatles were exempt. They're one of my dad's favorite bands, but they can be overrated."

"Even the Beatles are too overrated for you? God, you're one of *those* hipsters."

Comments like these would have been enough to start an argument a few months ago. Now? It barely fazes me. I even smile, just a little bit.

A laugh floats down from the living room. It's loud and unrestrained, audible even over the music, and we both look up at the same time, recognizing the sound. Sam grins. "Seems like Christian's still having fun."

"Yeah." I frown. "He's like a different person up there. Has he always been like this?"

"As long as I've known him, yeah. He kind of, like, *lights up* in front of other people. In crowds, I mean, places where he can talk to lots of people at once and nothing ever has to get too deep. I used to be jealous of him for that."

I look at Sam in surprise. "What, that he's friends with everybody? I thought that was your thing, too."

"I can talk to people, sure. But it takes work. Making friends is so easy for him. He does it without even trying. He doesn't *have* to try."

I don't think I'm imagining the slight edge to her voice. When I look over at her, her face is even, no signs of anger. Still, I know what I heard. I raise an eyebrow. "Is that a dig at Christian or yourself?"

She laughs quietly. "You know something? You're too smart for your own good sometimes, Ros. You're normally not supposed to just *say* those kinds of things to people, especially not someone you barely know."

"So we're not friends?" I ask.

Sam looks at me, startled. "I didn't say that."

"But you're saying we barely know each other. Friends know things. I know about Christian's family, and his older brother, and the things he likes to do when he's not at school."

"That doesn't count, you're—"

"You know about my dads. You know what I'm thinking of doing after graduation. You know I sometimes eat pineapple on pizza. But I've never asked you about yourself before. Why not start now?"

The silence that falls then is heavier than I expected. Without even trying, I've managed to strike some sort of nerve. Sam still doesn't look angry, though. Rather, it looks like I've made her think. That idea sends a tiny thrill up my spine.

"Whatever you've heard," she says slowly, "it depends on who you've heard it from. If it came from Christian, then it's all true. Even the embarrassing stuff. Other things, though, I can't guarantee. People talk. And sometimes I tell them different things to be safe."

"Why? I get acting a little different around certain groups, but completely changing yourself? If someone doesn't like the real parts of you, then what's the point of talking to them at all?"

Sam laughs again, just loud enough that I can tell she's faking, that nothing about my question or the thing she says next is funny. "And what if *nobody* likes the real parts?"

"I . . . don't think that's possible. I used to, though. I thought that it was fine that nobody liked me and that I was happy being alone. But Christian does genuinely like me, not just the things people assume about me. *You've* seen some of my real parts, Sam. Do you like any of it?"

She locks eyes with me. "Yes."

"Then there you go. There's probably nothing to be worried about."

For a second, I think she's about to laugh me off. It's a very *Sam* move, to grin and say something witty and completely ignore the heart of the conversation. I wouldn't even say I'd be disappointed. But instead, she looks down at her feet for a minute, chewing on her perfectly glossed bottom lip. For some reason, the motion is hypnotizing.

"You remember what Christian said on the track?" she asks. "About the little town in California my play was based on?"

I do, vaguely. I scramble for the name in my memories. "Loredo?"

"Yeah. I got defensive because I used to be obsessed with that town when I was a kid. For no reason, really. My mom and I went on a trip to LA once, and I saw it on a map and decided it seemed cool. But there's nothing there. Just a bunch of hippies raising chickens, probably. I've never been there." She sits back, sinking into the couch cushions, one hand running through her blond hair. "When my mom finally moved out to LA, I decided that the only places worth going were cities full of so many people that you could be invisible if you wanted. Places where you'd have to fight and *work* to be seen. Where if you did actually get noticed, it meant you'd earned it somehow."

There's a little bit of pain behind those words. I knew Sam didn't live with her mom, but I didn't know the circumstances. Suddenly, I'm wondering whom Sam is trying to get noticed *by*.

"But sometimes," Sam continues, sounding unsure of her words for the first time, "sometimes it seems like a good idea to get in my car, throw my phone out the window, and just drive. Find some middle-of-nowhere town, small enough that I could learn everyone's names, and . . . stay there. Raise chickens. Live a stupid, unimportant little life. Not *be* anything to anybody. Sometimes that sounds like the best idea I've ever had."

And for the first time in years of hearing her name come up in conversation, gossip passed around like trading cards, after months of talking to her on *her* terms, seeing only the pieces that she thought were acceptable, after so long assuming that those were the only pieces that meant anything, something unexpected has happened.

Sam Dickson managed to surprise me.

The silence is thick until Sam shatters it with a self-conscious laugh. "I, uh . . . I don't think even Christian knows that last part," she says quietly. "You might be the only one. I've gotta stop drinking before I spill any more secrets."

When she meets my eyes this time, though, I can tell that's a cover. She's stone-cold sober.

"Do you still talk to your mom, Sam?"

She shrugs. "She calls every Christmas, sure. And on my birthday."

"Does she know about your play?"

Sam smiles, and if it weren't for the conversation we've just had, I might not have noticed how it doesn't reach her eyes. "She will," she says. "Once it's worth something."

"You wrote it. You produced, directed, and starred in it. You put on an entire show at age seventeen. Shouldn't that be worth something?"

The smile drops just a little. Sam's right—she's a good actor—but I think I'm finally starting to see her tells. I'm not trying to hurt her, though. That's the last thing I want. Maybe this kind of conversation is too heavy for a party.

"Have you ever thought about taking a road trip there?" I ask.

"Loredo?"

"Yeah."

She frowns at me. "Why?"

"Just to see it."

"There's *nothing* in Loredo. What would I even do once I got there?"

"Whatever you want."

Again, I watch her resist the urge to laugh it off. She shrugs. "I don't know, maybe. I always thought road trips were kind of cliché, and I've already got plenty of plans for summer. But . . . maybe."

I think that's the closest I'm going to get to her admitting that it's something she wants. It isn't much, but for her, it's probably bigger than she's willing to admit.

"I won't tell anyone," I say. "If you don't want me to."

There's a tiny, grateful smile, a relaxing of her shoulders that I don't think even she notices. "Thanks, Ros."

I'm about to say something back to her—what, though, I'm not sure—when the light from the doorway is blocked by a figure. Christian. "There you are! Was it getting too loud up there?"

I nod, smiling, as I feel the moment between Sam and me pop like a soap bubble. "A little bit."

"I get that. Everybody's starting to go home now, though." He makes his way into the room, inserting himself between the two of us on the couch. I can tell he's feeling a little drunk.

Sam groans and shoves him. "*Move*, Christian. There's a whole other couch in here!"

"Maybe, but I want this one. I want to sit with my two favorite people."

"Gross."

"You love me."

They interact so naturally. There's none of the weird fumbling Christian has with me or the loaded, backhanded questions from Sam. Neither of them has to think about what they say to the other. They might not be dating anymore, but they really do love each other, in a way. This is just what that means for them.

"Did either of you submit a proposal for the Bellerose Assembly project?" I ask, interrupting their banter.

Christian says no at the same time that Sam says yes.

"Okay, well if you *both* had, what would you have said? How would you have answered the prompt?"

Christian wrinkles his nose. "What does love mean to you?"

"Yeah, exactly."

"I don't know, I—"

"Here." I remember that my phone's still in my pocket and pull it out, opening the camera. I start to record, holding the phone up in front of Christian's face. The lighting's bad, but that doesn't matter. It's not like it's *for* anything. "Pretend I'm interviewing you."

Christian blushes, camera shy. "What am I supposed to say?"

"Anything! What does love mean to you, Christian?"

He bites his lip and thinks for a few seconds. "Uhh . . . I think it's like being in the sun, kind of. This person's light is shining down on you, and it makes you feel warm and happy, and alive in a weird kind of way—"

"Incorrect," Sam interrupts, throwing an arm around Christian's shoulders and leaning dramatically into frame. "Love is making that light for yourself first and then finding someone else to give it to. Right, Chris?" She plants a kiss on his cheek, leaving a smear of lipstick, and then puts a hand on his face and shoves him sideways. He topples, laughing and swearing, and Sam turns to me. "What about you, Ros?"

I'm still recording, though I'm not looking at the screen anymore. I'm staring between the two of them, caught off guard and wondering what to say. I can't say what I'm really thinking: that I wasn't expecting to suddenly feel the world turning on its axis, to suddenly feel like I *belong* somewhere because of a few simple, casual words. I can't say that this dark room is suddenly one of the brightest places I've ever been. I also can't say that between the two of their responses, I'm starting to realize that the answer is a little bit of both.

"I think," I say, ending the recording and putting the phone back into my pocket, "that I'm not the one being interviewed here."

37

ROS

THE PARTY WINDS DOWN PRETTY QUICKLY AFTER that. Most people go home. Monty finds us, still talking. "All right, degenerates," he says. "Are you going or staying?"

Christian looks at me a little sheepishly. He was our ride here tonight. "I probably shouldn't drive."

I'm not mad, though. I wondered if something like this might come up, and I told Dad I'd text him if it did. He seemed fine with it, provided nothing "impulsive" happened.

"Me neither," Sam says. "You got room for all three of us?"

"There's a guest room down here, and then my dad's room upstairs. Also, the couches, obviously."

Sam jumps up. "Dibs on your dad's room."

Monty rolls his eyes. "Shocker. You guys figure it out on your own because I'm going to sleep. Night."

We mumble some "good nights" after him, and Sam stretches, arms over her head. "This has been fun," she says. "But now I'm going to leave the two of you alone and not think about what that probably means. See you tomorrow."

Christian goes beet red. "Sam, that's not—"

But she's already gone without a backward glance, heading for the stairs. I can hear her boots stomping their way up to the second floor.

Christian turns to look at me, still blushing. "She, uh—I can sleep on one of the couches. You can have the guest room."

"I'm not going to make you sleep on the couch, Christian."

"Uhhh—"

"That's not saying I want anything to happen," I add quickly, looking away so my face doesn't burst into flames. "Just making that clear. I don't think I'm—"

"No, I get it. I wouldn't if you weren't . . . you know. No pressure."

"We haven't even kissed yet, so I feel like that would be a pretty big leap."

That makes both of us laugh, and the tension eases. "I'll sleep wherever," Christian says after a few moments. "It's up to you."

"We can share the guest room."

He smiles. "Okay."

In the end, it's only a little bit awkward. The bed is big enough that we can both sleep there without touching, and apparently, the party tired Christian out, because he's asleep almost as soon as his head hits the pillow. He managed to stay awake long enough to kiss me on the cheek and mutter a "g'night," though. Thankfully, he was tired enough not to notice my flustered reaction.

It's almost three in the morning, and the party drained me enough to make me almost as tired as Christian. But something is buzzing in the back of my head, something that keeps my eyes open and my brain turning.

The conversation with Sam is replaying on a loop inside my head. She is so, so unlike the girl I first thought she was. I've seen hints, sure, in the way she reacted when Christian first mentioned Loredo, in the text conversations we've had over the last few weeks. That moment, though, before Christian came into the room, was the most *her* I've ever seen. "I don't think even Christian knows that last part," she said. There was no hint of her usual confidence, her invincibility. It feels like she willingly showed me a crack in her armor. She knew I could hurt her with that information, but she said it anyway. What does that *mean*, and why does thinking about it make my heart beat faster?

Maybe my curiosity is getting the better of me. Now that I've seen a piece of the real Sam, I want to know everything. To know how much of her act is really fake, how much is actually her, and whether or not it changes how I feel about her, though that last part I'm not even sure about to begin with. I thought I disliked her. I could have sworn I did. When I suspected she might be tricking me, I almost convinced myself that was true again. Now, though?

Next to me, Christian snores softly. I should be asleep, too. I know myself well enough, though, to know that I won't be able to settle down without doing something first. So I reach for the nightstand on my side of the bed, fumbling for my phone.

SAM

Sleeping in a stranger's house is weird. Everything is out of place, like it *should* be your house, but everything's been moved around. There's a picture of Monty as a little kid on the dresser, grinning with a couple of teeth missing and holding a soccer ball. I could say that the lack of familiarity is what's making it hard to sleep, but I'd be lying.

I think I said too much earlier. It's not that I don't trust Ros—her reaction to my confession was enough to reassure me—it's just that I don't really know *why* I did it. It's not like anything good is going to come of it. And now, Ros is downstairs, sharing a room with Christian. My chest feels tight and itchy just thinking about it.

Stop thinking about it, then.

That's easier said than done. I try to distract myself by playing games on my phone, checking Instagram, anything. It doesn't help. I just end up seeing a friend's picture from the party, and there in the background is Christian with his arm around Ros's shoulders.

But then my phone buzzes in my hand. I sit up, click through to the message, heart in my throat.

ROS: What's stopping you from going to Loredo?

The rush of relief I feel seeing her name on my screen is more than I want to admit. She's still awake, too, and clearly not busy with . . . anything else. Not that it's my business, but still. I type an answer, trying hard to sound lighthearted:

SAM: Well, money for one thing. Don't exactly have the
cash for a road trip right now 😜
ROS: Not what I meant. What's stopping you from
LIVING there, or somewhere like it, at least?

Ros is too smart. Maybe this is what I was afraid of: that she'd want to know more, know *me*, even the parts I don't like. Even the parts I wish didn't exist. But I can't ignore her now.

SAM: Because of all the things I have to do. You can't
exactly have a career like the one I want in the
middle of nowhere
ROS: Do you want it, though? That's not exactly the
impression I got earlier.
SAM: It's what I'm good at

There's a pause before she answers after that. For a second, I'm worried she fell asleep on me. Then:

ROS: "Good at" and "want" are two different things.
SAM: I know

ROS: So?

SAM: So what am I supposed to do besides the stuff
I'm good at? Better that than doing nothing with my
life and ending up a nobody

ROS: What does that mean?

SAM: Ugh, sorry. I know that sounded awful, I didn't
mean it to

ROS: No, I mean, what does "nobody" mean? What
would make you feel like that?

SAM: What is this, therapy?

ROS: Sam.

I'm trying to joke my way out of this conversation, but it's
not working. Ros is relentless when she thinks she's found out
something. I shouldn't have told her anything in the first place.
Too late now. She won't let go of this until I give her something.

SAM: Fine. Living in a place like Loredo means that no
one will ever know who I am. I wouldn't be important
or memorable. I wouldn't have made any impact on
the world. I'm not asking to be a superstar or anything.
I just don't want to die anonymous

We're really getting into the late-night sleepover conversations now. Ros doesn't seem to mind, though.

ROS: Your neighbors would know you, though. And
the other people in town. Maybe you do community

theater nearby, and somebody decides to join in, too, because they saw you act. Maybe you write a really good play and it gets produced in a big city. "Little" doesn't always mean "less."

ROS: Take Christian, for example.

Her next text is a dark, blurry picture of the guy himself, asleep with his face squashed in a pillow. It makes me laugh.

ROS: I don't know exactly what Christian wants to do with his life. Honestly, I don't even think HE knows. But if he goes off and does the same thing his dad does, lives in Worcester his whole life, doesn't cure cancer or end world hunger, does that make him any less important to you?

SAM: I see where your mind games are going

ROS: There's more than one way to be "known," Sam. You make an impact without even realizing it. I mean, I wouldn't even be at this party if it weren't for the two of you.

SAM: That's mostly Christian's fault

ROS: I don't think so. You had a hand in it, too. You influence him. Not in a bad way, I don't think. I just see you in him sometimes. Certain things he does or says.

ROS: Can I ask you something?

SAM: Nothing's ever stopped you before, so sure

ROS: Has Christian ever asked you for advice when he

was talking to me? Asked you to give him something
to say, even?

My heart lurches. This is the part where I should probably
confess. I *should*, right? Ros deserves to know.

But then I picture the look on her face, how angry she'd be—
not just at me, but at Christian, too. I could ruin everything
right here.

I like to think I'm brave, but apparently, that's a lie. The most
I can force myself to do now is give her a partial truth.

SAM: Yeah. A couple of times

There's a longer-than-average pause before she responds.

ROS: I thought so.
ROS: That's what I mean, though. You affect people.
   The people who matter know that you're worth
   keeping around no matter how "little" you've done
   with your life. And you're still in high school, by the
   way. I know you were shocked when I said I didn't
   know my college plans yet, but honestly, that's one of
   the most important things I've learned from my dad:
   We're both still really young. We're not out of time
   yet. Not even close.
ROS: That, and therapy. Therapy's a pretty big deal.
SAM: Who uses colons in text messages?
ROS: You're deflecting again.

SAM: Yeah, it's what I'm good at

ROS: You're good at a lot of things.

She's just trying to make me feel better. That doesn't actually mean anything. It can't. But she's still going:

ROS: Christian talks like you sometimes, or talks
ABOUT you like you're one of the coolest people he
knows. That's not the same as becoming a megastar,
sure, but that doesn't mean it doesn't matter.
Christian would thank you for the impact you've had
in his life. You're a good influence on him.

SAM: I hope so. I try to be.

ROS: He's more open about himself than most people
I know, too. It doesn't make anyone like him less. It
even made me like him MORE.

ROS: Maybe he should be a good influence on you,
too.

I'm frozen, staring at my phone as my heartbeat starts to echo in my ears. I know what she's implying—*open up to people, be more honest, more vulnerable.* She means it in general, not just to her, but . . . but . . .

I can't help feeling like this is a sign. If not from her, then the universe or whatever. This would be the exact time to say something. The whole conversation has been leading toward it. Ros doesn't know how I feel. I know she doesn't.

But would it really be so bad if she did?

SAM: Actually, I think he already has.

ROS: Oh?

SAM: Yeah.

SAM: If we're being honest, Christian's the only reason I started getting to know you in the first place. I never would have given you a chance otherwise. But I'm glad I did. If it wasn't for him, I wouldn't have gotten to learn that you're actually pretty cool.

ROS: "Cool" is a stretch, but thank you.

SAM: No, I'm serious. You were right about people always assuming something about you without actually getting to know you. If I'd stuck with assumptions, I never would have learned that you're funny, or that you're smart in a not-pretentious way. I wouldn't have learned how soulfully you play the violin. You're the first person I've actually WANTED to get to know in a long time. Do you know how weird that is for me?

ROS: Sam?

Say it. Say it. My fingers are shaking. I could back out, apologize, and say that I'm still drunk or something. But I feel like I've crossed a line inside myself, and past this point there's no going back. *Now or never.*

SAM: What I'm saying is, Christian's not the only one who's been falling for you.

ROS

I DROP MY PHONE.

It lands facedown on my lap, the glow of the screen extinguished, and I stare at the darkness, the image of that last text message burned into my retinas.

Sam?

Every conversation we've ever had suddenly shifts in my brain. Her willingness to admit something personal to me tonight. The quick banter that I just thought was Sam's particular way of speaking. The questions about myself that suddenly feel more pointed, more purposeful. Has it been this way the whole time?

Then another part of what Sam said hits me. *I never would have learned that you're funny, or that you're smart in a not-pretentious way. I wouldn't have learned how soulfully you play the violin.* She's never heard me play the violin. Not once. I don't even remember if I mentioned it to her. Hearing that I know how to play from Christian is one thing, but actually knowing what it sounded like?

The earbuds. *Christian's* earbuds. The ones he told me he used to listen to music when he was nervous. I took his reasons at face value—Christian wasn't lying about that; why would he?—but now that I'm thinking about it, I'm realizing he only started wearing them after that first date. Whenever he wore them, I got flashes of that other side of Christian—the confident, funny one, the side that could keep up with me in a conversation and had interesting things to say. The side I always thought reminded me of Sam.

Suddenly I'm searching my memories for every time I saw him wearing earbuds, as the world rearranges itself in my head. The day at school when he came up to apologize to me. The date at the art museum. That day at the park when I said I wasn't ready to kiss him.

In the university library, when I got brave enough to show him my project.

Sam was there. She was there the whole time, listening to everything, listening to *private conversations*, and telling Christian how to respond.

Has Christian ever asked you for advice when he was talking to me? Asked you to give him something to say, even?

Yeah. A couple of times.

It was more than a couple of times. It was *every* time. I don't know how often I was texting with the real Christian, but I imagine it's even easier to pretend over text than it is in person. They've been lying to me for *months*, and even though both of them are apparently in love with me, neither one thought it might be a good idea to confess.

Maybe I was right all along. Maybe it's better to be the outcast. This whole time I've been doubting my project, thinking maybe I was being too harsh, but of course, here comes life, proving to me yet again that nothing works out like the happily ever after you envisioned.

I'm angry. I'm so angry it feels like bile is rising up my throat, hot and choking and impossible to stop. It makes me want to get up and leave right now, call my dad to pick me up and then never speak to either of them again. Mostly, I'm embarrassed—the thought that I might have been lied to this whole time, manipulated, convinced I was falling for someone and putting my heart out there only for someone else to see it—but there's something else there, too. When I reframe events, all the messages Christian sent that made me smile, that made me think there was more to him than the obvious first impression, that made me feel dizzy in a strange, happy kind of way . . . when I rearrange the thoughts to make it Sam instead, my mind doesn't immediately reject it. In fact, the feeling barely changes, except that maybe it makes my heart beat a little faster.

Sam?

I feel Christian start to stir next to me. Maybe he senses something, because the first thing he does is turn to look at me. "Why are you still awake?" he mumbles, half-asleep. "You okay?"

I panic. I kiss him.

Christian almost pulls back, making a surprised noise against my mouth. One of his hands flutters awkwardly at my shoulder, like he can't decide whether he should touch me or not. He tastes like whatever he was drinking earlier. Dimly, I realize this is my first kiss.

I don't know what I was thinking this would do. Give me an answer, maybe? Help me decide if these feelings are for Christian or not, and if they're actually feelings at all? It doesn't help. I should stop this, pull back, and tell him it was a mistake.

Except now, part of me doesn't want to. Christian's lips are a little chapped, but they're nice. *He's* nice.

I like him, don't I?

When I break the kiss, Christian stares at me like I'm growing a second head. "What was that for?"

"Just wanted to," I say.

"Oh. Well, I—wow."

I could leave it at that. Having my first kiss with Christian—my first kiss with *anyone*—would be plenty. I know he doesn't expect more. Except Sam's words are still in my head, and now that there's space between me and Christian again, they're getting harder to ignore. I can see her smiling at me earlier tonight. I think of every conversation I ever had with Christian when he said or did something that reminded me of her, with his earbuds in, or over text, and who I might have *actually* been talking to. Who I might have actually been falling for.

I kiss Christian again, harder this time, more insistent. He makes another shocked noise and mumbles, "Wait—where is this going?"

"Where do you want it to go?"

"That's not really—"

I shut him up by pulling my shirt over my head. His jaw drops.

"Oh," he whispers. "Ros, you're—"

He's going to keep talking if I let him, so I decide not to. I press close against him, stop his mouth. I feel like I should be angry, and somewhere a part of me is, but right now, I need to not think. I'm not going to think about Sam's text. I'm not going to think about the fact that all the parts of Christian I've been falling for have come from her. I'm not going to think about how she lied, how both of them did. I'm not going to let this be a mistake.

I'm choosing Christian. I have to.

Christian pulls back, frowning at me. His hair sticks up on the side where he was sleeping. "Wait, hang on. Are you sure about this? I was serious earlier, we don't have to do anything till you're ready, I'm not disappointed—"

I cut him off. "I'm sure. Do you have a—"

"Yeah, yeah. In my wallet."

I move in to kiss him again, tugging at his shirt until he pulls it over his head. His hands on my back are big and warm—gentle, just like the rest of him. For a second, I imagine smaller hands, long fingers, nails dragging across skin.

Stop it. Stop it.

I'm here with Christian. I'm doing this with Christian. And I'm doing it because I want to, because this is what you do when you choose somebody. Because he is the person I've been falling for, been vulnerable with, been trusting enough to let in.

Because I can't think about the alternative. Not right now.

SAM

SLEEP WAS NOT AN EASY THING LAST NIGHT.

I stayed up for hours, almost until the sun came up, staring at my phone, waiting for Ros to answer me. There was nothing, not even the ellipsis that meant she was thinking about it.

So I wake up a scant few hours later, feeling more tired than I was when I finally fell asleep. Everything feels fuzzy and wrong, partly a side effect of the rough night and partly from waking up in an unfamiliar house. My first thought is to check my phone. I sit up, scrub at my eyes, and fish my phone out from under the blankets. The screen's blank, except for some notifications from Instagram and my email. I check my text messages just to be sure, in case maybe she said something late last night that I didn't see, but of course, there's nothing. Only that last message with my baring my soul.

Here's the thing: Knowing everything that I now know about Ros, I don't think she'd leave me hanging. She's not the shrew everyone thinks she is. Not to me, not to Christian. If she'd seen it, she would have responded, even if it was to shoot me down. I shouldn't agonize over what is, most likely, a case of someone falling asleep in the middle of a conversation.

But then, why was she so quick to respond before that moment? She was typing back to me almost as soon as she got my messages, not seeming tired at all. But as soon as I confessed? Nothing.

In a way, I guess that's a pretty telling answer.

I have to stop thinking for a few minutes. If I don't, I'm going to spiral, and that's the last thing I need. *Not now, Dickson.*

Checking my phone is a nervous habit, so to distract myself, I check the notifications from Instagram, keeping my hands and my attention far from my empty text inbox. There's nothing worth looking at in there.

What *is* worth looking at, though, is an email from the Greater New England Young Playwrights Competition. The subject line is pretty clear: "Greater New England Young Playwrights Competition RESULTS." The first few lines in the preview don't give much more info, either, just something generic thanking me for entering. There's no information that could tell me what's inside before I open it.

I'm scared to open it. I don't know why, but after everything that's happened in the last twelve hours, I don't feel as in control as I normally do. I need to get over myself.

I close my eyes and open the email.

It takes a couple of read-throughs for the full message to sink in. My brain keeps catching on the word *unfortunately* and sticking there, unable to move on to the rest of the email. I didn't place. Not only that, but the whole thing reads so generic, like they sent this same message out to everyone. If there were as many submissions as they're saying there were, then they must not have had time to personalize. My entry was nothing but an afterthought, the whole thing read and dismissed and forgotten about just like that. Hardly worth wasting time on, and then passed on for bigger and better things.

Semper ad meliora.

I can hear my heartbeat.

I force myself out of bed and head for the kitchen. If Monty's dad doesn't have coffee in the house, I'm going to burn the place down. As I hit the stairs, I hear a door shut softly somewhere ahead of me. I think it was the room Ros and Christian were staying in. I freeze, terrified for a second that it's going to be her, almost hoping that it is, but then a mop of messy blond hair comes around the corner. I relax.

Christian spots me on the landing and smiles. "Hey. Not too hungover?"

Right. There was a party last night. I was having fun last night. I force a smile. "Barely feel it. You?"

"I'm fine. You want coffee?"

"Sure."

I follow him to the kitchen, uneasy in a way I can't identify. The clock on the oven says it's 9:37. I should probably get home soon.

"Where's Monty?" I ask, thinking that maybe the odd feeling in my stomach is because I'm in a strange house without the person who lives there.

"Probably still passed out."

"And . . . what about Ros?" I almost don't want to ask.

"She's still asleep, too."

It's the *way* he says it that catches my attention. He always gets dopey whenever he talks about Ros, but this is different. Something about the confident smile, about his messy hair, the way he blushes. I dated Christian for five months, and we've been friends for a while. I know all his quirks; I know what each of them means.

And now I know why Ros didn't reply to me last night.

Christian starts hunting for coffee in one of the cabinets. I stare at his back, my head filling up with static. So that's it. Ros definitely saw my message. She read it, she was scared, or disgusted, or angry, and she made her choice. She made it pretty clearly.

I shouldn't be angry. She's not my girlfriend. Getting her to date Christian was the goal all along, and I can't pretend otherwise. I should be happy for them. I shouldn't be shaking like this, standing in the middle of Monty's kitchen and watching Christian spoon grounds into the coffee maker while my heart tries to throw itself out of my chest.

Was this how Ros hoped I'd find out?

Chris turns and sees me staring at him. "You okay?"

"I'm fine."

"Sam?"

Can he hear the catch in my voice? Does he see something in my face that gives me away? I try to smile again, but something about it isn't working.

I have to get out of here. I grab my bag and jacket from the hallway closet, only realizing as I nearly drop my purse that my hands are shaking. My vision's starting to fog up.

I'm nearly out the door when Christian stops me with a hand on my shoulder. For one fragile second, I almost turn around and slap him. My hand is halfway up, fingers clenched, and I have to force them down. He looks confused, concerned, and I don't have the heart to hurt him now, not when he looks at me like that. It's not his fault. The only person I have to blame for being unhappy is me.

"I'm fine, Christian," I say again, working to keep my voice flat since I don't think I can force any false cheer into it right now. "I just need to leave. I'll see you later."

"But you—"

"I said I'm *fine*." The front door unlatches with a loud click, echoing in the silence. "Go make coffee for your girlfriend."

His hand slides off my shoulder, and I slip out before he can respond, slamming the door a little harder than I mean to. It's sunny outside, well into the morning, and a light breeze rustles the buds of the tree near the driveway.

It's the chill of that spring breeze that makes me realize my cheeks are wet.

I throw myself into the car, slamming that door behind me,

too. In the back of my head, a voice says, *Drive. Don't think. Don't feel. Just run. Isn't that what Mom gave it to you for?*

I scrub at my face, trying to force the tears to stop, but they just keep coming. So I give up and drive home without looking back.

40

CHRISTIAN

I STARE AT THE CLOSED DOOR FOR A WHILE AFTER Sam leaves. What was *that*? I've never seen her act like that before. Usually, Sam's so cool and collected, and in the years we've known each other, I don't think I've ever seen her cry. Did something happen last night?

A couple of nightmare scenarios flash through my mind, and my heart starts racing. If somebody hurt her at the party last night, it's going to end *badly* for them. I don't think I can let her leave in good conscience if something did go down. Is she even okay to drive?

I check outside, but her car's already gone. I should text her.

Coffee abandoned, I head back to the guest room. I try to be quiet, but the door squeaks when I open it. Ros stirs, looking up at me with bleary eyes.

"Hey," I say. "Sorry for waking you up."

"What time is it?"

"Almost ten."

She groans. "I told my dad I'd be home by ten thirty. I should probably get moving."

"Yeah, me too." I pick my phone up off the nightstand, but it doesn't turn on. "Does your phone still have a charge? I need to send a message."

I don't tell her that I need to text Sam. Something about the weird exchange Sam and I just had was so personal, like she didn't even want *me* to see her like that. I doubt she'd be okay with my telling Ros about it. I'll have to be vague in my message, just so she doesn't read it and start to wonder.

Ros nods. "Yeah, the code's two-five-eight-four. I'm going to the bathroom to clean up a little."

She gets up and leaves the room, and I punch the pass code into her phone.

To my surprise, a text thread with Sam is open on Ros's phone. I don't mean to read it, I really don't, but the last message from Sam sort of . . . jumps out at me.

SAM: What I'm saying is, Christian's not the only one who's been falling for you.

Oh.

The text was sent around four in the morning, after everyone went to sleep. Ros never answered it. If I'm remembering

276

right, this happened a few minutes before I happened to wake up, before . . . everything else happened.

Math was never my best subject, but I don't like how this is adding up.

Somewhere inside me, I think I feel anger starting to surface. I don't know who it's for—me? Ros? Sam? Maybe all three. Sam didn't say anything and let me go on thinking she was okay with helping me when actually she was using me as a mouthpiece for her own flirting. And speaking of using, Jesus Christ, Ros. I feel like such a creep. I couldn't have known any of this was going on, but does that make it any better?

Did she even want to do it, or was she panicking because she felt like she had to? Even having to ask that makes me feel a little sick.

Giving your virginity to somebody isn't exactly a casual thing. That's huge. You wouldn't do that unless you were *completely* sure. Especially not somebody as logical as Ros. She wouldn't. The endgame of this whole scheme wasn't to get Ros to have sex with me; I'm not a monster. I wanted her to fall for me like I'd fallen for her, and something like what happened last night is what I'd consider a pretty big indicator that it worked. So Ros actually cares about me. Right?

I feel like I should be happier that everything worked out the way I wanted it to. Instead, I'm not sure what I feel.

I hear a door shut somewhere nearby. Ros must be coming back. I quickly put the phone back on the nightstand, trying to look busy by hunting for one of my shoes that I kicked under the bed.

I can tell the second she walks in that she remembered what was on her phone. She grabs it right away, pretends to be casual as she unlocks it, and sees the display still showing that text thread. She won't make eye contact, and the smile she gives me is gone just a few seconds too quick to be genuine. She knows I saw it.

So I wait. I wait for her to say something, to confess, to reassure me that it's fine, that it means nothing, that everything we did and the decisions she made last night were made with a clear head . . . that I was the one she *really* wanted to be with.

Instead, she looks around and says, "Have you seen my purse?"

A heavy rock settles in the pit of my stomach. "I, uh . . . no."

"Hmm. Maybe I left it in the hallway closet."

"Maybe."

She leaves the room again, and I go back to looking for my shoes. We're not going to talk about it, then. We're both just going to ignore it, pretend like we don't know the other one knows, pretend everything's fine and Sam's not secretly heartbroken. I wish I could say I was brave enough to bring it up, but I'm not. I never have been. I let my parents destroy all evidence of my older brother's existence, and I didn't say a word. Why would I grow a spine now?

ROS

HAVING A WEEK OFF FOR SPRING BREAK IS A blessing and a curse at the same time.

On the one hand, it means I don't have to see anyone from school. Christian goes on a beach trip for a few days with his family. I text him a little here and there, and he sends me pictures of the waves and his sister burying him in the sand. He seems happy. I wonder if he can tell that I'm not.

I don't talk to Sam. She's not the one I'm dating. As much as she tried to be, she *isn't* Christian. She's nothing but a liar, just like I suspected she was from the beginning. So I don't think about her. I try really, really hard not to think about her.

That's the bad thing about spring break: It gives me a lot of time to think. Dad's university has a different calendar, so he's still working in the mornings and afternoons, leaving me alone in the house most of the day. I have no homework to do that might distract me. I try to relax, but nothing sticks. I can't focus enough to read, and any movies I try to watch are just background noise to my already noisy thoughts. I end up taking a lot of walks around my neighborhood, watching people walking their dogs, kids playing in yards. It helps a little bit. I tried going to the park, but once I thought I saw someone who looked like Sam, and I ran back to my car.

I almost say something during support group. It's not even on topic—we have a guest speaker in to talk about the science behind surrogacy, to see if that helps any of us understand our feelings better or something. There's no way for me to bring up what's going on with Christian and Sam, but when May smiles and asks me how I am, I almost do it. In front of this room of strangers, I nearly break and start crying. I guess my expression showed, though, because May cornered me after the meeting to ask what was going on. I didn't say anything then. The moment passed. And besides, the group is about finding your family. They don't tell you what to do when the ones you found turn out to be the problem.

I tell myself that I'm angry. I *am*, I think: Everything that I thought was true about Christian was because of somebody else, someone with an ulterior motive and feelings they didn't have the guts to tell me about. That isn't fair, and I *should* be mad. I also tell myself that I should break up with Christian. He's not the person I thought I was falling for, and he's just as guilty as Sam.

Still, there's something painfully cathartic about the way things are now. If Christian thinks that something's off, he won't be brave enough to bring it up himself. I know that now. He'll just let himself suffer in the awkwardness in favor of avoiding a fight, and why not let him stew?

And as for Sam—well, isn't this what she wanted? She agreed to help Christian "win" me like an awful carnival prize, manipulated me into falling for a person who doesn't exist, and now it's worked out exactly like she intended. Mission accomplished. Good for her. Now she can live with the fact that she lied to me, that her little plan worked despite her feelings for me, and now there's no chance she can ever fix what she broke. Everybody gets what they want, and no one is happy.

How's that for a love story?

My violin sits in the corner of my room all week, untouched. I should practice my piece, make it happier like Mrs. Reagan wanted, but I can't.

I'm just going to play a cover of popular love songs over my assembly project. I can't put any more thought into it than that. If I do, I don't think I'll be able to perform at all.

SAM

Spring break is closer to a spring breakdown.

I stay in my room the entire time, blinds shut, leaving only as often as I have to so that Nana doesn't worry more than she already has. She's the only one I talk to the entire break. Nobody talks to me, either. Ros is avoiding me. So is Christian, which means she told him or he figured it out. No one else from school seems to be thinking about me. Not Aria, not any of my friends from the drama club, nobody. They've probably got better things to do. That's fine. It's fine. I have work to do.

Just because I don't have school doesn't mean I can't stay busy. I look up more playwriting competitions: There are others besides Greater New England Young Playwrights, better ones, *national* ones, and I have as good a chance at those as anyone. I start looking into requirements for universities I want to go to. They're all in big cities: New York, LA, Chicago, the only places that are worth going to. It's too early to apply for them, but the time is coming soon, and I have to be ready.

The map to Loredo stares down at me from my wall. It feels more like a threat than it ever has. Once, in a fit of panic, I almost rip it to pieces. Knowing that it's there makes it hard to sleep, because what else could I be doing to make sure I don't break my future any more than it's already broken?

Nana tells me to go outside. "It's gorgeous out," she says. "I know you've got friends who stayed in Worcester for break. Why don't you go see some of them?"

I tell her I'm busy.

"Busy with *what*? Sweet pea, you're starting to worry me."

So I put my actor face back on, promise her I'm fine, that everyone else is busy and I'm trying to fill my time. I don't think she buys it, but at least she stops asking.

I know I could tell her. She'd understand, be sympathetic, maybe even give me some advice. But I can't make myself face her. I can't talk about the fact that Christian hates me, that I lied to a girl until I fell in love with her, and that now she hates me, too. I can't talk about how I've failed in almost every aspect of my life and how I need to stay busy so I don't think about what that means, what it says about me as a person and where it'll land me eventually.

I can't talk about it because that makes it real. And if it's real, then there's no fixing what I've broken.

So I swear through clenched teeth that I'm fine and try to make it look as much like a smile as I can. I ignore the worried looks she gives when she thinks I'm not looking; it's easy to, once I get back to work.

CHRISTIAN

Spring break doesn't feel right this year.

Nothing's felt right since the party. I guess it's easy enough to figure out why. I don't know what else Sam and Ros talked about that night, but from the little of it that I saw, I know it wasn't good. I also know that it happened *before* Ros woke me up. That means something, and no matter which way I try to frame it, I don't like the possibilities.

Still, I've never been good at conflict. I just pretend that every-thing's fine, and Ros seems happy to do the same. I send her pictures from the beach, talk to her like normal, plan dates for when I get back, and even though I sense that same coldness in her tone from when we first started talking, I don't bring it up.

Sam doesn't talk to me the whole break. I think I'm okay with that. She should have *told* me something was happening in the first place. She shouldn't have agreed to help me if falling for Ros was ever a possibility. She should have . . . I don't know. Nothing about this situation is normal, and I have no idea how to handle it, other than exactly what I'm already doing. I know it can't go on forever, but what's the alternative?

Nothing feels right anymore. Not even at home. Now that Ros has asked about it, now that I'm actually looking, I can't help but notice the little things that bug me. Like how Dad always manages to talk over Mom. Like how they both *assume* I'm going to do something before they ask me. Like how Aimee gets shushed or criticized in a way that feels all too familiar. Like how Will's birthday comes and goes without so much as a mention. They're perfectly happy to act like he doesn't exist, and why did I never question that? Why did I never question *anything*?

I wish I could talk to somebody about it. But I don't want to make Ros angrier, and Sam isn't an option. Maybe Monty would get it. Maybe. Then Monty texts me to say that he's on a hiking trip with his dad and won't have service for a few days, and the last person I could have talked to about any of this vanishes.

During dinner, Mom tries to get us to watch a family movie, but I'm not in the mood, so I say no thanks. Dad says I'm disappointing her, and she looks like she might cry for a second. My gut twists with guilt.

"I'm just tired," I say, hoping the almost-lie works well enough. "I didn't sleep much last night. You can watch it without me, though."

I think they buy it, but Dad looks annoyed for the rest of the meal, and Mom still vanishes for a few minutes before coming back and pretending everything's fine again. She was crying and wants me to know it, but she won't say anything.

They don't end up watching the movie.

I stay in my room, selling the "tired" story by pretending to go to bed early. It wasn't really a lie—I haven't been sleeping well the last couple of days, for obvious reasons—but now that I'm in bed, my brain won't settle down. My sheets feel scratchy and hot. Sam is pissed, Ros is pissed, too, and Monty is busy. I feel like my head is about to explode. Nothing in my life feels okay anymore. Not my friends, not my girlfriend, and now not even my parents. I have no idea what to do about any of it, and there's nobody to help me except myself.

Is this what Will felt like when he left home?

It hits me then that I'm still blaming Will for what happened when he left. I don't think I'm doing it intentionally. Obviously, I miss him and wish he would come back, so I don't think he's completely at fault. But I've also spent the last two years trying not to turn into him. How am I supposed to do that when I don't even know what he did?

I barely remember the arguments now. At the time, I didn't want to hear about it. Now, though, I wish I'd paid more attention. How can I know whose fault it is, or if there's really fault at all, if I never see the full picture? I know that, toward the end, Dad told Will he'd better never see his face again, and I watched that hit my brother like a blow to the chest. But I also saw Will scream I-hate-yous in my parents' faces and listened to Mom crying about it later. How do you take sides in something like that?

I don't know if I ever will. But I do know that hearing only one side of the conversation isn't really listening at all.

I have Will's old email address. It's an ancient one, the kind with a joke name that you make when you're twelve. He probably doesn't even look at it anymore. But . . .

I get out of bed and head to my desk, booting up my laptop. The blue light from the screen makes a halo around me as I open a browser window.

Hey Will,

I don't know if you still have this email or not, so you might not even get this. I also wouldn't blame you if you see this and don't respond. I haven't tried to talk to you for years, so you might not want to hear from me.

I just want to know if you're doing okay. I don't know where you went after you left, or how your life is going. Mom and Dad don't talk about you anymore. They don't even know I'm sending this. Might get in trouble if they find out, but I wanted to try anyway.

I'm really sorry you had to leave. I don't know what happened, but if I did anything to make it worse, I'm sorry. I'm starting to think that our parents didn't treat you very fairly, even though I don't remember what you all fought about. You don't have to tell me if it was personal, I guess. You don't even have to reply to this. I'm not asking you to come back or talk to Mom and Dad if you don't want to. I just wanted to say that I'm sorry and that I hope you're doing well. That's all.

—Christian

I sit and stare at the cursor blinking at the end of the email. My mind swings between sending the email and deleting it. What's the point? He might not even have the account anymore, and I'll have gotten my hopes up for nothing. Or maybe he *does* see it, but he doesn't want anything to do with me. Can I live with that?

My hand thunks down on the desk, and something rattles. I look to my right. Sitting inside the halo of light, like it's been waiting for me to look at it, is the white Go piece. My lucky token. It's scratched up and a little dirty, but I've managed to hold on to it for four whole years and never lost it once.

I miss Will. I miss my older brother.

I hit the SEND button, and the email whooshes out of my sight.

42

SAM

WHEN SPRING BREAK DOES EVENTUALLY END, it's the first time I've ever considered faking sick for school. After a week of avoidance, the idea of having to go back, of having to see Christian or Ros in person—well, it gives me enough anxiety that faking sick might not be a problem.

But I've never been a quitter. Avoiding them now would be like admitting defeat, letting them know that they've scared me. And if they could see it, what might other people notice? Sam Dickson, scared of The Shrew? Not on your life.

So I show up early, head held high, dressed in my Doc Martens, an old band T-shirt, shredded jeans that might get me dress-coded—an outfit that makes me feel impenetrable. And I act like nothing's wrong, because nothing *is* wrong. Aria notices my attitude change during second period, at least a little bit. "You okay?" she whispers.

I nod, smiling and trying to look unfazed. "Sure. Why wouldn't I be?"

"You've just got this look on your face. And I didn't hear from you at all over break. Were you sick or something?"

I consider telling her that, in a way, I was. Aria would understand. I don't think she'd judge me for any of this, either. But that would require breaking the "casual friend" barrier we've set up, and getting close to somebody *else* right now doesn't feel like an option. Instead, I smile brightly at her. "I was busy writing my next masterpiece. There's a part in it for you, obviously."

She grins back. "You'll have to tell me about it at lunch."

I promise that I will, and it seems like that's enough to get her to drop the subject. I'm not exactly relieved that it was so easy to lie to her, but still. It's good to know that my disguise is working.

I do end up seeing Ros during the day. I hoped I wouldn't, since we don't take any classes together. But there she is, walking out of a classroom after the bell, eyes down on her open backpack. She hasn't noticed me yet. I freeze, then spin on my heels and make for a bathroom a few yards away. I think I duck through the doorway in time for her to avoid spotting me. Still, I stay plastered against the wall, heart hammering, waiting for her to leave. She passes my hiding spot, backpack closed and on her back again, and for the briefest second, I almost want her to turn and look at me. *I'm right here, Ros.*

But she keeps walking and meets up with a tall blond figure at the end of the hallway. My heart sinks.

"Sam?"

I jump and spin around. A girl from drama club is standing by one of the sinks. She's a freshman, so I don't know her that well yet, but she looks concerned, frowning at me as I hover in the doorway.

"Are you okay?" she asks.

I straighten up immediately, pushing my shoulders back and giving her a smile that even I can tell doesn't reach my eyes. "Yeah. I'm good."

She doesn't believe me. I can see pity in her face, pity I didn't want or ask for. She's going to tell somebody else in drama club that she saw Sam Dickson acting weird after fourth period, and soon enough, it'll be all over the place. Everyone will be watching me to see what's keeping me so on edge, and I can't. I *can't* live with that right now.

I don't wait for her to ask me if I'm sure. I just leave the bathroom, trying to put a confidence in my walk that I don't feel, hoping nobody else sees what that girl saw, and resolving from that second on to be *truly* impenetrable.

Based on that one near-encounter with Ros, I'm going to need to change tactics. Running away didn't work, and it only made

290

me look more suspicious. I can't handle that kind of scrutiny right now. The best defense is a good offense, after all. I can't let Ros know she's won. In fact, I have to prove exactly the opposite.

Which is why, the next day, I actively look for Ros. I know where some of her classes are. I can catch her between two of them and make sure she has to talk to me. If I knew where she lived, maybe I could have gone to her house to do this, but I don't have that option. And maybe it's better for people to see the confrontation.

I catch Ros coming out of a classroom after second period. Christian's class is all the way across the building, so there's no chance he'll interrupt us, either. When I stand directly in her path, she freezes, looking me up and down with a guarded expression.

"We should talk," I say.

She frowns. "Now's not really a good time."

"I'll make it quick."

Ros looks at me like she's worried I'm about to start a fight. That stings, but I don't let it show. "Fine," she says. "Can we get out of the main hallway, though?"

We move to a bank of lockers out of the way of the crowd of students. She leans against one of the lockers and crosses her arms. "What is it, Sam?"

The distance in her voice is the same I heard in our first conversation, when she called my play fake and tried to take me apart.

I reach into my backpack. "I wanted to give you something."

"Give me—"

She stares at me in confusion when I hand her the beat-up old map. When she takes it, she handles it like it might be a trap. Once she opens it and sees the clumsy circle and the writing in Magic Marker, though, it clicks. She looks back up at me. "Is this . . . the map of Loredo?"

"Yeah."

"Why?"

I shrug. "I don't really need it anymore."

"You don't . . . what?"

"Yeah. I mean, you sounded so interested in the story the other day, and I don't need this old thing hanging around anymore. I thought you might want it instead."

"Sam."

The way she says my name is like a blow to the chest. It isn't as harsh as I expected—there's ice in it, sure, but not nearly as much as I thought there would be. It sounds more like she doesn't believe me. Or, worse, she thinks she knows why I'm *actually* giving it to her. I can't let her have that. I can't let her read me again.

I force myself to look at her, bite out a "What?" in the steadiest voice I can manage.

Ros holds out the map. "I can't take this from you."

"Sure you can."

"But it's *yours*. There's no reason for me to have it."

"It's just going in the garbage anyway, so you might as well."

"I don't have to take anything from you, Sam. You want to give me something? How about an apology?"

I bite the inside of my cheek. She's right, but I don't know how to give that to her. Maybe a part of me was hoping she'd accept the map as an apology. Stupid.

I try to keep my voice light. "I really did try to make sure it was still Christian you were talking to, you know. I never made him say something he wouldn't say anyway."

"You *thought* you did. But that doesn't matter because, in the end, I wasn't talking to Christian. Not really. That's an awful thing to do."

She's right. She's right, and I don't know how to fix it. "Yeah, well, sorry to disappoint you."

"God, Sam, can you stop pretending you don't care for two seconds?"

I look up at her. She's glaring at me, but it doesn't feel malicious. This is another one of many times when Ros has seen something in me that I wish she hadn't.

"I get it," she says with a scoff. "We're in public. You have a reputation or whatever. So why would you try to have this conversation with me now instead of asking to talk privately— because you think you can get away with it? Were you even paying attention when you spied on me?"

"That's not fair."

"You know me better than that, Sam. I know *you* better than that."

I don't like the way she says it, like she's about to drop some sort of truth on me that she knows I don't want to hear.

And then it comes: "Giving me the map isn't going to magically make me forgive you, you know. Just like it won't save you from ending up there."

That's it. Something inside me breaks. Did she mean for it to hurt? I'm not sure, but right now I don't care. I meet her eyes and take a step forward, not backing down when she flinches.

"You know something, Ros? You're *right*. Giving you the stupid map *isn't* going to stop me ending up there. But you know what *is*?"

She doesn't break eye contact, just stares as I gesture down at myself. "Me. I won't let myself end up in a town like Loredo or stay in Worcester for the rest of my life, or anywhere else not worth my time, because I *know* I'm too good for it. I've got better things to do, and I actually care enough not to settle for second best."

"Sam—"

"*Don't.*"

I'm almost shouting now. Out of the corner of my eye, I see a few other students turn to look at the noise. I notice Callie, one of the other girls in drama with me. She's the worst gossip I've ever met. Everyone else in that club is going to know about this argument by tomorrow.

"Just shut up and take the stupid map, Ros. I don't need it. If you want to go on some pretentious art house movie road trip for self-discovery with it, then fine, but I've got better things to do. Things that are actually worth doing."

Part of me hopes Ros will get mad right back, shout at me, even though lots of people are watching us now. A tiny, stupid part is holding on to the idea that she'll somehow admit she was wrong, that she didn't mean to straight-up ignore me and she does have feelings for me. Weirdly, I don't think any part wants her to let me win in this conversation. It would be too easy.

It wouldn't be her.

But she just keeps staring at me, so I keep ranting, louder and louder, until plenty of the people nearby have stopped to actively listen. I can feel my heart climbing up my throat, aware of the eyes on me and Ros's most of all.

"I am not a failure," I spit at her. "And I'm never going to be. Because I'm actually willing to *do* things, instead of sitting around judging other people for doing them. I don't need that map, and I definitely don't need people in my life who tell me I'm going to end up there."

"I never said you would, Sam."

"You *didn't have to*." I pull my shoulders back, forcing myself not to bow under the weight of *so many people* watching me lose my composure. I have to leave before this gets worse, before anyone starts figuring out what's going on.

"Keep the map, Ros," I say with every last drop of anger I still have. "Where I'm going, I won't need it."

Then I turn and leave before she says another word. I can feel Ros's eyes on my back all the way to the end of the hallway. Once I'm around the corner, I don't stop walking, passing my next class, heading for the back door that leads to the student parking lot. My vision is starting to fog up. Better hold it together until I'm in my car, until no one else can see or hear me.

I skip classes for the rest of the day. Maybe that'll hurt my grades in the long run, but it doesn't matter. There's no point in pretending I can do anything right.

43

ROS

I DON'T HAVE THE HEART TO THROW THE MAP away.

I really should. Sam gave it to me for all the wrong reasons. She's too full of pride to take it back, and there's nothing I can do with it anyway. It's not my responsibility, not my problem. *Sam* isn't my problem.

I still can't throw it away.

It stays in my backpack, tucked carefully between two textbooks, untouched. I ignore it as much as I can, as if it'll go away if I stop thinking about it every five minutes, if I focus harder on whatever the teacher is saying, if I actually commit myself to this test I'm about to fail. It doesn't help, but I still don't touch it. So it follows me home. This whole day has been a disaster. I want to lock myself in my room for a few hours, enjoy the silence of an empty house for a bit until Dad comes home and I have to pretend that nothing happened.

Except, when I get there, Dad's already home. I hear him clattering around in the kitchen as I come in, and with a guilty shock, I remember. It's April Thanksgiving—Dad's and Charles's joint birthday party. I've been so distracted by everything else that I forgot it was coming up. I didn't even remember to get Dad a present.

"Hey, kiddo," Dad calls from the kitchen. "How was school?"

It takes me a second to pull together enough thoughts to answer. "Fine."

"Can you come in here and help me with the potatoes? I've been procrastinating because you're better at it than I am."

"Sure, Dad. Just let me put my stuff away."

He sounds so happy. Even though his birthday is still partly a sad occasion, he always manages to find things to be excited about. I know he likes the tradition. I can't ruin this for him. I head to my room and put my backpack down, not opening it, not even thinking about what's inside and how that makes me feel. I allow myself one deep breath, then two, before heading back down, leaving both the map and any thoughts about it upstairs behind a closed door.

Cooking is a good distraction. Dad keeps up a steady chatter about things that happened in one of his classes the day before, and it's easy to lose myself in a conversation with him. It feels as if almost no time passes while we're cooking, but when I look out the window, I realize that it's gotten dark.

We set the table and then settle in to eat. We cooked enough for a family of five, easy, so there's definitely too much food. But that's half the fun of big holidays or celebrations. All the food makes the table feel bigger than it is, like it's more than just me and Dad sitting here. Maybe that's the point. We eat until we're both too full to move, and then Dad takes a store-bought cheesecake out of the fridge for later.

The third part of the tradition is Dad's favorite. *Cinema Paradiso* is the first movie Charles showed him when they started dating, and even now, it's still his favorite. He only watches it once a year now, though. "To keep it special," he says.

I settle in on the couch while he pulls out the old, scratched-up DVD. We both know this movie—and every comment either of us could make about it—like the backs of our hands by now. I usually complain my way through the teenage romance in the middle, and Dad tells the same story about how it was around this point in the movie when Charles reached over and took his hand and how that instantly made this his favorite movie. "It didn't hurt that Charles looked a little bit like Salvatore when I first met him, either," he says with a wink.

Except this time, everything feels different. From the moment the title theme starts playing, I feel fragile in a way I can't explain. I know this movie backward and forward. I don't speak Italian, but there are lines I can quote. Nothing about it should surprise me anymore. But somehow, it's as if I'm watching it for the first time, and suddenly, everything is different.

Young Salvatore pesters the projectionist to teach him how the projector works, and I don't smile at it like I used to. Salvatore's father is declared dead, and the air in the room gets heavy. Dad still cries when the projectionist is blinded by the cinema fire.

I don't complain through the teen romance part. In fact, I can barely breathe. That girl smiles like Sam, with the same light in her eyes. I want to yell at teenage Salvatore to run, to get out before she hurts him, but instead, I bite my tongue as hard as I can. I don't crack when Salvatore starts writing letters to her that never get answers. I stare at the screen until it blurs so I don't have to see the look of disappointment on his face, so it doesn't start to remind me of Sam staring at her phone in the middle of the night, waiting for my answer.

I never understood the ending of this movie. To me, the biggest part of the story was always the relationship between Salvatore and the projectionist, and everything else was embellishment. The romance in the middle didn't make sense, and the choice to include the old, rejected clips of film reel confused me. Why not end at the projectionist's funeral? Why include the reel at all?

But now.

Now, I'm watching it along with the older Salvatore, those kiss scenes that the village bishop wouldn't let Alfredo or Salvatore include in the screenings, and something *clicks*. Connection. Actual human connection. *Belonging* with another person. Salvatore ran from it his entire life, abandoning the projectionist, his mother, his sister, never marrying anyone for long. The only real romance he ever had broke him, and he decided that meant that love wasn't worth it. It's only now, at the end—too late—that he figured out what a mistake that was.

I don't realize I'm crying until Dad puts an arm around my shoulders. The screen in front of me has gone so blurry I can't see anything anymore, and my breath is stuck in my chest.

"You okay, kiddo?" he asks.

I try to say yes. I try to say I'm just tired, stressed out from school, sad that he and Charles didn't get to have the life they were supposed to. I try to say so many things that aren't quite the truth. Instead, the dam breaks, and I bury myself in his shoulder, sobbing so hard my whole body trembles.

"Hey," he murmurs, "hey, it's okay. I know, Ros. I know."

I cry for every time I haven't in the last seventeen years. I cry for all the moments I convinced myself I was better off on my own. I cry for the people in my support group who've known me for years, who I never bothered to know in return. I cry for *Salvatore*. I cry for Dad and Charles. I cry for Christian, and for Sam, and for me, and somewhere along the line, I manage not to cry for long enough to tell Dad every single detail.

When the storm finally settles, Dad says, "You've had a busy couple of months, huh?"

I laugh-sob. "Yeah, I guess so."

"I wish you'd told me sooner, kiddo. I might have been able to tell you what a *teenager* you were being."

"I didn't really know there was anything to tell. It all just kind of . . . hit me."

"I understand." He frowns. "I'm gonna be 'Dad' for a second, and then we can go back to talking about this. When you and Christian got together at the party, did you use protection?"

"Jesus, Dad, yes."

"Okay. Good to know." He sighs, then shifts so he can face me a little better. "And how do you feel about . . . everything that happened?"

"I feel like an idiot. I can't believe I fell for it. And I hate that I still miss both of them, even after this."

"Feelings don't make sense, Ros. The sooner you figure that out, the happier you'll be."

"Are you sure? Because I think I figured it out, and I still feel pretty miserable."

Dad pulls me into another hug, both arms around me, and for a second, I feel like a little kid again. "Yeah, well, that's part of it, too."

"Can you just tell me what to do?" I say into his shoulder.

His laugh rumbles through me. "I don't know how well that would work out. But I can give you my opinion on things, if you want."

"Yes, please."

He releases me and sits back, giving me a perceptive look. "From the way you described it," he says, "Christian and Sam lied to you. And that was wrong, and I know it hurts. But all of you ignoring the hurts isn't going to fix anything. It only makes things worse. If it were me, I'd talk to them, or at least try to. If they apologize and mean it, try to make things better. You'll all be stronger in the long run, and so will your connection."

301

I bite my lip. My voice sounds small when I ask, "And if it doesn't work?"

His smile goes sad. "Not every relationship works out. Not every one *should*. But that doesn't mean every connection is destined to hurt you. Sure, some of them might, but isn't it worth a little hurt to find the ones that make you happy?"

I shrug, eyes welling up again. "I don't know."

"God, kiddo, what have I been sending you to counseling all this time for?" There's a laugh in Dad's voice, and it makes me laugh, too, even as the tears start up for the second time. He hugs me through that storm, too, then gives me a friendly nudge on the shoulder. "The cheesecake's probably stale by now. Want to see if it's still worth saving?"

"I don't like this metaphor, Dad."

"It wasn't supposed to be one, but now that you mention it—"

"Please, no more!"

I shove him off the couch, and we both get enormous pieces of cheesecake and cry a little more about the relationships that hurt. In the background, the movie starts itself over again.

44

CHRISTIAN

PRACTICE WORKOUTS WITH THE REST OF THE TEAM feel like the only part of my life that makes sense anymore. It's comforting, in a way—my body is the part of me that never lets me down. I can make wrong assumptions all day long, I can try to be nice and screw things up, I can say the wrong thing and hurt somebody, but in the end, if I need to go somewhere, my legs will take me. If I have to run, my lungs will keep me going. If something's hurt, it'll tell me. It makes *sense*, in a way most other things don't. It's not doing so great at keeping me distracted today, though. On top of everything else in my life to freak out about, the universe decided to add one more thing, and it's kept me so on edge that I haven't been able to focus on school all day.

There's an email sitting in my inbox. A reply, with Will's name at the top. It's been there for days, but I got the courage to open it only this morning. I had to lock my door and make sure Dad left the house for work before I felt brave enough. Honestly, I wasn't expecting him to write back. And if he did, I thought it would be a rejection. He'd be right to reject me. But what I actually got was a lot more confusing.

Hey Christian,

First, I wanted to say that I'm really glad to hear from you. I was kind of hoping you'd reach out, but I know it's complicated because of how I left. And just to get this straight right off the bat: I don't blame you. I never have. The way things ended between Mom, Dad, and me was never your fault. If anyone's apologizing here, it should be me.

I'm not gonna get too much into what happened with Mom and Dad, since it's taken years and a lot of therapy to figure it out, but I think you deserve the basics. Honestly, it was never just one thing that we argued about. It was anything—my grades, the friends I hung out with, what I wanted to do for college, if I wanted to go to college at all. Whatever they didn't like about me, basically, and there was always something they didn't like. Nothing I ever did was enough. No matter how good my grades were, what classes I was taking or clubs I was in, there was always something I was doing wrong. I get that they wanted the best for me, but it wasn't just that. Anything about me that wasn't like Mom and Dad, or went against what they saw for me, they took as a personal insult. I was an "ungrateful brat" for not wanting to go to Babson, and "lazy" for not getting into soccer like you or Dad did. Do you remember that one really big fight, about a month before I left? I disagreed with Mom on some tiny political thing, and she called me a disappointment. Dad was pissed. He told me that if I didn't do what they wanted or believe the things they wanted me to believe, after everything they'd done for me, then I was going to ruin my life. I told Dad that him talking about me like I couldn't make my own decisions was hurtful. He laughed at me and said, "You don't get to have feelings."

I don't mean to rehash this stuff, I'm sorry. I want you to understand what it was like for me back then. Mom and Dad were always harsher to me than they were to you. I don't blame you for that, either—some kids are the favorites. But I was never going to be happy with them trying to control my life. I had to stand up to them. Maybe

I didn't exactly do it in the best way, but hey, I was a kid. And I'm glad I did it. I had to leave so I could find a way to make myself happy, and they weren't going to let me do that if I kept them in my life. Just because somebody raised you, it doesn't always mean they're good for you.

I never wanted to cut you and Aimee off, too. I wanted to keep you guys in my life, but I never found a way to. There was no way to keep in contact that didn't involve being in contact with Mom and Dad, too, and I . . . couldn't do that. I still don't plan on talking to them, for what it's worth. But I do want to talk to you. You've been a victim in all this as much as I have. And honestly? I've really missed you.

We've got a few years to catch up on, huh? How are you? How's school? You seeing anyone? Are Mom and Dad treating you guys okay? I want to hear everything, if you're willing. It'll be nice to talk to you again. And hey, if you're ever in my area, maybe we could meet up! You don't have to tell Mom and Dad, don't worry.

Miss you, little brother.
—Will

I haven't replied yet. If I leave it much longer, I feel like my chance will have passed, but the problem is that I have no idea what to say. How are you supposed to reconnect with a lost family member after years of no contact? What am I supposed to say about how Mom and Dad treated him? And how am I supposed to feel about all this?

The easiest option would be to leave it alone. Then at least I don't have to worry about my parents finding out about it. Will seems like he's been fine without me for this long, and wasn't I fine without him? Wasn't everything fine?

You know it wasn't, whispers a voice in my head. *Something's been wrong with you and your family for a long time.*

I force it to be quiet and try to focus on the workouts with everyone else. Keep my muscles moving. Breath moving in, then out. Monty's noticed the change in my mood. I told him about what happened with Sam and Ros. I'm grateful he hasn't given me any "I told you so"s yet. He's too nice for that. He doesn't know about the email, so I'm assuming he thinks my bad mood is just about girlfriend drama.

Still, I catch him watching me closer than usual during warm-ups. When Coach starts us running laps, he jogs up next to me. "You want to talk about it?"

I shrug, eyes fixed ahead of me. "What's there to talk about? I've barely seen Ros today."

"Yeah, and you're flagging hard enough that even Coach is starting to notice. I heard Adam talking about it earlier."

Anger flares up in my chest. "Adam can say whatever he wants."

"He could beat you out for the forward position, too."

"So?"

"See, this is what I'm *talking* about, Chris!"

"Powell! Wells! Less talking, more running," Coach Branson shouts from the other side of the pitch.

Monty shoots me a look, then lets one foot drag on the Astroturf and pitches forward, skidding hard on his knees.

I stop dead. "Monty!"

A couple of other players notice, too, and Coach calls out, "You good, Wells?"

Monty gets shakily to his feet, hissing in pain. "Twisted my ankle."

"Let's go to the nurse's office." I give him my shoulder to lean on and call out, "We're going to get him some ice."

Coach gives the thumbs-up, and together Monty and I hobble off the field.

As soon as we're past the doors, though, Monty shrugs me off and starts walking normally.

I stare at him. "What are you doing?"

"You think I don't know how to fake an injury? We play *soccer*, Chris."

"Okay, but why?"

"Because I needed to talk to you." We round the corner from the gym, just far enough that no one will accidentally see us hanging around, and Monty finally stops and turns to face me again. "Are you ever going to start fighting for things you want?"

The question takes me by surprise. I blink at him. "I . . . I don't know what that—"

"You really like Ros, right?"

"Of course I do."

"But you're going to let both of you stay miserable?"

"What am I supposed to do? I can't go back in time and make their conversation not happen."

"No, but you *can* talk to her about it!" Monty runs a hand through his hair. "Stand up for yourself, Chris! Start saying what you want from people, and then actually try to get it."

"I *want* everyone to get along! I don't want Sam and Ros to hate each other, and I don't want them to hate me, either!"

"Then *tell* them that!"

I wish I could get angry, but right now, I only feel tired. I don't even know who I'm talking about anymore. "Yeah, because arguing with them is a great way to make sure they don't hate me."

Monty frowns. "You . . . asking for what you want isn't arguing, Chris."

I don't have a response. My impulse is to deny that that's what I was saying, but I can't. Monty barely knows half of what I've been dealing with the past couple of weeks, but it doesn't feel like that at all. It feels like he knew exactly what to say to punch me in the gut, to leave me winded and speechless and hurt. He found something I wasn't ready to hear.

I think he notices how unbalanced I'm feeling suddenly, because he steps forward and puts a hand on my shoulder.

"I don't know where you got that idea from," he says quietly, "but it's not true. You're a really cool guy, Christian. People will still like you when you stand up for yourself—they might even like you *more*."

There's a tremor in my voice. "Thanks, Monty."

"Except me. I'll probably start hating you anyway."

That forces a laugh out of me. "Shut up." But I pull him into a hug, and he returns it as hard as he can. "You're the worst."

"Ouch, is this what the new, confident Christian sounds like? I take it back, actually. Keep being a doormat."

"I will twist your ankle for real if you don't stop."

"Fine." He pulls back and grins at me. "We should get some ice, though. So Coach doesn't think I was faking."

"Probably."

We both turn and head for the nurse's office, Monty bumping my shoulder affectionately as we go, and, to show him I'm willing to fight, I bump him back.

Maybe it's Monty's pep talk that makes me aware of something Dad says to me later that evening at dinner. We're talking about finals, about summer plans and possible vacations, when he looks over at me and says, "You know, Babson has tours this summer. We should schedule you one before availability fills up."

I nod and start to agree with him, but suddenly the new little voice in my head, the one from earlier today, whispers again.

Is that what you want?

"Sure," I say carefully, measuring every single word. "We can do that. I should probably schedule a couple more college tours then, too."

Dad frowns. "Why?"

"Well, it'll be a pain if the tours are spread out all summer. If they're closer together, there's more time to—"

"No, I meant why would you want to look for other schools?"

Mom frowns, looking confused.

I take a deep breath. "It's always good to have options. The school guidance counselors say we should apply to at least three colleges, and to have a safety school in case—"

"Your grades are fine for Babson," Dad interrupts. "They'll accept you."

"Okay," I say. "But it's still good to have options."

He stops eating and looks at me hard for a second. "Don't you want to go to Babson?"

He doesn't make it sound like a question. Mom gives me a warning look, like she thinks I'm about to start a fight. Next to me, Aimee hunches down in her chair slightly.

Inwardly, I wish I could do the same thing. My heart is pounding. All I hear in my head is old fights, my parents screaming and Will screaming right back. Everything in me is begging me to shut up. I still could. I could just say that he's right and leave it at that, and we would move on.

What would somebody else do in this situation? Sam would fight back, of course. Monty would probably make some kind of joke. Ros would use logic to argue her own side. None of those sound quite like me.

But maybe, somewhere between the three, is the thing *I* would do.

I reach into my pocket, where a little round piece of plastic rests next to my skin.

"Babson's a really good school," I say, keeping my tone light. "It's obviously going to be on my list. But Massachusetts has a lot of great schools, so I want to do some research and make sure I'm making the best choice for me."

Mom flicks her gaze between my dad and me.

He narrows his eyes. "Did that Ros girl say something? Is she trying to get you to go to the same school she is?"

"No, Dad. She doesn't even know where she wants to go to college yet, remember?"

That stumps him for a second. Meanwhile, I'm holding on to the Go piece in my pocket for dear life. I'm being so, so careful not to sound angry—not raising my voice, not saying anything confrontational. No reason to argue, but still telling them what I want in the safest way I can. This may not technically be fighting for something I want, but it sure as hell feels like it.

Mom tries to change the subject. "Aimee, are you almost done eating? You can't push your food around your plate—"

"Where's this coming from, Christian?"

That's the third time he's spoken over me or Mom in the last couple of minutes. I do my best to make my expression look pleasant. "What do you mean?"

"You've always wanted to go to Babson."

You assumed *I wanted to go to Babson.* "I still do. I'm just being careful. I want to make sure I know about my choices so that I can make the best one for my future. Isn't that what we both want?"

I'm waiting for him to yell at me. He and Mom never needed much reason to start in on Will, even though he never exactly tried to avoid it. If there's a part of the conversation to turn into an argument, then this is it.

I don't know what makes this different. Maybe it's that I tried to keep everything as nonconfrontational as possible. Maybe neither of them is in the mood to fight. Maybe it's because it's me.

Whatever the reason, after a long silence, Dad breaks eye contact and shrugs. "I still think we should schedule the Babson tour first."

"We can. I'll look into it after dinner tonight."

The energy at the table relaxes. Mom goes back to eating, and Aimee gives me a relieved look.

I grin at her, still shaky, not sure if that was victory, but happy that I did it anyway.

My email's open again. A cursor is blinking in an empty text box, and I can't say I have the words to fill it just yet, but I'm going to try. Will deserves that much from me, at least.

What would talking to Will again look like? I don't know where he lives, or if I could even visit him. I ignored him for so long. Is it even possible to be something like friends again, let alone siblings?

I run my fingers across the Go piece in my pocket and think about having more of my big brother to hold on to than a little piece of plastic.

Is that what you want?

I still don't know who that little voice belongs to. It's not Sam, or Ros, or Monty. It's not me, I don't think. Not yet. But maybe someday it could be.

What's that phrase Sam uses? "Fake it till you make it"? I guess it means that if you pretend something long enough, that makes it true.

I don't know how well that works, but I'm definitely willing to try.

45

CHRISTIAN

I TEXT ROS AND ASK HER TO MEET ME AT THE
park. It's short notice and it's late—nearly dark out—but I don't
think this can wait. It's waited long enough as it is. I wasn't sure
she'd agree, but thirty minutes later, she's there, at one of the
benches under a tree that's starting to grow new leaves.

When she sits down next to me, her posture is stiff, and she's
being careful not to touch me.

"So . . . I know about the message Sam sent you," I tell her.

Ros nods. "I figured you did."

"I'm not mad," I say.

She laughs, but it doesn't sound like she thinks it's funny.
"Yeah?"

"If anything, I feel like *you're* the one who should be mad."

"Why, because you and your ex-girlfriend *Cyrano*'d me?"

I frown at her. "We what?"

"*Cyrano de Bergerac*. It's an old French play."

When I stare at her for another few seconds without figuring it out, she sighs.

"I mean, because you both *lied* to me?"

Oh. I wince. "Yeah, because of that."

"I am mad. I've *been* mad since the party."

"So then, why are we still together?"

Ros pauses, chewing at her lip. "I don't know."

"Yes, you do."

There's a heavy silence. In the twilight, the hollows under Ros's eyes look even darker.

"If I'm being honest," she says, "I think part of me wanted to hurt Sam a little. Make her feel as embarrassed as I did."

She doesn't say anything about wanting to hurt *me*, and somehow, that makes it worse. "And how's that working out?"

She looks away, twisting her shirt hem in her hands. "Not great."

"Doesn't feel great on this side, either."

"No, I know, I . . . sorry."

"You're not the one who should apologize first."

She quirks an eyebrow. "Oh?"

"Yeah. Listen, you're right—Sam and I lied to you. Pretty much since the beginning. We tried not to make it too obvious, and I felt bad about it sometimes, but that doesn't excuse anything. Sam was . . . there for most of our conversations. She heard a lot of private things she probably shouldn't have. Sometimes you thought you were talking to me when actually you were talking to her. That's a crappy thing to do to someone. I was scared, and an idiot, and I shouldn't have done it. I'm really sorry."

Ros sighs. "I don't get *why* you did it, Christian. What was the point?"

"Because . . . I was nervous. I screwed up that first meeting so badly I thought I didn't have a chance without some kind of help. I wanted to impress you."

"So you lied?"

I wince again. "Okay. That one's fair."

"You know what, Christian? I'm not as mad as I thought I'd be. Maybe I should be angrier. But also, I shouldn't have brushed you off so quickly the first time. I . . . assumed you didn't want to know me for the right reasons, and if I'd taken the time to actually talk to you, I'd have figured out I was wrong."

"I mean, yeah. But you also don't *have* to give somebody your time."

"True." Ros laughs quietly. "You know, I told my dad about what happened."

I freeze. "Should I be worried?"

"No! No, he's not mad."

"Even about the—"

"Not even about us having sex. Promise."

I let out a shaky breath. "Your dad is . . . really nice."

"Yeah, he's great." She looks down, frowning at the now-wrinkled hem of her shirt. "He gave me a lot of good advice about what to do."

"Care to share any of it?"

317

"He said I should try to figure out if our relationships are worth saving. If they're making me happy."

"And . . . what did you decide?"

I'm trying really hard not to show on my face how nervous I am about her answer. Sure, I need to fight for myself more, but right now, Ros is the one who got hurt, and her opinion matters here, too.

Ros takes a deep breath and finally looks back up at me. "I don't want to lose you, Christian. Not all the way. We both messed up the relationship part, but you still make me happy. I *like* hanging out with you, I like talking. You're a great guy. I'm not in love with you, but . . . I don't want that to mean that I have to lose a friend."

The feeling that washes over me then isn't entirely disappointment. It feels more like relief. There's a bittersweet edge to it, of course—Ros doesn't love me, and that stings. It stings a lot. It's going to take time and effort to get over her. But I definitely know I don't want this to end with the two of us hating each other.

"I understand that," I say after a while. "I said the same thing when Sam broke up with me. I care about you a lot. I'd like to keep that in whatever way we can." Then, after another pause, "Speaking of Sam."

Ros tenses up. "Yeah?"

"Where are you and her at right now? I haven't talked to her since all this went down, so I wasn't sure."

"I haven't talked to her, either. Not much." Ros goes back to fidgeting with her shirt. "She gave me her map of Loredo."

"*What?*"

"Yeah. Said she didn't need it anymore. Got mad at me. I baited her, though."

There's a lot Ros isn't saying, but I decide to go for the most obvious. "You never replied to that last message she sent you. Was that because you didn't feel the same, or you were mad, or . . . ?"

The silence is lead-thick. Ros can't look at me. I give her time to answer, but as the seconds drag on, I watch her eyes get more and more glassy.

"I'm sorry, Christian," she whispers finally.

"Don't be."

"All the parts of you I thought I was falling for, everything I saw that made me interested—"

"It was her."

She presses her lips together, hard. "Yeah."

She starts to cry, and for a second, I panic, unsure if I should hug her or stay where I am. I settle for a hand on her upper back, thumb brushing across her shoulder. She doesn't pull away, and secretly I'm relieved. After a little while, I say, "Are you upset because she's a girl?"

"No!" Ros makes a sound that could either be a laugh or a sob, and I'm too awkward to ask which. "I don't care that she's a girl."

"Didn't think so. So what's up?"

"I just didn't plan for any of this. And now I don't know what to do."

"I mean, it kind of seems like the next step is talking to her."

She gives me a watery smile. "You sound like my dad."

"He obviously gives good advice, so I'll take that as a compliment."

"Sure, that's the only reason. Definitely not because he was cool with my giving my virginity to you." She cringes. "Sorry about that, by the way."

"You weren't lying when you said you were sure, were you? I did ask—"

"No, I wasn't. Promise."

I sit back, not bothering to hide how relieved I am this time. "Good."

"I just wasn't thinking as much as I should have been. I regret the circumstances, but not you." Ros looks at me. "What are you going to do, Christian? We keep talking about *my* issues."

"Yours are a lot more interesting." I give her a self-conscious smile. "I'm not sure. But I'm kind of okay with that. I've had a lot to think about over the past week or so, and I'm not done figuring it out." Then I add, "I emailed my brother."

Ros sits up straight. "You did? What did he say?"

"He was happy to hear from me. I think he wants to keep talking. I wouldn't blame him for not wanting to, since I never bothered all this time, but I figured I'd . . . I don't know, try."

"I'm proud of you."

I don't know why that simple sentence makes *me* feel like crying. "Thanks."

"That's a big step."

"Yeah." I take a deep breath. "And I disagreed with my dad yesterday. Just a small thing, and he didn't get as mad as I thought he would, but still."

"Wow, such a rebel."

"Whatever."

Above us, the streetlamp flickers on. We both jump, then laugh, tinted orange in our own pool of light.

"We should probably go home," Ros says.

"Yeah, probably." But before either of us can get up, I ask, "When are you going to talk to Sam? I need to as well, but I don't want to steal your thunder."

She frowns. "I'm not sure. I don't even know if she'd *want* to talk to me at this point."

"I could help, if you want."

"Maybe. It probably won't be until after the assembly. The project is taking too much of my brainpower, and I—" Ros stops, staring into space.

"What?" I ask.

"I think," she says slowly. "I just had an idea."

"Spill!"

"Sam likes theatrics, right? Grand gestures?"

"She's the most dramatic person I've ever met."

"In that case, I'm definitely going to need your help. Are you okay with that?"

Is this what you want? the voice in my head whispers.

I grin down at her. "Say the word, Ros. I'm on board."

46

SAM

I'VE DECIDED I'M PLAYING HOOKY TOMORROW.

Attendance at the Bellerose Assembly is mandatory. The entire student body piles into the auditorium to listen to whatever speakers they've invited that year and then sit through the student speaker presentation. This year, I think that's a little more than I want to deal with. It's not that I can't, obviously. I just don't want to.

Of course, if I'm going to make it look like I'm sick enough to miss school tomorrow, I need to start laying the groundwork ahead of time. Any good actor knows that the work you do behind the scenes is what makes the performance believable. So I have to convince Nana that I'm not feeling well. It doesn't take much—keeping quieter than usual, not finishing my dinner, making passing comments that I feel "weird." That's enough to get her worrying about me, at least. I brush her off and say I'm fine, though.

So now, I've ended up in the living room with her, on the opposite end of our couch that sinks in a little too far, watching some kind of cooking show. Nana loves this stuff—she's not much of a cook herself, but she loves pretending she'll make these needlessly complicated recipes someday.

There's a lot more I could be doing right now—anything that could keep my mind busier than watching this French guy on TV make a roux. But I still need to make Nana think I'm not feeling well, and this is part of it. That, and I also . . . miss her.

I've been avoiding Nana a lot lately. At first, I was busy trying to get Christian and Ros together, and after everything fell apart, well, I just couldn't face her. She could already tell I was upset. If I'd stayed around her, the truth would come rushing out. I know she'd be supportive if I told her what's going on, but that would mean admitting it to myself, too. Admitting that I was wrong, that I'm hurt, that I care about Ros way more than I planned to. None of that is an option.

Now, though, I think I'm safe. It's been long enough that I can say Ros's name without feeling like I might cry, right?

Nana's pretty engrossed in the show, but about halfway through it, she turns and looks at me, frowning. "I'm not keeping you from homework, am I?"

"Nah," I say. "Tomorrow's an assembly. There's nothing I really need to get done."

"Okay, good. You've been working too hard lately."

"Just trying to stay out of Loredo," I say lightly, adding a slight rasp to my voice and clearing my throat. In a few minutes, I'll cough and see if she notices.

"Oh, come on, you know I hate that old joke," Nana says. "That was you and your mom's thing, not mine." She pauses. "Have you heard from her lately?"

I snort. "Is it my birthday already?"

"Hmm." She doesn't say much more than that and keeps her eyes on the TV, mouth fixed in a straight line. She gets weird when we talk about Mom. Not that we do very often, but every time it comes up, I get the vibe that she's waiting for me to say something. I have no idea what, though.

After a few more seconds of silence, Nana says, "Speaking of Loredo, I saw that you took the old map down."

Ah. So she noticed that, too. I shrug. "Yeah. Wanted to change up my decoration a little."

"You want me to hang on to it, make sure it stays safe?"

A hot spike of guilt lodges itself in my gut. *Actually, Nana, I appreciate it, but the map's already gone. I spite-gifted it to the girl who broke my heart. Oh, I didn't tell you about that? My bad.* "That's okay. I can take care of it."

"Sure thing, sweet pea." She smiles at me when she says it, perfectly trusting, and it makes me want to curl up and die.

I shake my head, forcing my eyes back to the TV. I can't think about this right now. Not if I want to avoid bursting into tears in front of my grandma.

Of course, the universe seems to have other plans. My phone buzzes in my back pocket, and I pull it out.

CHRISTIAN: wanna sit together for the assembly
  tomorrow?

I stare at the message for a few seconds, blinking hard. Christian hasn't talked to me in almost two weeks. Not since the party. No messages, no meeting up between classes, nothing. I assumed he figured out what happened between Ros and me, or she told him. But this message is so . . . casual. Like his completely deliberate ignoring of me was just a passing thing. Like there's never been anything wrong.

Looks like we're pretending nothing happened, then. I'm fine with that. But I'm still not going to the assembly.

SAM: I'm not feeling very good. Probably won't be at
  school tomorrow
CHRISTIAN: oh yeah? what, food poisoning or
  something?
SAM: Something like that
CHRISTIAN: sounds pretty convenient
SAM: What?
CHRISTIAN: pretty convenient that you're planning on
  being sick tomorrow, that's all
SAM: You know I don't fake sick to miss school, Chris
CHRISTIAN: do i know that?

And it's moments like this when I swear that Nana's psychic, because right then she looks at me and says, "Why don't you invite Christian over sometime soon?"

It takes a lot of effort not to stiffen up when she says his name. "He's been pretty busy lately," I say, aiming for breezy. "He and his . . . girlfriend have been hanging out a lot more often."

"Well, invite her over, too! If the two of you get along, that is."

If we get along. I force out a laugh. "It's complicated."

Nana frowns. "Complicated how?"

There's no good way to explain this to her. There just isn't. So I dodge the question. "I'll tell you later. Aren't you trying to watch this show?"

She glances over at the TV again, where the French guy has moved on from making a roux and is starting to prepare some kind of bird. "I suppose so," she says, but I can hear the doubt in her voice.

I take advantage of her distraction to look back at my phone. Christian has been sending me more messages.

CHRISTIAN: you should come tomorrow. i think it'll be worth it

CHRISTIAN: unless you're too scared or something

God, he knows exactly how to mess with me.

SAM: I told you, I'm not feeling well

CHRISTIAN: right, sure you're not

SAM: Are you planning something? If you're trying to get me to go just to embarrass me, we are done

CHRISTIAN: i wouldn't do that. you know i wouldn't

CHRISTIAN: just promise me you'll show up?

I bite my lip. Something about this feels like a trap. Christian has to know about what happened between Ros and me, but now he's trying to get me to go to the assembly. An assembly where she'll be presenting about love and what it means. I'd be stupid not to see how bad this could go.

But it's Christian. Even if he's mad at me, he wouldn't try to pull some kind of prank. Not on his own, at least. But what if Ros put him up to it? A part of me still thinks she wouldn't, even after everything I've done, but is that worth the risk? It's better if I just stick to my guns and don't go. It has to be.

Nana speaks up again, and I almost jump, remembering she's still in the room. "I'm assuming you're texting Christian?"

"Yeah."

"Tell him hey from me, then. And tell him I miss seeing him around."

"I will," I say quietly, staring at her even as she keeps her eyes fixed serenely on the TV.

It's too much of a pointed comment to be accidental. She knows I'm lying about what's been going on lately. And more important, she knows what I'm like. I'm not going to just tell her what's up. I *can't*. But the thing is, Nana's always been pretty good at dropping subtle hints. Like right now, as she keeps watching the French chef and pretending she can't feel my staring at her. She's not going to pressure me into giving a straight answer—she knows better than to try—but this is her way of reminding me that she sees it and that she'd be willing to talk if I ever wanted to.

Nana might not know exactly what I'm going through, but she definitely knows what she's doing.

I look down at my phone again.

SAM: Fine. I'll be there

CHRISTIAN: you won't regret it 👍

It's hard to believe that one. Something about this still feels off, like Christian's keeping something from me or planning some kind of intervention. I don't like being the one in the dark in this situation, but I guess I won't know until I'm already there. I have to admit, a part of me is curious. Besides, even if he and Ros are setting up some prank to humiliate me, it's not like I'd blame them.

I think I'd probably deserve it.

47

CHRISTIAN

IT'S FRIDAY, AND CLASSES ARE ENDING EARLY
for the assembly. The whole day usually leads up to this, and
even though almost no one is actually *excited* for a mandatory
assembly, they're at least taking it as an opportunity to check
out and mess around on their phones for an hour and a half. I've
never really cared much about the Bellerose Assembly myself,
but now, things are different. I'm invested.

Plus, there's a good amount of pressure riding on me to make
sure Ros's plan goes right.

Students file into the auditorium in messy lines, some grum-
bling about how boring this is going to be, some already on their
phones. Sam looks like she wishes she could be anywhere else.

I bump her with my shoulder. "You still here?"

She shoots me a smile, but it's not as confident as usual. "Do I have to be?"

"It's an assembly. You'll live. Plus, I think you'll like it."

"I've already heard what her project sounds like, Christian. Do I really have to be there for it?"

"Yes. Trust me."

"And remind me why I should do that?"

"Because you love me, and I'm *extremely* trustworthy."

She scoffs. "Right."

She does pale a little, though, when we enter the auditorium. The stage is set up with a projector screen and a lectern, and a couple of people mill around up there. One is the vice principal, Mrs. Reagan, talking to another woman, who must be this year's guest speaker. Near the back, almost in the shadows, Ros sits in a chair with her violin on her lap, tuning the instrument and looking anywhere but at the audience.

I bump Sam again. "You can do this. Let's go get a seat."

She nods and follows me.

I'll admit, I'm a little nervous. Not that I *should* be—it's not my project, not my presentation. But it is my friend's, and a lot is riding on this plan going well. I agree with what Ros said the other day—I don't want to lose either of these girls in my life, and no matter what happens today, I don't plan on it. It would just be a whole lot easier if they could stand to be in the same room with each other.

Almost on reflex, my hand goes into my pocket. My lucky Go piece is still there, like always, squashed into the seam by my phone. A different kind of relief comes with feeling it now, after Will's reply. It feels more present, somehow. It feels luckier.

Sam and Ros can make up. Weirder things than that have happened in the last couple of weeks. Sometimes, all people need is a shove in the right direction.

SAM

Christian is being entirely too cheerful right now.

I don't know what his plan is, but he seems excited, and somehow that makes me even more nervous about going to this assembly. I almost considered hiding in one of the bathrooms until this is over, but he tracked me down before I got the chance. Now, I'm stuck with him—him and that all-American smile that's tinged with just a little bit of mystery.

He insists we sit at the front of the auditorium. I make him settle for the second row; being front and center for whatever is about to happen is too much for me right now. I'm still ready to fake sick and duck out of here the second it gets to be too much, though; it's a cruel joke of the universe that this year's theme is love and that Ros is the one giving the presentation on it after everything that happened.

Mrs. Reagan steps up to the lectern to start the assembly. There's some very half-hearted applause, and I check out before she even starts speaking. The only thing worthwhile about these assemblies is the student presenter part, and even then, only if you're the one presenting. The guest speaker comes up to the mic and starts telling some sort of anecdotal story about her life that's supposed to teach us about the meaning of love, and like most other people in the audience, I bury my face in my phone and ignore her. I'm more than happy to stay that way, too, except all too soon I hear Mrs. Reagan speaking again.

"And now it's time for a presentation from our student speaker at this event, Miss Rosalyn Shew!"

More half-hearted clapping. My shoulders immediately tense up. I keep my eyes fixed on my phone, but Christian squeezes my forearm. "Sam?"

I look up at him.

He's smiling, and it's the same puppy dog look he always uses because he knows it works. "Please watch," he says. "I think you'll like it."

I sigh and force myself to look at the stage. Ros is approaching the center, violin in her hands. Behind her, the projector screen goes blue as the machine starts up. She looks nervous; that's the first thing I notice. There's the tiniest shake to her hands that I've never seen before. Her dark hair almost covers her face as she checks her violin's tuning one last time. She doesn't go over to the lectern; instead, she stands off center stage, letting the projector screen be the focus of attention. It lights up with a still frame, the image of an older guy with curly hair who, if I'm remembering the draft of her presentation right, must be Ros's dad.

I already know how this goes. I heard the whole thing before, when I was spying on Christian and Ros during their study date. Except, to my right, I can feel Christian grinning at me. Something's about to happen, but I don't know what. My heart starts to race.

The image on the screen starts to move, and Ros's dad looks into the camera. "When I first met my husband," he says, "*before* he was my husband, I mean—I didn't think I'd ever meet someone I'd want to be with. It was barely an option for people like us back then. I'd almost accepted that I would be alone. But these kinds of things always sneak up on you."

I frown at the screen. This isn't the way I remember hearing it start.

What's going on?

"It's always the person you're *not* looking for," Mr. Shew continues, "the one you'd least expect. But once they're in your life—well, you can't imagine it being anyone else."

I glance over at Christian. He's grinning up at Ros and at the screen, and when he catches me staring at him, he jerks his head back in that direction. "Keep watching."

The image on-screen changes. Now it's not Ros's dad at all. In fact, it looks like a video of another student. A senior, Hannah Winthrop. She and I have talked a few times, but not enough to say we're friends. She looks directly into the camera with a smile.

"To me," she says, "love is something that nobody in this world can live without. It can be any kind of love, not necessarily romantic—love from your parents, your siblings, your friends—but no matter where it comes from, it's incredibly important."

A new face pops up. This one is a younger guy I don't recognize. He says, "Love is sacrificing for the people you care about. It's giving them your time or your money or something else valuable. Not expecting anything back, because that's not what it's about."

That's when I realize what this is. These are the speaker proposals—every student who wanted to be where Ros is right now, giving their own presentation, had to send in a video proposal detailing their project idea and explaining what love meant to them personally. How did Ros get ahold of these?

I also realize, then, that Ros has started playing her violin. It's not the same song I heard over the phone, either. That one had a heavy, somber tone that felt almost too dark for the story her dad was telling. This one feels . . . romantic. And familiar, though I'm not sure from where.

My friend Aria's face appears on-screen, and I laugh in surprise. "Love, to me, is being willing to talk," she says. "You can't assume the other person loves you and then leave it at that. There has to be communication there. That's how you make the relationship the best it can be."

"Amen!" someone shouts from the audience, and a few people laugh. I look over and realize that Aria's actually sitting in the same row as me, closer to the aisle. She catches my looking at her and winks.

Then there's a new face on-screen, then another—student after student, all of them explaining what they think love means, while Ros plays. Her eyes are closed in concentration, a frown on her face as she sways slightly to the swell and ebb of the music. It sounds so familiar.

After a few more students, the videos change slightly. These look like more candid interviews, not submissions. Some are teachers, some students, but they're all still answering the same question.

"Love is something you have to have for yourself, first and foremost," one of the social studies teachers says.

"Love is being willing to try, again and again," says Mrs. Reagan.

"Love is putting up with the other person's crap," says Monty with a grin.

I hear him whoop from somewhere behind us.

Christian's little sister beams up at the camera, missing tooth on full display. "Love is liking all the same stuff as somebody else!"

A bunch of people laugh at that, and there's a couple of scattered *awww*s. I laugh, too, but as I look back at Ros, Aimee's words still rattling in my head, I realize something. The music. The reason it sounded so familiar. Lifetimes ago, Christian came over to my house to watch a movie, to do *research*, because how could he possibly think about dating this girl without knowing about her favorite things first? We barely paid attention, but this . . . *this*, I remember.

Ros is playing the theme from *Cinema Paradiso*.

It feels like a hand closing around my chest. Ros's dad is back on-screen. He looks teary-eyed. "Losing Charles to cancer wasn't what either of us had planned for our lives. It wasn't fair, and I still miss him. I think I'll always miss him. But because of him, I got to have some of the happiest years of my life. I got to have a *daughter*. No matter how painful the rest of it was, I'll never regret any of that."

The violin music swells. On-screen, new faces pop up, nobody talking, but each with something to share. Two junior students from my year, pride flags wrapped around their shoulders, give each other a sideways hug and grin at the camera. A freshman girl I recognize from drama club holds out her phone, showing an image of her and her little brother. Mrs. Reagan shows off a photograph of her and her husband on their wedding day. Mr. Shew holds up a framed photo, showing him, a man who must be Charles, and a little girl of maybe two years old with dark, curly hair.

Then, suddenly, it's Christian's face on-screen. The lighting is bad, and the camerawork is shaky, clearly not taken at the same time as the other clips. He's sitting on an old, beat-up couch, and in the background, I hear the thump of music.

"What am I supposed to say?" he asks.

"Anything!" Ros's voice pipes in from behind the camera. "What does love mean to you, Christian?"

Oh.

The Christian sitting next to me puts a hand on my forearm and squeezes. On-screen, the Christian from the night of the party bites his lip. "Uhh . . . I think it's like being in the sun, kind of. This person's light is shining down on you, and it makes you feel warm and happy, and alive in a weird kind of way."

"Incorrect." And then there I am, leaning into frame, throwing an arm around his shoulders. "Love is making that light for yourself first and then finding someone else to give it to. Right, Chris?"

I'm used to seeing myself on camera. We don't get to do much film work in drama club as high schoolers, but it's happened once or twice, and I've taken enough pictures for Instagram to know exactly what I look like through a lens. Usually, though, I have some kind of control over what gets seen by the public. I can make whoever's looking at the picture think I'm smart, or scary, or gorgeous, or intimidating, or whatever else I want to feel, because I'm the one in charge of who gets to see those sides of me.

This video isn't that. This video is a random, ridiculous moment I thought would never see the light of day. I wasn't trying to be anything to anyone—I was just *being*. And as much as it scares me not to have control over how I'm perceived, in this situation, it almost doesn't feel so bad.

Is this how Ros sees me?

In the video, I plant a kiss on Christian's cheek. A few people in the audience whistle. I shove Christian away, and both of us (and Ros, quietly, almost surprised behind the camera) laugh like nothing in the world could ever be wrong again.

Then, the me on the recording turns to the camera, still grinning, and says, "What about you, Ros?"

The image freezes there, on my face, smiling, and very slowly fades into black. The last few notes of *Cinema Paradiso* hang in the air. Ros lowers her bow and violin, taking a deep breath. There are wet spots on her cheeks. She turns, instrument by her side, to face the audience, and for the first time in several minutes, she opens her eyes.

And looks directly at me.

Around me, the rest of the auditorium applauds. I'm frozen, staring at Ros, at the expression on her face, paralyzed by what I'm starting to realize it means.

Mrs. Reagan walks back onto the stage, still clapping, and congratulates Ros. She breaks eye contact with me, giving a quick smile to the vice principal before nodding out at the crowd and walking offstage. Like a spell has just been broken, I realize I can move again.

Christian nudges my shoulder. "What are you waiting for?"

I stare at him. "What?"

"Go talk to her."

I glance around at the rest of the auditorium. "But—"

"What, are you *scared*?" There's a sparkle in his eyes and an angle to his smile that I know he learned from me. "Get out of here, Sam."

"Are you sure?"

"Really sure."

Right at this moment, I am so, so glad he persuaded me to be friends with him. "Thank you, Christian."

"Don't worry about it. Go."

I stand, surprised that my legs still know how to carry me. Mrs. Reagan is giving the closing remarks for the assembly, but it's easy enough to stand and make my way to the back of the auditorium, whispering an excuse to the teacher who tries to stop me. Once outside, I book it around the corner. I know where the stage doors are. I know my way around. The only thing that could stop me from finding Ros would be if she didn't want to be found.

And right now, I don't think that's going to be a problem.

48

ROS

I KNOW WHO'S BEHIND ME AS SOON AS I HEAR the footsteps. Turning around almost feels scarier than the performance was, but I do it anyway, and there's Sam.

She looks like she ran back here. Her hair's a little wild, and she's breathing heavily, eyes fixed on me.

The first thing she says is, "I'm sorry."

"Me too," I tell her.

"No, seriously, Ros. I'm sorry." She swallows, takes a deep breath. "It was my idea to try to fool you in the first place. It was a terrible thing to do. You're right to be angry."

"I was, and you're right. You shouldn't have done it. You made me think I was falling for Christian when really it was somebody else."

Sam nods, eyes going down to the floor.

"Can I just ask you one thing?" I say softly.

"Sure."

"Was that you?"

She glances up. "What do you mean?"

"You like to pretend, Sam. Show people what you think they want to see. I saw parts of you through Christian, and bits and pieces whenever the two of us talked. So . . . was that you?"

Sam looks lost for words for a minute. When she laughs, it's breathy, like it's the only sound she can think to make. Her eyes are shining.

"Yeah," she says. "It was. Maybe not at first, but eventually . . . it was as real as I know how to be. It's not much, but I'm trying."

I nod. "Okay."

I think Sam expects the conversation to end there, because she nods back and almost turns to leave. She looks surprised when I step forward and say, "Here," as I reach into my back pocket and pull out a carefully folded piece of old paper.

She doesn't realize what it is when I first put it in her hand. Once it clicks, though, her head shoots up. "My map."

"Still want to go on that road trip?" I ask.

"I . . . yeah, but—"

"Then I'm coming with you."

"What about—summer work, Ros, and college tours? We're gonna be seniors next year. There's so much we need to—"

"Sam."

I have a whole speech prepared—about how she takes herself too seriously sometimes, about how pointing that out probably makes me a hypocrite but doesn't change the fact that I'm right—but Sam doesn't need it. She takes one look at me, and her face splits into a huge smile, even as tears pour down her cheeks. I'm grinning, too, so wide that my cheeks hurt.

She's the one who pulls me into a hug. I return it as hard as I can, laughing a little even as I feel my own throat start to close up. I don't think I've ever been this close to her before, and I can smell her shampoo and some kind of spicy perfume that she wears. She's warm and surprisingly soft, and it makes my heart thud hard.

Sam pulls back. "I—sorry, can I kiss you?"

"Yes."

"Really?"

It kind of sounds like she doesn't believe me, so I close the distance and answer that for her. She gasps against my mouth, hands immediately going up to my face. I can feel her smiling through it, and I'm sure that I am, too. I don't know who the happy tears on my cheeks belong to anymore.

We pull apart after a few seconds, both of us laughing and crying at the same time, still holding on to each other.

"Is this happening?" Sam says.

"Everything I thought I was in love with Christian for was actually coming from you," I tell her. "I just panicked when I found out. I'm sorry I didn't talk about it sooner."

"But Christian—I mean, is he *okay* with it?"

"He literally persuaded you to come and see the presentation. He's okay, Sam, I promise."

"Right." She laughs again, louder, wilder. "For some of the

smartest girls in the whole school, we've really been acting like idiots, huh?"

"I think my GPA's probably lowered *itself* in protest at this point."

"Does that mean I have a shot at valedictorian next year, then?"

"Not on your life, Sam."

She kisses me again, and distantly, I hear the sounds of more applause and then people getting out of their seats, chatter rising from the hundreds of other students as they're dismissed for the day.

Sam looks alarmed. "Christian! We should go find him! Thank him, I mean, for—"

"God, you're right. He helped me put this whole project together."

"He's probably waiting to see if we murdered each other or not."

But Christian isn't waiting outside the auditorium. I don't see him in the crowds of other students, and he's not in one of the hallways nearby. We rush out to the parking lot, but his car is already gone.

"I'll text him," Sam says, phone already halfway out of her pocket. She takes one look at the screen, then bursts out laughing. "Oh my *God*."

"What?"

"Check your phone."

I pull out my own and check my messages. There's just one, from Christian, sent to both of us about five minutes ago.

"He's quoting my play," Sam says, grinning. "I guess his memory isn't that bad after all."

I wouldn't have remembered it unless Sam pointed it out, but looking at it now, I see it. Christian's last line, the one he stumbled on at the performance. The one, Sam explains, he messed up because he was too busy staring at me. But now he's nowhere in sight, off doing God knows what, and it's just the two of us standing here, staring down at our phones and smiling.

CHRISTIAN: so long, dum dums 🖤

♥

TWO
MONTHS
LATER

49

ROS

THE GROUP MEETING IS FULL FOR THE FIRST TIME in a while. I'm sitting in the same place I usually sit, near the windows that look out onto the park. I can't help but keep glancing out there every now and then. I catch glimpses of my car in the parking lot a little farther off, waiting for me. I've got somewhere to be, but right now—

"Ros?"

I turn my focus back to the rest of the room. Everyone is looking at me, including the people on Zoom. I recognize one of them: Kadan, who I've been messaging with online lately. They've actually got a pretty similar family situation to mine. Sitting next to the screen is Brooke, and then Victoria on her right. We sometimes get coffee together after meetings. A few seats down from me, Michael is giving me an amused smile. They've all caught me daydreaming.

The group leader, May, smiles patiently. "You seem distracted," she says.

I shake my head. "Yeah, sorry. I promise I'm here."

"All right, then. We're discussing the word *family* and what it means to everyone here. Do you have anything you'd like to add to the conversation?"

I can't help giving one glance back out the window. I'm not ignoring May—not this time. I'm just thinking.

I turn back to the group, looking around at everyone, at all the faces and names I recognize now, at my friends. "Yeah, actually," I say. "I think I do."

I've got a packed suitcase in the trunk of my car.

It's not staying there long—long enough to make the drive to Sam's house, and then it'll be shoved into a different trunk next to other pieces of luggage, on the way to somewhere exciting.

Dad joins me by the car. "You about ready?"

"I think so," I say.

"You're taking your camera with you?"

"Obviously."

"You know, I'm a little mad you're about to have so much fun without me."

I grin at him. "I'm pretty sure no one would mind if you wanted to come along last minute."

He shakes his head. "No, I'm not stealing your thunder. Besides, no matter how much I say it, summer courses don't *actually* teach themselves."

"Okay, Dad." I give him a long hug. "I'm going to miss you."

"You too, kiddo. Call as often as you can, okay?"

"I will."

As he pulls away, Dad says, "Oh! By the way, I talked to Aunt Rhetta this morning while you were out. Said to wish you luck on your big adventure."

"Tell her thank you for me."

"I hope this doesn't awaken anything in you. Soon you'll be running around across the globe, like her."

I laugh. "I *have* always thought about backpacking around Europe."

"Oh God, maybe you do have some of her DNA."

"I'll be sure to learn plenty about the Byzantines while I'm there, just for you."

"That's all I ask." He hugs me again. "Get going, Ros. Sam's going to be antsy if you're late."

I close the trunk and climb into the driver's seat as Dad closes my door for me. He waves at me until the car disappears around the corner, and I head for Sam's house.

Despite the joke I told Dad, I don't think I'm much of a traveler. I've never felt like I needed to fly to other places to be happy or to find some sense of purpose. That, and flying makes me nervous.

Still, I can't help but feel a rush of excitement now. There's nothing wrong with something *new*, with feeling out of your depth sometimes. Maybe I haven't always felt that way, but it's something I've been learning to accept over the past couple of months.

Besides, it's not like I'm going to do any of this alone. I'm going with friends.

SAM

Everything's ready by the time Ros pulls into the driveway.

I run out in front of her car, waving my arms. "Don't block my car in, idiot! We'll never make it out of here!"

She parks behind Nana's car instead, grinning at me through the open driver's side window. "I know which one's yours, Sam. And I'm not an idiot."

"Debatable, but sure. You got everything?"

"If I don't, it's too late now."

"We'll pick up anything we forgot on the road." I turn back toward the house. "Nana! You ready?"

Nana pokes her head out the door. "Two minutes, sweet pea! Go ahead and get the car cooled down."

That's something I'm more than happy to do. While I lean into the driver's seat, turning on the car and plugging in my phone to get the music started, Ros drags her bag over to the open trunk.

"You didn't leave me that much room," she calls.

"What, do you *need* room? I thought you were all hipster and *minimalist*."

"I've literally never described myself as either of those things." She shuts the trunk and then walks around the car, hopping into the passenger seat. "What's first up on shuffle?"

I press PLAY and let the music start, something fast and bright with an electronic beat.

Ros wrinkles her nose. "Are we going to listen to this the whole time?"

"You at least have to let me have my own music until we're out of Massachusetts. Then you can play whatever you want." I brandish a finger at her. "But I *will* get you to appreciate modern pop music one of these days, Ros Shew. Mark my words."

"Keep dreaming." Ros grins at me, the fake arguing slipping away for a moment. "Are you excited?"

Just hearing the question makes something thrum inside my chest. "Yeah. I really am. I'm glad you're coming, too."

"I wouldn't miss it, Sam." She gives me a quick kiss over the center console, which I'm more than happy to lean in for. "Let's do this."

Behind me, I hear the front door shut. Nana locks up, then makes her way over to the car as well, settling herself in the back behind Ros.

"Everybody got everything?" she asks.

"Yes, Nana."

"Then let's get this show on the road."

We're going on a road trip. Destination: Loredo, California, and wherever else we feel like along the way. It's over a week's drive to California from Massachusetts, so it's unlikely we'll get that far, but it's nice to think that we might. The old map is sitting on the dash, Magic Marker scribbles facing up, just in case. Nana's coming with us, since two seventeen-year-olds can't exactly rent a hotel room, but I'm glad she's coming. Besides Christian, this is almost all the people I care about in one car.

Mom might not have had a problem with running off on her own, but as of right now, I do. This car isn't a chance to run away anymore—it's a way to bring everyone with me. And who knows? If we make it all the way to California, maybe we'll avoid LA altogether. Maybe I won't even tell her I'm there. The thought gives me the same thrill as the moment before the curtain goes up on a stage.

I have GPS pulled up on my phone, but I don't know how much I'm actually going to use it. Maybe we'll get lost halfway through Pennsylvania. Maybe we'll find something cool enough there that we have to stick around a few days. Maybe I'll find another town like Loredo, tiny and close, where people raise chickens and know everyone else's business, and where nobody's important but they live happily anyway. Maybe they'll help me figure it out.

Either way, I'm not looking for answers on this trip. I'm just looking for a good time.

"Sorry I'm going to be slowing you girls down," Nana says as I put the car in gear and start to back out of the driveway. "We'll probably have to make a few more stops than you want to since my terrible bones can't be in the car for too long."

Ros smiles. "Gives us more chances to explore. Right, Sam?"

"Yeah," I say. "I'm not in a rush."

CHRISTIAN

New York subway maps are actually pretty easy to understand, once you get the hang of them.

I definitely wouldn't say I'm an expert—I only made it into the city late last night, but after a good hour or so getting lost on a bunch of different lines, I've at least figured out the difference between the downtown and uptown trains, and that's been working out well for me so far.

This isn't the way I pictured my first time in New York City going. I figured I'd be here with friends, or maybe my parents, that I'd be scoping out all the stereotypical tourist spots, not hunting down an obscure corner of this giant city based on some vague directions I got via email. Still, I can't help being excited.

Nervous, too, obviously. But excited.

My phone is on silent in my pocket. If I need it, I'll look at it. I'm not expecting messages, anyway. The last ones I got were two separate good-luck messages from Ros and Sam, one including a lot more party emojis than the other, and a short, dry text from my mom. She and Dad haven't contacted me much over the last couple of days, mostly checking in to see if I'm okay. I've been replying every time, but not pushing for much more conversation. If they want space from what I'm doing in New York, then I can give them that.

I did think it would be more of a fight when I first brought up the idea. I expected to have to argue, and it definitely got close. But in the end, they kind of . . . agreed with me. Well, *agreed* isn't the right word. It's more like they accepted that I was going to do it, whether they wanted me to or not. Maybe I'm really good at convincing them. Maybe they realized they don't want to lose another kid. Whatever their reason was, it got me here. This might make me the "problem kid" now. Mom and Dad might start whispering about everything wrong with me when I'm not in the room. The thought makes my heart speed up a little.

But, realistically, what can they do? I turned eighteen two weeks ago; I'm a legal adult, free to make my own choices. I'm not in New York to stay, either. I'll be back in Massachusetts before the month is over, taking a tour of Babson's campus— along with a few others. I'm doing everything I can to keep the peace without being a "doormat," like Monty said. And even if my decision to go on this trip does go south once I get back home, I think I'll still be glad I did it. It feels important, more important than anything else I've done with my life so far, because it's *mine*.

I wanted to come here, to do this, so I said I would, and I didn't ask permission. No matter what happens, that makes this worth it.

The park I'm walking through now is hot and muggy—not Central Park, just a small patch of grass and some trees in the middle of more tall buildings. Still, most of the people around me don't seem to mind the heat. Kids play on a jungle gym nearby, their parents fanning themselves on the benches, and across from them, under a shaded awning, a group of people sit around picnic tables with board games in front of them.

My heart thuds. One figure sits apart from the others. His head is down, but as I get closer, he must hear me coming, because he looks up, locking eyes with me for the first time in over three years.

Will looks different. Older. There's a streak of blue in his hair now, and some scruffy beard that he *definitely* wasn't capable of growing the last time I saw him. He looks a lot like Mom, I realize. I can't remember if that was always so obvious before.

"Hey, Chris," he says.

"Hi, Will," I answer.

Will grins at my awkwardness. "Been a while, huh?"

"Yeah, I . . . it has."

"Come on, sit down. And stop being weird."

I sit, folding myself into the picnic bench across the table from him.

"So," I say, with a glance around, "is this why you moved out? To play Go in the park with a bunch of grandpas?"

"Don't be a dick."

"We're the only two people here under sixty; don't tell me you haven't noticed it."

Will laughs, throwing his head back. "All right, fine, you got me. Where did this sass come from? I didn't teach you that."

"I learned from the best."

There's a pause then, like both of us are trying to decide whether to say the thing that's in our head. I speak first. "Will, I . . . well, sorry I never tried to talk to you. After."

He shrugs. "Sorry I never did, either. I don't blame you, you know. It's not exactly like I left on the best of terms. And, well"—he gives me a sad smile—"Mom and Dad probably didn't want you talking to me, did they?"

"Not really."

"I figured." He looks me up and down. "What changed?"

Now it's my turn to shrug. "I did, I guess. Decided I needed to figure some stuff out for myself, instead of being told what to do."

Will beams. "Good for you."

"I don't blame you, either, you know."

There's a smile in his voice. "I know. I could talk about some of it, though, if you want. We've got a lot of catching up to do."

"I'd like that."

"Cool." He gestures at the Go board in front of him. "But you have to play this with me again before I spill my guts. That's my only condition."

"Deal." I pull a little round circle of plastic out of my pocket. "Missing any pieces?"

Will stares at me. "Is that from the old Go set?"

"Yep. I wanted something to remember you by."

"Did you at least get another full set to practice on? I'd hate to start wiping the floor with you again."

"No, but I guarantee this is the game where I beat *you* for once."

He grins, and I see the old competitiveness resurface. "Very confident for a future loser, Chris."

"Oh, I don't know." I slip my lucky piece back into my pocket, giving it one last comforting squeeze. "I think I might surprise you."

ACKNOWLEDGMENTS

This book was both an unexpected gift and a complete beast. I never expected to write anything like it, and it fought me every step of the way. But in the end, I think I'm proud of it, and that's good enough for me. To quote a line from *Cyrano de Bergerac*, "My garden's small, my fruits and flowers are few, but they are mine." I couldn't have grown them alone, though, so here's thanks to the people who helped:

Firstly to my agent, Alyssa Jennette, for being generally fantastic and also for dropping this opportunity in my lap at the exact moment I needed it; to John Cusick, for championing this book so brilliantly; to Adam Wilson, for helping me craft a story that felt true; to my editor and editor's assistant, Janine O'Malley and Melissa Warten, for whipping this thing (and me) into shape; and to anyone at FSG who has touched this book and left it better than they found it.

To French playwright Edmond Rostand, for the source material; to Nita Tyndall, for being a friend and answering my frantic debut-author questions at one in the morning; to Kadan, for the insight, feedback, and endless support; and to Ken and Sue, for your belief.

And also to any reader who finds a piece of themselves in Sam, Ros, or Christian. Know that we have something in common and that I wrote this for you.